CAMELOT

OF THE

ROADS

Written by
Eric Loren

Book 3
Ways of Camelot

Reader Hill
Yucaipa, California

Published by
Reader Hill
PO Box 490
Yucaipa, CA 92399
readerhill.com

Dedication

To my beloved wife. You are such a blessing in my life, enriching my days and filling them with laughter. Thank you so much. I will love you always.

ONE

Alone

Thomas sat on the edge of a cot in the lifeless suite that had belonged to his now-dead master. Levitanus had been a powerful wizard and one of the three Founders who crafted the enchantments that protected Camelot and the routes to it. Because of his position, Levitanus was given one of the best suites at the guild house, which included this extra bedroom for any servants or students. Although the students' sleeping room was spare in furnishings, the rest of the suite was richly and tastefully furnished. It was a suite where a wizard could comfortably rest, study, entertain visitors, or craft new enchantments. Nonetheless, Thom's mentor had never enjoyed the opulence of Clas Myrddin; Levitanus had preferred a simple cottage on the edge of a wilderness, cooking for himself and often grubbing herbs and magical elements from the land around him.

To Thom, the plush chambers seemed cold and cavernous without the warmth of his teacher to fill them. He had avoided the rest of the suite and had kept to the students' bedroom. As he sat on his chosen cot, he looked around the room. He had left the other two beds undisturbed, keeping his few items confined to the night table and the dresser.

He was done with tossing-and-turning, now that dawn was just starting to reveal the room's spare furnishings. Anxiety's gnawing had kept sleep away, for today he was going to appear before the magicians' council. The leaders of the guild had ignored him for days, but then yesterday they had sent word that he was to appear before them this morning. Why the sudden change? What had moved them? Most likely, it was because they were nervous about having a student underfoot who had no master to keep him in line.

Apprentices sometimes died during their years of training- after all, magic can be deadly if mishandled- but it was rare for an apprentice to outlive his master. Although Thom was officially a journeyman now, he knew that most still viewed him as a mere apprentice, for he was so young, so fresh to his higher rank, and so new to the larger community of magicians. Levitanus had kept him apart, isolated in that little cottage and far from the guild house. So now the other wizards seemed doubtful of his talent, no matter what tales they had heard about his exploits on the Roads. They seemed to look down on him whenever they even noticed him. Not just the wizards, but even the other journeymen he encountered seemed uninterested in him.

No apprentice or journeyman could be left without a teacher… not unless they had been released from the guild as a failure. It wasn't Thom's fault that his master had been killed while they were traveling within the Road of Waters, but would the council see it that way? Might they blame him for not sacrificing his life

1

to save his teacher? Thinking back, he wondered why he hadn't.

He frowned at such morbid thoughts. There had been no way he could have saved Levitanus from his fiery death. He hadn't even been in the same room when it happened.

Instead, he turned his thoughts back to the council. Apparently, they wanted to make some kind of formal ruling about him, most likely assigning him to a new master. Who would that be? How would he be treated?

Thom wasn't afraid of hard work; Levitanus had worked him relentlessly. He wasn't afraid of abuse; his own father had beat him regularly. What Thom was afraid of was contempt from his new master, a refusing to acknowledge what he already knew. It would also be hard if the man insulted the training of Levitanus. Call Thom a dullard, but don't insult his first master. That would be difficult to endure.

He stood up, the cot creaking as it was relieved of his weight, and walked across the cold stone floor in bare feet, to open the shutter of the small window. His master's rooms were on the second floor of Clas Myrddin, so the view was that of an empty side court and the outer wall beyond. Of the city, he could only see the peaks of some higher roofs and hear the muffled traffic on the street beyond the guild's outer wall.

He set his hands on the rough stone sill and leaned out the deep window to look straight up. Almost directly overhead was the Road of Clouds, its billowy underside still gray-dark even as its eastern face gained color with the coming day. Thom wished his master would have taken him on that magical route just once, for it must be enchanting to walk within ethereal mists, but it had never happened. He wondered if he would ever master the skills of magic required to walk the route alone, for only wizards had the ability to take that Road. Or would today be his last day as a magician?

"Enough of this despondency," he muttered, pushing off the window sill and turning back to the room. He needed to get dressed and find some breakfast before the meeting because he hadn't eaten much yesterday. It would do him no good to be faint or have his stomach rumble with hunger while in front of such an intimidating group. So he dressed in the formal attire of his rank, straightened his bed, and then walked through the dark sitting room and exited the suite. He left his knapsack and journeyman's staff in the room for now.

He ate in the Student Hall, the dark blue of his journeyman's robe gaining him courtesy from the servants but not companionship. The workers knew better than to try bantering with any magician- that was frowned upon in Clas Myrddin- so he merely heard a few polite greetings and an explanation of what was being served that morning. Only two other students were eating so early, both journeyman magicians. They gave him no greeting and it was clear he would not be welcome at their table, so he sat on his own. To them, Thom was a stranger who had never been schooled here. But worse, they knew he was without a master, which Thom surmised was the reason why no journeyman ever wanted to strike up a conversation with him.

When a pair of apprentices came in, they gave a respectful nod toward him and the other two, but they made no attempt at conversation. Thom had once tried talking with some of the apprentices, but the guild discouraged mixing of ranks and the newer students were assiduous in following the guild's expectations. He wouldn't be finding any companionship among them.

It was a quiet meal.

He finished and left, returning to the luxurious suite. The servants had stopped attending the suite as soon as they had learned of his master's demise, so it was shadowy and silent when he entered. No one came to open the shutters, refresh the linens, or set out fresh fruit. Such was only done for wizards. They had given it one last cleaning and then thrown protective coverings over the furniture in here and in the grand bedroom, for they certainly weren't going to leave expensive upholstered chairs available for a mere journeyman's buttocks, and Thom was not one to rebel against their judgment. These were not rooms intended for the likes of him, a thief's son who had lucked into getting half of a magician's training.

The only piece of furniture that they hadn't covered was the large wizard's cabinet that stood to the right of the cold hearth, for the servants knew better than to get near any of the locked dressers set aside for the wizards to store their excess magical elements and various supplies. Thom had no idea where the cabinet's key was and really had no interest in gaining entrance. He knew that his master had kept most of his cache of elements elsewhere, in a hidden room that Levitanus had revealed to Thom during their first stay here, after his adventure on the Road of Leaves. The door to the hidden room was along the back wall and unnoticeable by either sight or sound, for it wasn't disguised by magic. Thom thought it creative, to hide a magic cache behind a mundane door, one that blended into the ornate wood paneling so well that no one could see its edges. The room beyond was a long, narrow one that ran the length of that wall. He had gone in there only once since his master's death, and that had been to add to the supplies stored there, not to take anything. He had put his master's magician box on a shelf along with the man's mixing bowl and pestle. It was Levitanus' stores, not his, even though his master had given him permission to use any of the supplies in here.

The main cache of elements was still there as far as he knew. He wondered who would inherit that treasure. Would it go to whoever took over his training or would it be divided among the other wizards? It was not something he planned to bring up at today's meeting, though he would guess such a hidden room wouldn't remain unnoticed for long once this suite was assigned to another guild leader.

Thom felt a bit tempted to peek inside the hidden room and verify that all was still there, but he resisted. Now was not the time. Instead, he went to the one small room he was allowed to use and washed up from breakfast, using the water pitcher that he had filled last evening. He dried his face and hands, then hefted to his shoulder the knapsack containing his magician's box. He also retrieved his journeyman's staff, though he didn't know how to use it beyond kindling the light of its jewel.

It was still early, but he had no desire to dawdle here, so he set off for the council chamber.

* * *

He walked along the carpeted hallway, past doors of a half-dozen other suites that were assigned to the wizards who were at the guild house this week. As he understood it, some magicians were here almost all of the time, but most only came for a few weeks each season. Others showed up at the guild house far less often- his own master had been that way. As Thom started down the wide stairway to the ground floor, he passed two servants carrying covered food trays for some of those master magicians who were in residence. The two men gave him a polite nod of the head, appropriate toward a journeyman, but made no attempt to greet him. They were focused on not sloshing the food and drink they were delivering.

Downstairs, he strode to the waiting area in front of the council chambers. A pair of tapestries hung on either side of the closed door. Beneath the right-hand tapestry sat a long wooden bench with a dark-purple cushion. On that cushion lounged a youngish journeyman; he seemed a mere ten years older than Thom so he was likely new to the rank too. The man's knapsack was tucked beneath the seat, within easy reach. His magician's staff lay on the bench beside him to the left. Also on the bench, to his right, was a tray containing a half-eaten breakfast. He looked up when Thom approached, grimaced at him, and then returned to cleaning his fingernails with the tip of a knife.

Since the fellow was working so hard to ignore him, Thom decided to return the favor. He kept walking toward the closed door, intending to knock and make his presence known.

"Close enough."

Thom stopped and turned. The man pointed the knife like he might try throwing it at him.

"You are to wait here until I let you enter. Understood?" He jabbed it into the air in a mock throw.

Thom refused to be intimidated. "Why should I?"

The man sat up straighter. He used the knife's butt to tap his own chest. "Because I am Journeyman Sarlic, favored student of Wizard Varus, and I am assigned door duty this day. No one enters unless I say so."

Thom had no desire for a silly cock fight, so he swallowed the first words that wanted to come out and chose others. "So be it. I am Journeyman Thomas, student of the late Wizard Levitanus. I was summoned by the council."

The man made no reply, but instead returned to cleaning his nails.

Thom wasn't so dense as to miss that he was being baited. He couldn't afford to strike out at the pompous man but he also wasn't about to retreat across the room or just stand there like a dismissed dunce. Instead, Thomas walked closer and sat down on the other end of the same bench, ignoring the tray of dirty plates and the nail-cleaning twit.

A few minutes later, Thom heard a magician's box being opened within the council chamber. Shortly thereafter a small greenish light squeezed under the door and then flew to the middle of the room. It gave off a distinct chiming sound that Thom heard both normally and with his inner ear, then the enchantment dissipated into nothing.

Sarlic calmly stood up, taking his knapsack and placing it over his left shoulder and picking up his staff as well. Without a word or glance toward Thomas, he sauntered to the door and slipped inside. A few minutes later he came back out, carefully closing the door behind him before walking over to loom in front of the still-seated Thomas.

"You must go before the magicians' council now. I would suggest that you not expect any favoritism merely because who your dead master was. That is in the past and now you are merely a masterless student."

Thom didn't reply. Instead, he stood and strode quickly toward the door.

Sarlic had to hurry to get ahead of him.

Thom knew his haste would anger the other, but the man had already shown his dislike.

Sarlic opened the door and announced his entrance. He motioned Thom in and followed after, closing the door behind him.

Eric Loren

TWO

Judged

He felt the silence as soon as he entered. His last time here, the room had been full of bustle. This time there were no other magicians about, neither wizards nor students. And there certainly weren't any element vendors hawking their goods or nobles looking for a court magician. The only occupants were two elderly men and an older woman sitting at the head table. Their black robes proclaimed them master magicians, but Thom already knew that; no one else would dare sit at that table except a guild leader. The other two seats at the head table were empty, as was the side table that was meant for the three Founders but had only held Merlin and Levitanus the last time he had been in here. His eyes caught on that empty seat where his master had once sat. For most of his decade of training, Thomas had never known that Levitanus was one of the three who had established the guild and the enchantments that protected Camelot. To Thom, he had been a caring teacher and second father, not an esteemed Founder.

He caught himself, realizing now wasn't the time to be reminiscing about his apprenticeship, for the three were watching him.

Thom strode into the large room and stopped at what he considered a respectful distance, bowing in respect toward the trio of magicians.

"Come closer, Thomas of York," said Wizard Thallud, a thin man with a shock of white hair that almost glowed in the dim room. He sat between the other two. Thom remembered him from his first visit to this chamber, when Merlin had chastened him to seal his magician's box to stop the sound of the elements he had just purchased. "Stand near us, in that pool of light. We want to be able to examine you without squinting."

Thom complied, wondering if the master magicians could hear his fast-beating heart, for it seemed as loud as a thundering waterfall to him.

"I am Wizard Thallud." He indicated the man on his left. "This is Wizard Varus." Then he gestured to the woman on his right. "And this is Wizardess Una."

Thom gave each another respectful nod as they were named.

"Three are enough to make a ruling on behalf of the whole council as long as we are in agreement, and what we are about to pronounce is something in which we are certainly united."

Thom swallowed, fearing the worst. He couldn't have responded even if they were to demand it; his mouth was too dry.

"Wizardess Una will explain why you are here." Thallud motioned toward his fellow master magician.

Thom looked at her and tried to smile in hope, but her countenance remained serious.

"Thomas, you are now master-less, as you obviously know. As such we must decide what is to be done with you. None of Levitanus' past students are willing to take you on."

Thom's eyes widened at that. He hadn't known that there were other students besides the one that had been murdered and the notorious one named Gwier who had killed both that student and, later, Levitanus. But then again, his master had lived many decades, so he must have had other apprentices before them; it just wasn't something that Levitanus had ever talked about.

She noted his reaction. "Yes, there are three others who were once his students- all three vaunted magicians in our guild now. But two already have students and the last is serving us in a capacity that keeps him from acquiring any. No, that door is barred to you.

"We have the added problem of you being a journeyman by title but a mere apprentice in training and age. It is an awkward position to be in. I am certain that your late master had planned to bridge that gap in your training, but it is there. Now someone else must commit to the hard labor of bringing your education up to the robe color, so to speak. It is a chore that causes others to hesitate to take you on."

She paused for a long time, gazing at him as if she could see inside to his thoughts and emotions. "You are a burden for us, Thomas of York."

"At least he is no brawler or braggart," stated Thallud. "I will give him that. He causes no trouble in the guild house nor in the city."

"But that does not justify him running wild until a master takes him on," argued Wizard Varus. "Idle time could easily corrupt even the most innocent, and this hunt for a new teacher will likely take some time. He'll dirty his robes in more than one way without a strong hand of a master to keep him controlled. That is the way of all youth. Everyone knows that. He must have a master, yet we have none for him. Maybe we would be better to dismiss him now, before he sullies the guild's reputation."

Thom couldn't help sagging at the mention of throwing him out of the guild. What would he do? Where would he go?

"I said nothing of letting him loose to pillage Camelot," said Thallud, "but it would be an injustice to Levitanus' memory to turn out his last student to the life of a pauper. And have no delusion on that truth, Varus. He would be a beggar if we ran him out of the guild at this age. He's too old to apprentice any other trade. Starvation might drive him to true rebellion and maybe even to the dark arts. Would you want that on your conscience?"

"We have already argued this," stated Una, sounding tired of her fellow leaders. "Are you now backing away from our agreement, Varus?"

The other shook his head. "No, but I still have my doubts and wanted to make sure the youth heard them."

"So be it, but let us get on with our pronouncement. Only for the memory of Levitanus do we even bother to convene for an official judgment." She turned her attention back on Thom. "Hear our ruling, Thomas of York. The council, in its benevolence, will grant you shelter here at the guild house until a new master is found to take you on. However, until such time, you are forbidden from practicing any magic. We'll not have any rogue enchantments hurting others or damaging the keep. So, no magic until you have a new master to oversee your work, is that understood?"

Thom thought that unfair, considering how Merlin and Thallud had treated Vivien when she lost her teacher. "But Journeywoman Vivien was granted her teacher's library and notes. Will I at least get those for future use?"

"She is nearly a wizardess herself," replied Thallud. "Your situation is very different. We cannot place such things in your hands. It would be too great a temptation, what with our ban on practicing or studying any magic."

"We will consider placing Wizard Levitanus' personal writings and books in secure storage. Once you receive a new master, we can reconsider your request for his things," stated Wizardess Una.

This seemed to upset Varus. "But Levitanus was no ordinary wizard. His writings and books should not go to this youngster. They deserve a better, stronger owner who can step into that great man's boots. Such a legacy would be wasted in the hands of this whelp. It is…"

Thallud interrupted, "I think the fate of Levitanus' belongings should be decided by the full council once we have consulted Founder Merlin." He glanced at Thomas, then added, "This is not the place to talk about the legacy from his dead master and who should possess it."

Thom gritted his teeth, understanding what wasn't said. They still saw him as a mere apprentice, no matter the color of his robe. His eyes burned with tears over the unfairness of it all, but he refused to show any emotion in front of these uncaring people.

"I agree with Thallud," said Una, cutting short another protest from Varus. "The placement of Levitanus' belongings is a matter for the full council to decide. Now, can we get back to telling the boy our decision?"

When neither wizard objected, she turned her focus back on Thomas. "As we have already said, you are not to practice or study any magic until a new teacher has been assigned to you. Nonetheless, we expect you to behave like a well-disciplined student in the meantime. Though you are free of instructor, that does not mean you can become a louse or a layabout. Stay clear of the taverns and other places of ill-repute…"

"And away from Theobold's shop," added Varus.

She frowned at the interruption, but agreed. "Yes, you are to stay away from Theobold's shop of magic, the Golden Unicorn, since you have no reason to be in there eying the powders and vials. And there is another place of temptation that is out-of-bounds, and that is Castle Camelot. Some noble might try to cajole you into his service in the hopes of gaining his own pet magician. We will have none of that, so you are to keep clear of the king's keep. Is all of that understood?"

Banned from the castle? Adele resided there as one of the queen's maidens. He wouldn't be able to visit her there any longer. What about their planned meeting in two days? He wouldn't even be able to go there to explain why he now had to avoid the keep. Would she think he had forgotten? Thom swallowed his new fears; he needed to respond to the magicians in front of him. "Yes, I understand your restrictions."

"Also, you are to wear your journeyman's robe at all times. We want to make sure all know who you belong to, even if you are currently master-less. Whether in the guild house or out about the city, you will be in your dark-blues. And since you have no master, it will be one of us who will discipline you should we hear even the whisper of misbehavior."

"You are no longer at some hovel in the wilderness, running about with country ragamuffins," added Thallud. "You are now in the finest city in the realm, the seat of our benevolent king. You will act becomingly or face severe punishment. Our offer of shelter and promise of a new master is not given unconditionally, young man. You will behave or we will have you thrown into the gutter for the street-sweep to toss into his garbage wagon."

Although relieved that he could stay, he realized now how precarious his place was. One error could cost him his way of life. One false claim could easily bring banishment from the guild. It was not a good situation.

Una continued, "While you await a new master, you will be given a room among the servants. We have decided that it would be best to keep you away from the other students. The temptation would be too much if you had to hear their discussions about magic and watch their practice sessions."

"You are to stay away from the other students, apprentices as well as journeymen," interjected Varus. "Keep away from their rooms, the classes, their dining halls, and even the library."

She frowned at the second interruption, but didn't disagree. "Yes. That will be best for now. You will live and eat with the servants. It may be humbling, but it is only until a new teacher takes you on. Hopefully, another will be found soon."

So they were banishing him to the lower levels to keep him away from the others who were still actively learning their craft. Thom knew it would be futile to argue, but he didn't like the idea. It would be convenient for them to forget about him once he was out of sight.

"Do you understand and agree to these terms, Thomas of York?"

He had no other choice if he wanted to continue his guild training, so he gave them a firm reply, "I do."

"Should we seize his staff and magician's box?" suggested Varus, "Then he would have no temptation to fiddle with either."

Thom's breathe caught. His eyes widened. If they took his box, he would lose all the elements he had worked so hard to earn.

"You act as if he has been apprehended mixing love potions for some of those foolish noblewomen," stated Thallud, "which he has not done. No, he keeps his cache of elements and his staff, for those are only seized when someone is banished from our midst. We aren't doing that, Varus."

"Not yet," muttered the other master magician, "but there are enough who will try to bribe him to do deeds that will get him banished."

"Then he is also ordered to keep away from the houses of nobility, from the better inns, and from the shops around Ilson Square where the lords and ladies tend to congregate," said Wizardess Una. "That should be simple enough for the lad; he's not of noble birth and is most likely not comfortable amongst such folks. Neither would he have the coin to take on the lifestyle of such expensive shops and market stalls for long, despite the coins the king awarded him for his heroism on the Road of Leaves. I think these restrictions will be enough to help him avoid the lure of any unscrupulous lordling, do you not agree my fellow masters?"

Varus spoke up. "If he is to keep his cache of elements, then we should at least inspect it and note what it contains and how much. We can then check on it at any time and know if he has been dabbling in magic."

Una gave him a curt nod. "That would be wise on our part." She held out her hand toward Thomas. "We will inspect your magician's box. Have no fear; you will get it back, but we will note what elements it contains and the quantity of each."

Thom swallowed, knowing his cache was a rich one that would raise more questions, but he had no choice in this. He swung off his knapsack and pulled out the magician's box. He stepped forward and handed it toward Wizardess Una, since she had extended her hand.

As he stepped back to his place, the wizardess opened the lead-lined lid and the sound of the elements whispered throughout the room to any ear who could hear it.

Una's face showed some surprise but she didn't seem upset. She carefully pulled out one glass vial and observed its contents, giving Thomas a brief questioning look, but she said nothing.

Varus grabbed the box and glared at Thom. "You were just raised to Journeyman; you should not have so many elements. Did you steal from your dead master?"

Thom was shocked at the accusation. "No! Of course not. I would never have stolen from Levitanus. Those are all mine, harvested by me, purchased with permission, gifted by Keeper Cruthen, or gained in victory over a sorceress. My master knew about all of this."

Una chuckled. "He has you there, Varus. Not many journeymen have battled even one sorcerer and lived to tell about it, yet this youngster has quite the victory trove that he could justifiably boast about. As much as you disliked Levitanus' training methods, he was obviously successful with this one."

"Training is not finished until the black is earned," mumbled the wizard, turning his attention to the vials in front of him, pulling out and holding them up to the light. Thom was sure the man would remember exactly the contents and quantity in each vial.

"His mix certainly has the sound of a sorcerer's mix," noted Thallud with a frown as Varus handed the cache to him. "Maybe we should remove some of the … more questionable elements. For his sake, so that he isn't tempted to dark magic."

"We should leave that for his new master to decide," argued Una. "That is how the guild has always done it."

Thallud grumbled in grudging agreement. For a brief moment, Thom wondered if the man was coveting the elements for himself, but he dismissed that thought. Surely, a master on the council had no need to confiscate supplies from a mere journeyman.

Eventually, all three were satisfied with their inspection and Thomas was given his magician's box back, which he carefully stowed in his knapsack.

Wizardess Una spoke as soon as he had his knapsack back over his shoulder. "Be aware, young man, that we could ask to see your cache of elements at any time. Guard them well, because if any go missing you shall face the consequences. Now, are there any other objections to be raised?"

She waited to see if the other two had any more arguments.

"Maybe Varus was right when we talked earlier," said Thallud. "Maybe he should be confined to Clas Myrddin until he gains a new master. That cache might tempt others to steal from him."

"I think not," argued Una. "No one knows of his unusual cache and none of us will telling anyone about it. You will vouch for your student, will you not, Varus?"

"Sarlic is discreet; he will tell no one."

"Then I think a month's confinement to the keep will be long enough," said Una. "That will give Journeyman Thomas enough time to adjust to his new place here at Clas Myrddin. After a month, he can go out into the city, as long as he respects the other limits we have imposed. Do you two agree to only a month's confinement at the guild house?"

Once they gave their nods to her further suggestions, she turned to Varus, "I am done with my lecturing. Can your student now take him and see to his relocation to the lower rooms?"

He nodded and motioned Sarlic over. "Take him back to the room where he has been sleeping. He is to gather his belongings- and only his belongings- and then take them down to the steward's office. The steward is expecting him."

THREE

Sent Below

Journeyman Sarlic led the way back to Levitanus' suite. He didn't speak until they were in the suite's sitting room, and then he held out an open hand toward Thom and demanded, "Give it to me now."

"What do you want?" asked Thom, confused.

"The key to the cabinet. I will not allow you to steal any of your late master's supplies." He thrust his hand closer, insistent.

"I have no key," said Thom, shaking his head. "Maybe your master lets you rummage through his things, but Levitanus prized his privacy." Thom wasn't about to reveal the hidden room that was full of elements and money.

Sarlic sniffed, pulling back his extended hand and then crossing his arms. "Wise of him to keep your grubby hands out of there. I do not know why he would ever have thought you would be a good prospect for the guild. Maybe he pitied you like some do the mangy mongrel sniffing at the rubbish in an alley."

Thom sensed the other man was purposely provoking him, but he had no desire to fight back. If he did so, the council might change his lodging from servants' quarters to horse stall or simply throw him out. So Thom ignored the other's defiant stance and instead walked into the side room that had been his sleeping chamber.

Sarlic followed and stood right behind him, carefully watching as Thom gathered his few remaining belongings, taking out the clothes hanging in the dresser and laying them on the bed to add to his knapsack. But when Thom took off his knapsack and placed it on the bed to fill, Sarlic snagged it and looked through what was already packed to make sure he hadn't already stashed a candlestick or an ornate hair comb in there. For a moment, it looked like the arrogant man might dare something so scandalous as to search through Thom's magician's box, but he didn't. He merely hefted it, as if he could determine which elements were inside by its mere weight, and then tossed it onto the cot so he could rummage through the clothes already packed beneath it. Finding nothing, he tossed the knapsack back; it was up to Thom to repack everything. Through it all, Sarlic made snide remarks about the shabby state of Thom's clothing and other belongings.

Thomas didn't respond to any of it, even the comment that he had an apprentice-quality box. Despite his condescending tone, Sarlic's remarks had some merit. Maybe he should have replaced some of his worn things, for he had the money now. But he hadn't thought to replace either clothes or tools; he had been too shaken from his recent adventures on the Road of Waters. Now with the council's ruling, he doubted that he would get the chance to improve his instruments for crafting magic until he gained a new master.

Packing did not take long; Thom didn't have many possessions.

When they came back out to the sitting room, Sarlic again confronted him. "Are you certain that you have no key? They will learn if you have kept one hidden from us."

"I have no key to Levitanus' supply cache. If I did, I would still not dare to violate my master's things. Why are you so heated to get it? Did you want to look inside?"

Sarlic grabbed Thom's robe and pulled him close. "How dare you insult me so? I am no thief like you."

The other's breath smelled of mint, when it should of stank like his heart. Tom suspected that theft had indeed been the plan and then pinning the crime on Thom, but he dared not say so.

He made sure to keep his hands down so that he couldn't be accused of brawling and replied calmly. "I said nothing about thievery, just about wanting to look inside. But you're right. Surely, an accomplished journeyman such as yourself wouldn't stoop to rifling through a master's supply closet. Besides, my master would have guarded his supplies with more than a mere lock and you're smart enough to know that. My master knew many enchantments that don't need to be regularly reinforced. I'm sure he used such magic here and at his cottage, enchantments that could survive months or even years without his attention, enchantments that sang so low or so softly that they would be hard to detect."

"Magical trap," muttered Sarlic. He seemed unsettled by the thought. The man fell silent and Thom wondered if he was trying to hear the sounds of any enchantment in the suite.

Thom hoped the threat would be enough to keep him from trying to break into the cabinet. He waited, the front of his robe still bunched up in the other's fist, and made no attempt to break free. He was determined to be as docile as a lamb to avoid being banished from the guild.

Suddenly, Sarlic left go by shoving him away. "Get going. You are to report to the steward within the hour. Fail to do so and I will report it to my master. Or even better, you should just go out the front gates and keep walking. You are not meant to be a magician, not a commoner like you who could not even keep his teacher alive."

The words stung, but Thom still chose not to respond. Instead, he left. He didn't like leaving Sarlic in the suite where he might damage things and blame Thom for it, but he had no choice.

* * *

He found the house steward in his office, where the middle-aged man was reviewing figures written on a piece of slate. It was Cleo, the same man who had once met Levitanus and Thom at the keep's door the night of the king's banquet. He looked up when Thom entered.

"I was told to report to you, sir."

"Ah, the masterless journeyman. You have my condolences on the loss of Levitanus. He was a great wizard and an excellent teacher."

Thank you, sir."

There was a moment of silence as the man stared at Thom, then he continued, "I've been expecting you. However, I wonder… why is it that *they* have dropped this burden on me? Hmm?"

Thom didn't know how to answer so he stayed silent.

"Quite unusual. Sometimes apprentices are sent down here to work as punishment, but never has anyone been sent to live among the servants, especially not a journeyman. What would cause them to punish you so? Hmm?"

"It was thought best to keep me away from the other students until a new master could be found for me."

His eyebrows rose toward his thinning hair, showing his doubts. "I'm not one to question them. Most assuredly not. If you are to eat and sleep among the servants, so be it. I only ask that you not disturb the staff. They have their work to do, young man, so don't expect them to be waiting on you."

Thom nodded, "I don't expect any special treatment."

The steward set his slate down and stood. "Well then, come with me. I'll show you where your room is and the way to the servants' dining room. You will be housed along the men's corridor. Be sure to learn the route, for all men are forbidden from the women's corridor. No matter your rank, I'll not have any fondling of the staff."

He took Thom down a hallway, past the warmth and smells of the kitchen that came through a set swing doors. The steward pointed through a doorway across from the kitchen but didn't stop his fast stride. "That is the servants' dining hall. If you want to eat you must be there when food is served: at dawn, two hours past midday, and three hours after sunset. Don't try bothering the cooks for food at any other time, for they've been told to report it if any do."

He took Thom down a wide stone stairway. The next level down was for storage, according to the steward. He didn't stop at this landing, but continued down to the bottom floor. The stairs ended in a small hall, its walls adorned with old tapestries too worn for the halls above ground. The floor carpets were similarly old. The room held a motley mix of furniture and a large hearth that burned low at the moment. Thom imagined this was some sort of gathering room for the servants who weren't working, but right now it was empty. There were no windows this far down.

The steward paused to point to a passageway that led off to the left. "That way is the women's corridor. As I've said, it is forbidden to men." He turned to the right and led him down another corridor that was dimly lit, until they came to one of the last doors. The steward entered and used a striker from his pocket to light a candle on the side table. The room was so small that Thom could barely fit in behind him. The light revealed a bare cot with a blanket folded at its foot. The only other furnishings were a wash basin and pitcher beside the candle on a small, battered table. Looking over the steward's shoulder, Thom could tell that both had once been fine pieces but had been banished from upstairs due to wear. There was also a night pot under the table, but it looked to be made of inexpensive earthenware.

The steward turned in the tight room and then stepped back at the closeness of Thom. He jarred the table and the candle wobbled, making the shadows dance across the walls and ceiling. "'Tis small, I know, but it's the best I can provide. I'll hear no protests from you, for this is the ruling of the council. The guild house has nicer guest rooms, of course, but I was clearly told to find housing for you down here, young man. I am merely following the commands of the guild; if you have a complaint, take it up with the council."

Thom made no protest since he knew it would be futile. Besides, his room in Levitanus' cottage was nearly as spare as this place.

"The room was cleaned for you and that blanket is freshly laundered, but don't expect such care after this. I've been instructed that you will be doing your own laundering and taking care of any other necessities, since you have no other duties."

Thom nodded his understanding.

"Now, if you let me out, I'll show you the way to the lavatory and laundry."

FOUR

Across the City

It was still midmorning when the steward finished with his hasty tour, leaving Thom back at his assigned room. He stood there, unsure what to do with himself now. On previous days he had often lingered in the guild's library, reading about the history of the land, about magic, and memorizing entries from *Gauntley's Guide to Elements*. He could no longer do that, not when he was supposed to avoid any study of magic.

He was supposed to meet Adele in three days, but now he was confined to Clas Myrddin and was forbidden to approach the castle at all. Somehow he would have to send a message to her to explain his absence, but he didn't know yet how to arrange such a thing. He dared not ask anyone in the guild house about sending anything to the castle, for that would likely get back to the council and raise suspicion.

Thom felt imprisoned, even if it was in the rambling guild house and not some tiny prison cell. He laid down on his hard bed and to nap, since he hadn't slept much last night.

A few hours later he gave up trying to sleep and headed out for the servant's dining hall. He would be early for the midday meal, but he had nothing else to do with his day.

* * *

It took two days before he was able to get word out about his confinement, which he did by passing a short note to a visiting monk. It was a note to his friend Francis, explaining his confinement and asking him to relay the information to Adele. The brother insisted on reading the missive before taking it and then asked numerous questions about how Thom knew Brother Francis and why he would impose on the monk to communicate with a woman. It took some quick talking and the monk didn't seem fully convinced, but he did promise to pass the note to Francis.

* * *

The month of confinement passed slowly. In that time, Thom explored the keep's towers and gardens, its servants' section and courtyards. He was assiduous in avoiding the areas where the magicians lived and worked but he still had random encounters around the keep. None of the students even tried to talk with him, so he just ignored them in return. He found out that there was always a magician assigned guard duty at the main gate, either a wizard or an advanced journeyman, who wore a red cape like the guild guards and added a red cloth wrap around the head of their magician's staff.

When the month was finally over, he was eager to escape the guild house, even if it was just for a day. He ate an early breakfast with the servants and then hurried to the front gate, ready to leave as soon as it opened with the coming of morning. He had decided that his first destination would be the Monastery of Saint Barnabas, where his friend Brother Francis resided... at least he did whenever he was in Camelot. For days now, Thom had worried that Francis might have left on another of his book hunts and had never received his note about being restricted to the guild house.

When he walked out Clas Myrddin's front gates the guards didn't stop him or question his right to leave. Either they didn't recognize him as the masterless journeyman or they knew he was now allowed a longer leash. The mage-guard was in a conversation with some shopkeep and didn't even look over as he passed.

Thom headed across the just-awakening city. He aimed for the monastery, which lay at the far eastern end of the city, almost all the way to King's Haven harbor. He would miss the midday meal at the guild house, but he had more than enough coins to afford something from a street vendor. It would be a long day of walking, to go all the way across the city and then back here before the gates closed for the night, but it would be worth it.

It was midday when he arrived at the square in front of the monastery, still eating the last of a trio of roasted chicken skewers he had purchased from a food vendor. He paused to look at the high roof of the chapel and the mature trees peeking over the gray wall. The thick, tall stone wall surrounded the monastery and the smaller convent attached to it. From outside, it looked more like a fortress than a spiritual refuge.

Thomas had been to the monastery three times during his time in the city between his adventures on the Road of Leaves and the Road of Waters, so he knew that the Saint Barnabas Monastery of the Benedictine Order was a sprawling compound with many buildings among lush gardens. Its green areas were rich with flowering shrubs, vegetable patches, and rows of fruit-heavy trees. Francis had taken him on a tour of the grounds once, pointing out dormitories, a forge, a carpenter's shop, a chandlery, and many beehives. But the monk's favorite place was the scriptorium where they stored the monastery's important texts and where the scribes did their copying.

Thom noticed a steady flow of people were coming and going through the unguarded front gates, folks who either had business with the monks or who were going to the chapel to pray. Francis had told him that on certain days there would be large crowds, the days when the brothers would share of the bounty of their gardens, offering produce to the city's poor. But today was apparently not one of those days.

Thom walked through the gates and across a cobbled courtyard, entering the chapel. He paused to show appropriate reverence, then stepped out a side door. He had been here enough times to know the most direct route to the scriptorium where Francis usually worked. He had learned to stride purposefully whenever crossing the grounds; as long as he walked fast no one would question what he was doing there. He stepped out into a small courtyard with a gurgling fountain, surrounded by lush flower beds, but he didn't pause to admire any of it. Instead, he took the path that led to the library, which he could just spy beyond a smaller storehouse.

When Thom stepped inside, he was still awed by this hushed world. The quiet made the courtyard's fountain seem loud. To one side, a half-dozen monks sat at desks, focused on their copying. None of them noticed his intrusion; they were too focused on their work. The only sound heard from them was the scratching sound of their quills on parchment and one muffled cough. That end of the scriptorium was well-lit. The monks were no mere copyists as they reproduced writings. They were artists as well as scribes, creating beautiful illuminations with colorful pictures and gorgeous lettering.

In the other direction was the library, with shelves of bound books and stacks of scrolls. It was dimmer in this area and even more still. Thom couldn't see Francis, but he was probably at the back where Brother Colwyn kept all the new additions to the library until they could be assessed and assigned a home or a copyist. Francis kept the librarian well supplied in new volumes, for he spent many months each year traveling the country with his mule, Ears, and conniving books from nobles who had little use for them. Some tomes he borrowed with the promise to return them once they were copied, others he won as gifts. A few he purchased but, from what Thom understood, the abbot didn't provide Francis with much money for that. The monk seemed to enjoy his assigned role nonetheless.

Thom walked down one of the rows, searching for his friend. Instead, he found only the head librarian sitting at a table and studying a worn book. A neat pile of scrolls rested nearby. It appeared that he was reviewing some of the library's newest acquisitions, deciding which were worth copying. Brother Colwyn's sheared pate was ringed by disheveled gray hair. But his robes were neat and clean, hanging loosely on his thin frame. He looked old and just a bit frayed, but still well-kept— much like his books.

Brother Colwyn recognized him and gave the slightest nod toward the back wall. "You can wait on the bench, Journeyman Thomas. He will be back shortly."

Thom sat where indicated and waited patiently for almost an hour, but when Francis showed up he sprang to his feet.

The monk reacted with a warm "Thomas! It is good to see you."

The two embraced, then Francis held him at arm's length. "I received your note and passed it on to Lady Adele. You have new burdens, don't you?"

Thom nodded, suddenly feeling a bit of moisture in the corner of his eyes. Must be the dust from all the old books.

Francis turned to his supervisor. "Brother Colwyn, may I take an hour to talk with the young man?"

Colwyn didn't look up from his book but waved his hand. "Do so, but no longer than that. I need your help deciphering that one scroll you found in that seaside church. The writing is too crabbed for my old eyes."

Francis led Thomas back to the fountain courtyard, where the two sat on the pool's stone lip. Soon the younger man was telling the monk all about the council's judgment. When he finished, he looked to his friend and asked, "What can I do now? I feel almost exiled. I'm forbidden my craft, severely limited on where I can go or who I can be around, and I feel like I'm just one bad report away from complete banishment."

"You know my view about magic; I see no punishment in avoiding it completely. However, I know it is still your craft, so I understand your hurt there. Didn't they give you any idea about how long you would have to wait for a new master?"

Thom frowned and shook his head. "None, and I get the feeling that they have no urgency to find one. I fear that I'll be forgotten now that I'm isolated away from them."

"Maybe you should reconsider the Father Abbott's offer. The League of Barnabas still does magic, but they are at least better than the guild or the sorcerers."

"No. I owe my loyalty to the guild. If Levitanus hadn't found me and taken me on as an apprentice, who knows where I would be now."

"That sounds more like a debt to the man and not to the whole guild."

"I can't repay a dead man. I'm left with the guild as my only family. Would you have me turn my back on them just because I'm not getting what I want?"

"You've more than repaid them and the kingdom, my friend. You rescued the queen and the king! You stopped Dalrake's plot to take over the Roads. I doubt your teacher would have claimed there was any debt in the first place, but if there had been, your deeds have more than cleared it."

Thom disagreed but he could tell that Francis wouldn't see it that way. "What do you want, Francis? For me to denounce the Magicians' Guild?"

The monk chuckled. "If only you would. I wish that all journeymen and apprentices would do so. But I know that you are committed to your craft and doing right. I respect you, Thomas, even if you are a magician."

He smiled back. "Thank you. I know you can't solve this for me. I just needed someone to talk with."

Francis put a hand on Thom's shoulder and leaned close to catch his eyes. "I'm here whenever you need me. You're a good man who has done much for his land. You owe nothing to the guild, but I respect that you want to stay with them in honor of your late teacher." He let go and stood. "Now, what about Adele? She needs to learn about your new restrictions or else she'll suspect you of neglecting her. Would you like me to pass the details to her?"

Thom stood as well, with a bounce to his step. "Can you?"

"Of course. Although I avoid the league, I do know where they train their budding magicians. I will make sure word gets to her. Even better, you should write her a letter. Come with me back to the scriptorium and you can compose it today."

"Thank you!" Thom couldn't resist giving his friend a hug as his eyes became misty from relief. Adele would know why he had to avoid the king's castle. Maybe they could arrange for some other place to meet, someplace that wouldn't raise the ire of the council nor upset the sensibilities of the matron who oversaw the queen's maidens.

It took him another hour to decide on what he would write but he finally set quill to the scrap of parchment that Francis had provided and wrote a short note to his beloved. He briefly explained his restrictions and then concluded with words of affection and asked that she would meet with him soon. He left the day and time up to her, but suggested they could meet at the monastery's chapel and then go to a nearby market for a meal. He asked her to send word back to him through Francis.

When done, he asked Francis to review it and make certain that it made sense. The monk did so, his eyebrow rising over something, most likely the use of the chapel for a romantic meeting, but he said nothing disparaging. "You wrote well; it is legible and concise. And I will be glad to play the intermediary. It might take a day or two for this get this to her, but I'll make sure it ends up in her hands." He set it on a shelf above his usual work table so that the ink could dry. "Now, let's put you to work. I've fallen behind with all these disruptions, so I can use your help with some the tasks Brother Colwyn has for me. Please give me a few hours of help and then you can start your trek back to the guild house. You needn't worry, none of these texts have anything to do with the craft of magic."

Thom smiled at that and gladly agreed to help.

* * *

He stayed at the monastery until late afternoon and then hurried back across the city to reach Clas Myrddin before the gates were closed for the night. He crossed the cobbled courtyard just inside the gates and entered by the main doors that were used by visitors and magicians alike, but was careful to not get any closer to the areas that were off limits to him. He turned to the left, following a corridor that led away from the masters' wing. He passed the grand stairway that led to Sky Tower, where a bored guard kept watch to make sure no one tried to climb to the Road of Clouds. He entered a servant's passageway nearby and made his way to his assigned room. Not knowing his way through this warren of alternative ways, he kept to the route he knew, which passed by the very busy kitchen. It was time for the evening meal for the magicians, so servants were hustling back and forth, both human and pixies. Thom was surprised when one of them hailed him.

"Thomas! What brings you down here?"

He instantly recognized the garish clothing of another friend, the one they called Deranged because he imagined himself to be a prince of the pixies.

"What are you doing at the guild house, Dorthos?"

He smiled. "Many of my people have taken temporary employment in the city, waiting for the Road of Waters to calm down. I was at the king's castle for a time, but the head of the staff declared my cheerful attire too bright for the eyes of their dreary courtiers. Something about maintaining decorum. So I was sent to join the staff here and told to stay in the servants' area only. Apparently, your fellow magicians also deplore anything festive."

Thom had to laugh at his description. "You do look bright and festive, and I find that a pleasant change to the place."

"What brings you down here into the bowels of the servants' wing?"

"You'll likely see more of me now, for they also want to hide me down here."

Dorthos nodded, as if it was something he had expected. "My clothes are too brilliant and yours are too stained and worn by your hard-fought deeds. They judge by our garments instead of considering the man who wears them…"

At that moment another pixie came out of the kitchen and motioned for

Dorthos to keep moving.

The small man took no offense, but complied. Over his shoulder he finished his thoughts, "We will talk more, but I need to get this platter up to the students' dining room, not that they would actually let a mere pixie prince deliver food to them; a human servant will take it from me at the end of the servant's corridor. You would think I was a threat to those youngsters."

FIVE

Out of the Clouds

Thom awoke very early the next morning to a room that was pitch black. It took a moment for him to remember where he was. His first thought was to create a light with magic- it was a simple enchantment and he could find the right elements simply by sound- but then remembered the reason why he was down here. He was to keep away from magic. So sat up, fumbled for the cold candle, and then slipped out into the hallway to light it from one of the lamps burning there. He quickly slipped back inside before anyone caught him walking around in his small clothes.

He set the candle down and then considered what to do today. He wouldn't hear back from Adele for at least a few days, so there was no need to rush to the monastery. He looked at his journeyman's robe sprawled out at the foot of the bed and remembered Dorthos' remark about looking shabby. Maybe he should do his laundry today so that he could be presentable again. Yes, that would be a good way to spend the morning. And maybe a bath too.

He walked past the other servants' rooms, being careful not to make any noise that might wake them. Only the bakers would be up this early, stoking the oven fires and kneading the day's bread. He turned down another hallway and made his way to the servants' washing room. He found it empty but garments were still dripping on one of the clotheslines, so someone had already been in here. The large water kettle was still warm, so he took it behind one of the privacy screens and disrobed. He gave himself a sponge bath, for there were no large bathing tubs for the servants, and then dressed in his spare clothes, garments that he had outgrown two years ago. They were threadbare and tight, but at least they were reasonably clean. No one would see them, since his journeyman's robe covered all.

With the remaining water, he set about cleaning his clothes. He had no second robe, another thing forgotten in his quick rise to journeyman and then fast fall to teacher-less student, so he had to do his best by spot cleaning it. He dared not soak it or he would have to wear it sodden all day. Once the worst of the stains were out, he turned to the rest of his clothes, using the last of the now lukewarm water in the kettle and the water that was left over from his bath, to clean three shirts, two pairs of trousers, and his undergarments. When done, he hung the garments up to dry on a free line nearby while draining the dirty water from the catch tub.

He looked at the limp garments hanging there, dripping on the stone floor, and reconsidered. It was too damp down here; his clothes would take days to dry and would end up smelling dank. Thom thought it would be much better if he could set them out in the bright sunlight. Even though there were clotheslines in a small courtyard where the servants washed the clothes of the masters and journeymen, he dared not go there. It was too close to the forbidden area. But surely he could find some out-of-the-way place to set out his clothes to dry in the fresh air.

He considered, deciding against using any window sill or wall, for then others would complain he was treating the guild house like some commoner's hovel. That wouldn't do. Instead, he thought there had to be some sunny place that was also out-of-sight of the masters. Maybe he could climb up to an area where most of the magicians and servants never bothered to go. They hadn't banished him from the keep's half-dozen towers, so he would try there. He would lay his clothes on the stones of a tower walk and let the sun dry them. It should be safe to leave them there for the morning.

So he put on his still-damp robe, bundled up the rest of the wet clothing, and headed upstairs. He chose to climb Farview Tower, the guild house's second highest spire. After what seemed like hundreds of steps, he came out to a partially cloudy morning, sunlight just starting to touch the city laid out beneath him and brushing the clouds with color. This high up, the enchantment surrounding Camelot was a strong hum to his inner ear. A peaceful whisper, but one that brought him new sadness.

He missed crafting magic, even if his enchantments were far simpler than the complex magic that created a dome over the city. His own training in the craft was now on hold by order of the magicians' council until a new master was found for him. It wouldn't be easy to stop from dabbling with his cache of elements, but he was determined to resist such temptations because he didn't want to be thrown out of the guild.

Thom walked around the tower's walk to the side that would first catch the morning's sun and laid out his wet clothes there. As he straightened up, the Road of Cloud caught his eye. The magical path soared over the city to end at nearby Sky Tower, the only thing so tall that it actually pierced Camelot's shell of magic. There, above the city's covering, the tower and the Road met. Because it was outside of the enchantment he was in, Thom couldn't hear the magic of the Road, but it was obvious to anyone who looked up into the sky. Normal clouds didn't act like that.

Although Sky Tower loomed well above him, it still seemed almost close enough to touch. He could see it so clearly as he looked up at the clouds lapping against the gray stones. It was like a stone finger pointed at the heavens, so tall that he wondered how the masons were able to build it so high and straight. It was said that Sky Tower had a ring of three tower walks, one within Camelot's magical covering, one just beyond that enchantment, and a final walk at the tower's very top that was within the Road of Clouds itself. Thom could only see the bottom two walks.

Only master magicians were allowed to climb that tower and take the Road, and it was said that the Road would lead to wherever a wizard wanted to go, stretching across the skies of kingdom as required. Thom couldn't grasp how that could be, for it didn't look like a seething snake up in the sky. But maybe it altered its course once it was farther away from the city. However it worked, he wished that Levitanus would have taken him on that Road at least once. This particular

Road, more than all the others, was the pinnacle of the magicians' craft. To walk it, to hear its rhythms up close would have been an unforgettable journey.

Staring up at the Road, he sighed in wonder at the complexity of the crafting that he saw overhead. Magic— great magic like the enchantments encircling the city and the roads that led to it— was something he longed to learn, even while he was also greatly disturbed by the truth that magical beings like pixies and centaurs and merfolk had to die just to keep these greater enchantments going. Even when they surrendered their lives freely for the magic lands that benefited the rest of their society, it still disturbed him.

His thoughts shied away from rendering dead magical beings; it was a morbid subject. He wanted to look elsewhere. He leaned on the tower's walkway wall and looked over the city, gazing down at the main courtyard and the street in front the guild house, watching the people milling about. All seemed normal out there, in spite of the recent attacks by sorcerers on the Road of Waters. He wondered if any of the strife had even touched the lives of the denizens of Camelot. They went about their days as normal as can be in an enchanted city where all normal people had to leave occasionally or face the sickness that came from constant exposure to magic. If Thom stayed in Camelot much longer, he would also have to start the regular treks along the Short Roads to spend a day away from the magic. He had heard that the city council kept records of how often each citizen left the enchantment and would help the elderly and infirm to make sure they weren't exposed to the magic for too long.

Just then, he heard the whisper of a new enchantment. At first, he thought it was just his imagination, but he heard it again. Faintly. It was a type of fire magic and it came from above.

Frowning, he looked up at Sky Tower and saw a blaze of light on the second landing, the one between the Road of Clouds and Camelot.

It wasn't a faint enchantment; it was one so powerful that he could hear it through the city's enchantment.

Thom's heart sped up. His stomach felt queasy. Memories of sorcerer attacks clawed to the surface of his mind, unsettling in their vividness.

Then he heard another enchantment— again it was some form of fire— and saw a flash through a window in that shadowy spire. This time it was much louder and obviously happening within the larger enchantment surrounding the city. Soon after, four men strode out onto the tower's lowest walk. Men in black robes.

Thom thought them to be wizards but then he doubted his first impression. Maybe he was being too suspicious, but he ducked down so that they wouldn't notice him.

He was glad that he had when he heard the distinct scream of a griffin.

Thom dropped all the way to the stones, as he frantically swung the pack off his back. But before he could get out his magician's box, he heard the beast take flight. He looked up as the griffin flew past. He saw only the tip of the monster's wing and was thankful that it hadn't flown directly overhead.

The beast was loose on the city and there had been no way he could have stopped it. And if the men on Sky Tower had let it loose, then they were no wizards. Those men were sorcerers.

25

SIX

Griffins in the Air

Thom's heart pounded in his chest and his body wanted to run at the same speed, but he knew better. Any sudden movement might attract the griffin's attention. Instead, he carefully crawled back to the tower's doorway, no longer concerned about trampling his newly laundered clothes. Once through the open doorway, he paused. Should he go warn somebody? Should he hide? Or, was it time to pull out his magician's box and prepare an enchantment?

He heard another griffin's cry, this one a bit higher in pitch, and had a sudden fear that there might be a pair of them loose above Camelot. He crept to a window that faced toward Sky Tower and peeked out; he saw three of the monsters perched on Sky Tower's outer walk. The black-robed magicians had moved farther along the wall walk to let them squeeze out of the tower's doorway. The three lion-eagles didn't have much room on their perch and one of them was complaining about it to the others, giving a warning peck when the other pressed too close.

A griffin had once fallen on Thom in its death throes, so seeing three of them nearby brought back horrible memories. They were fierce monsters, with the wings and face of an eagle and the body of a lion. They were also hard to kill and Thom had no dryad poison to coat his blade. He kept low as he peered at the winged monsters.

The magicians ignored the beasts as they leaned over the wall to look at one of the courtyards far below. Their lack of concern further convinced Thom that the four were sorcerers.

Whatever the sorcerers saw caused them to step back and kneel out of sight, but he could tell what they were doing for he suddenly heard a cacophony of raw elemental sounds. They had opened their magicians' boxes and were crafting magic. Thom realized it would be foolish for him to open his own cache now, not with such powerful magicians on the next tower over. They could too easily engulf the top of Fairview in flames or ice or deadly winds.

His attention turned back to the griffins as another one pressed out of the tower door behind the trio, screeching in protest at finding its way blocked. The other three screamed back at it, then each one sprang off the wall in quick succession, taking flight.

Thom pressed against the stone wall in sudden fear that they might see him, but thankfully none did. He heard their feathered wings as they labored to catch air inside Camelot's enchantment. Griffins were vicious monsters; Thom could imagine them soon swooping down on people. Somehow the sorcerers had enough control over the beasts to bring five of them here and then let them loose on the city.

From somewhere below, Thom heard more magical elements, so he wouldn't need to warn anyone within Clas Myrddin; the wizards were already reacting to the attack. But that raised another problem. He felt very vulnerable up here, only one tower away from the invading sorcerers.

He decided it would be best to go back down, but first he quickly gathered his wet clothes. Some might have called him foolhardy for crawling back out on the wall walk just to get clothing, but he didn't know when he would ever get back here. Maybe it was because of the uncertainty and poverty of his early childhood, but he couldn't leave his clothes behind. He shoved them into his knapsack around his box a magical elements and then he crawled back inside the tower. Rising on shaky legs, he started down the stairs. As he descended, he heard and felt a series of explosions. The wizards and sorcerers were fighting with magic now.

As he kept going, he kindled the jewel at the head of his magician's staff. He had no idea how to use the staff to enhance his magical crafting but he felt better having it lit.

When he was nearly to the ground floor, the tower shuddered from an explosion outside. He paused and set his free hand against the wall to keep from stumbling. When the shaking stopped, he hurried on.

The stairway came out in the guild house's western end, only a few halls from the now-forbidden-to-him wing set aside for his fellow journeymen, but the area was deserted. He wondered if he should go through the forbidden area and raise a warning, but surely every magician would have already heard what was happening. The magical noise was so great that even those with the dullest of inner hearing would notice. He decided there was no need for him there.

If anyone needed warning it would be the servants, for most of them wouldn't have an ear for magic, but then he saw two maids hurrying around a far corner, obviously already in a rush to find safety. Hopefully they would tell others, for Thom decided he could best help by heading toward the battle and not fleeing from it.

He turned toward Sky Tower, for the invaders were coming down that spire, and quickened his stride. He thought the council surely wouldn't enforce their ban on him today; this was an invasion. He was hurrying through a long reception hall— a room eerily empty for this time of day— when another explosion struck the guild house.

Thom staggered as the building shook.

A row of windows suddenly shattered, and he covered his head as glass shards flew everywhere.

When the air cleared, he looked toward the tall, now-empty window frames. He saw nothing unusual outside— just a normal morning sky— but he heard the cacophony of enchantments being crafted.

Glass crunched as he now ran onward.

He ran through more hallways, until he rounded a final corner and started running down a wide, long corridor, a hallway with a set of richly-carved double doors at the far end that were ajar, revealing his goal. The stairway up Sky Tower. He saw no guard at the foot of the stairs, or anyone else for that matter. He kept running.

He was only halfway across the room when a horrendous attack came down the stairwell. Fire magic.

Flames roared out of the stairwell and blazed through the double doors.

Thom was thrown back by the rush of air, even though the flames didn't reach him.

He sat up to find the entry to Sky Tower burning and flames licking the frame and lintel of the doorways in front of him, black smoke starting to hide the ceiling of the corridor he was in.

He quickly retreated, wondering where else to go. He decided to head for the great courtyard. At least he would be able to see Sky Tower if he went outside. He became a little disoriented as he tried to find the nearest exit, but he eventually came on one. It was already thrown open and no one was in sight. Cautiously, he stepped near and looked out on the large courtyard that lay between the guild house's main entry door and the gatehouse. The sun wasn't high enough, so the cobblestoned courtyard lay in shadow. Nothing moved out there.

It was empty, except for two burnt bodies.

It was also silent, at least to normal hearing, but his inner ear picked up the sounds of numerous enchantments being crafted.

He heard a sorcerer forming something far overhead, still up in Sky Tower. He couldn't see the spire from where he stood but, if he stepped outside, he would be exposed to anyone looking down. He could also hear a trio of enchantments being mixed off to the right, in the heart of the guild house— maybe at the foot of Sky Tower, though he couldn't imagine anyone having survived the firestorm that had roared out of that stairwell. Maybe he should have lingered at the foot of the tower after all, for it sounded like the magicians were trying to take the spire back.

Thom was about to step away from the door and find some other route to go join the counter-attack, when he realized that they were on the move and not charging up the tower. They were coming toward the courtyard. He dared to peek outside and saw a door across the courtyard slam open, the grand entryway that was on the other side of the base of Sky Tower.

A band of magicians and pixies came rushing out. As one of the wizards exited, he threw a powder into the air and it coalesced into a magical covering that hovered over the courtyard at that end. To Thom's eyes, it seemed like a haze, too ethereal to offer any shelter; but to Thom's inner ear, the covering had a complex rhythm— loud and strong. He was uncertain of its purpose but he knew it was far beyond anything he could craft.

The group of four wizards, three journeymen, and two apprentices strode across the cobblestones, hurrying toward the guild house gates. One of the wizards still had his mage-guard cape and staff wrap, so he must have abandoned the gate to help this group get away. Ten pixies hustled to keep up, running carefully alongside the humans and trying to stay under the protective covering. The covering moved with them.

When Thom heard a fireball being formed up in the tower, he ducked away from the door, expecting a loud explosion when the two enchantments collided. With his inner ear, he could hear the fireball searing toward the magicians nearby.

He cringed in anticipation, but there was no explosion. Instead, he felt a rumbling like deep thunder and the enchantments seemed to meld and turn into a jangled mess of sounds.

He cautiously looked outside. The wizard's shield was aflame and slowly melting, sending a cascade of fire down the sides and back. The clash of enchantments was indeed causing both to falter, but it was happening as slow as ice melting in hot water. Thom could see it was a strain on the wizard maintaining the enchantment, but it held long enough to deflect the flames. When the enchantment collapsed into a smoky cloud of sparks, a second wizard threw up more elemental powders and another shield replaced the one that had melted.

Through all of this, the group kept marching toward the gate. They were fleeing the guild house.

Thom felt a sense of panic. He didn't want to be left behind, so he tucked his staff under an arm and ran toward them, hoping to join the others under that magical shield.

He only made it halfway to safety.

SEVEN

Escaping Clas Myrddin

Thom sprinted across the cobblestones, dodging one of the burnt bodies. As he ran, he heard another fireball being formed. He tried to run faster but he wasn't quick enough. He was still exposed when the fireball hit the wizard's shield.

He stumbled, covering his eyes against the glare. Even though there was no explosion, the power clash was intense. The protective covering went from clear to a grubby gray, like smoked glass. Another sorcerer threw a fireball and it too hit the wizard's enchantment. Suddenly, the shield over the magicians became a fiery waterfall as it melted and poured down around the sheltering group.

Thom staggered back as droplets of fire splattered on the cobblestones in front of him.

Some of those under the shield noticed him and maybe even recognized him, but no one tried to help. They were steadfastly moving toward the gates and they weren't going to wait for a master-less journeyman. The only one getting any aid was the wizard straining to maintain the shield- two apprentices were carefully leading him.

Thom was on the other side of the flowing fire and the cascade was increasing. The heat and brightness were too intense. He staggered back, coughing at the foul smoke of burning elements. Yet he stayed as close as he could and waited for the attack to end. He knew that he was dangerously exposed but he was desperate to join his guild brothers. He didn't want to be left behind.

Hope rose when the group stopped moving and he thought they were waiting for him. But then he realized that they had paused for a pair of wizards who were kneeling over mixing bowls in the middle of the party. One man was crafting a replacement shield for the one that was disintegrating over the group. The other was making his own fireball. The barrier shield over their heads was almost gone.

While they hadn't stopped for him, Thom saw his chance to reach them and started running; he needed to get there before a replacement shield could be crafted. He ran through a thick, acrid cloud of smoke, holding his breath and nearly closing his eyes. But when he could see again, he realized it was too late. The wizard who had been mixing a replacement covering now stood and tossed a powder into the air, which coalesced into a shield that was a bit smaller in circumference than the previous one yet somehow denser. No sooner was it in place, when the first fireball slammed into it, starting the waterfall of fire all over again. There was no way for him to get past a cascade of flames.

The second magician also stood, a fireball in each hand, but he didn't throw them. Instead, he just moved with the rest of the group, slowly fleeing the guild house. It was dangerous to try restraining magic right at the point of release, but somehow the wizard was doing so and not burning himself- at least not yet.

The wizards' party sped up to a trot, still aimed at the gate, keeping close together as they moved. Their protective shield was once again sloughing off a heavy flow of flames but for now it held. Frustrated, Thom followed them; he expected a fireball from the sorcerers to slam into his back at any moment, but what else could he do? If he dared to stop and try to mix his own magic, he would surely be killed before he could ever craft anything, so he kept his pack on his back and followed after.

The wizards were nearly at the half-open gates when Thom heard a new enchantment directly behind him. He looked back and saw Sorcerer Dalrake standing at Sky Tower's bottom door. Thomas recognized him from their encounter on the Road of Waters. The sorcerer held a giant fireball over his head, the heat of it setting the door lintel to smoking.

Thomas stumbled to a stop, realizing that he was in Dalrake's path. The sorcerer heaved his enchantment toward the magicians.

Thom threw himself to the rough cobblestones and the fire roared past him. The rush of power rolled him onto his side, his knapsack keeping him from rolling all the way over onto his back. Somewhere behind him, he heard another fireball thrown in response. He threw his arms over his face and curled up in a ball, afraid of what was about to happen.

The two enchantments collided not far from him.

The concussion skittered him across the stones like a fallen leaf pushed by a strong wind, scraping his arm raw. Then fire rained on him.

He screamed in agony as he burned.

* * *

"Thomas! Thomas!"

Someone was shaking him.

"Up to your feet, lad. I know it must hurt, but we need to flee."

He opened his eyes, trying to see the small man leaning over him. At first, he only saw a smear of colors, glaring in their brightness. He closed his eyes and reopened them, but the harsh colors were still there. Only then did he realize that it was Dorthos the Deranged urging him to move.

Thom's body throbbed with pain, making it hard to focus. He tried keeping his attention on the pixie's face because the man's jarring attire was causing his eyes to water. "What... what happened?"

Instead of answering, Dorthos helped him to sit up. Thom gasped as pain shot through his side. The explosion must have sent him sliding across the rough cobblestones. Gently, he felt the ripped side of his journeyman's robe and reached through it to pull down his shirt and cover the abraded skin. His arm screamed with pain but at least he could move it.

Once he had caught his breath, he looked around. There was no one else in the courtyard and the fires had died away. The main entrance gate was destroyed, as was part of the wall to either side. There was just a pile of jagged and charred stone.

"Where are the others?" he asked, wondering what had happened while he had been knocked out.

Dorthos was still trying to pull him to his feet. "They are all gone, Thomas. I think they have fled to the king's castle. We need to get away too or the sorcerers will take us. To your feet, lad."

Confused, Thom still complied. Fighting through the pain, he stood and took the staff that Dorthos handed him, leaning heavily on it for support. Confused, he started limping toward the ruined gates of Clas Myrddin.

"Not that way. You are in no shape to clamber over that pile of rubble, even if we had the time."

Thom stared dumbly at what had been the keep's main entrance. The pixie was right; the opening was blocked by a heap of stones.

"Come on, lad. We need to find another way out."

Dorthos led him around a corner and through a simpler door, entering a servants' passageway. The short man did his best to offer support, making sure he used his magician's staff to keep erect.

Thom let the pixie decide on their route, for he was still too rattled and in pain to think clearly.

They crept through the rambling guild house, always keeping to the servant passages when they could, descending to the lower level of the keep. They didn't encounter anyone else until they reached the main kitchen. There they found many of the human servants huddling in fear. Most of them didn't even make eye contact with the two, but the head cook stepped up and confronted the pair with a meat cleaver in his hand. He was a large, sweaty man whose countenance showed his anger. His focus was on Thomas.

"Out of my kitchen. We will not let you hide here, magician. I know who you are, you abandoned journeyman who no master will claim. You will not bring the sorcerers' wrath down on us."

Still confused and hurting, Thom struggled to understand why the man was so angry with him.

Dorthos answered. "He has been hurt. Show some pity. We only need some cloth for cleaning, some water, and maybe a bit of bread, then we will move on. Surely, you have no qualms with such measly aid."

The pixie grabbed a chunk of bread from a nearby basket, ignoring the cook's hiss of warning, and handed it to Thom.

"While he eats, you can tell us of the house's other gates. Are any of them still open?"

The cook glared at the pixie. "I've had enough of your kind. Take him out of here or else I'll retrieve a sorcerer to take you both away. I'm sure you are worth more to them dead and rendered than alive, you abhorrent midget."

Dorthos stared up at the red-faced man. Even in his confused state, Thom realized it was a look of condemnation.

"Among humans, I've found that many commoners are braver than the shiniest of knights," stated the pixie. "Sadly, in this kitchen, that is not the case." He pulled Thom away. "We will leave you to stew in your fears, cook."

The cook brandished his cleaver toward them.

Thom stepped back from the threat, but Dorthos ignored the cook as he grabbed a half-filled water skin from a hook near the oven and snagged a clean cloth from a nearby counter. "Come along, Thomas. We will find our own way out of this den of cowards."

* * *

They tried the Stable Gate, but found it held by two centaurs and a sorcerer. Thom was surprised to see the horse-men helping the invaders, but Dorthos only muttered that another of the Roads had been taken, claiming that the centaurs would never have come here by the Road of Clouds. They had probably come by river galley the pixie surmised.

Even in his fog of pain, Thom realized that was bad news.

Dorthos pulled Thomas back and led him to the one remaining exit, the Garden Gate that only the servants ever used. Thom drank some of the water and tried to chew a bite of bread as he walked, but he found that even his jaw ached. He gave up and let the piece of bread fall from his opened mouth; pain had robbed him of any hunger.

They made it the guild house gardens and could see that the gate was unguarded, so they hurried to make their escape. Unfortunately, a sorcerer was standing watch on one of the guild house's towers. The sorcerer spotted them and began a hasty crafting of magic.

Thom heard it clearly, in spite of his pain and shouted a warning to the pixie.

They rushed along the garden path and under the boughs of mature fruit trees just as the sorcerer released the enchantment. A fireball roared at them, but the entwining tree branches saved them, taking the brunt of the flames.

As Thom and Dorthos staggered out the unlocked gate, the trees behind them turned into an inferno. The resulting smoke screened them from the sorcerer up in the tower and they took full advantage of it, running down the nearest side street and away from Clas Myrddin.

Thom was distracted from his pain by the horrible sounds he heard with his inner ear: clashing enchantments everywhere and magical explosions. Something else was wrong but it took some time for him to realize what it was, because its sound was so subtle. Softly, in the background of everything else he was hearing, was the soft hum of the city's encompassing enchantment and there was now a stutter to that rhythm. For some reason, that decades-old enchantment was now unstable, and they were caught inside that magic. Should it fail, all would die. Thom swallowed hard when he realized that, but he said nothing to Dorthos since there was nothing they could do about it.

EIGHT

Closed Roads

They stopped in an alley so that Dorthos could tend Thom's injuries, pulling out the cloth he had taken from the kitchen and pouring some water on it from the waterskin. He urged Thom to sit down on an old crate that lay in the alley they were in. "Let me see your wounds, Thomas. I should at least clean them before we go any farther."

Thom gave into his ministrations. It hurt as the pixie thoroughly scrubbed the grit out of his weeping side and arm, but at least they found no broken bones nor any cuts bleeding profusely. The pixie had him bow his head so that he could look at the large bump on the back of his head. It hurt terribly as the pixie touched and prodded his skull, but Thom held still.

"You are thoroughly battered, but nothing seems broken," Dorthos declared, letting go of Thom's scalp. "You should be most careful with that bump on your head, and let me know if you grow dizzy or your vision becomes blurry. As for the other wounds, they should heal well as long as infection is kept at bay. You'll have a goodly amount of bruises everywhere for some time, but I think you will mend well."

Thom was glad to hear that, though he didn't feel so well. He considered getting rid of his ripped journeyman's robe, but the pixie suggested he keep it on for now. "It intimidates the commoners and might gain us some aid. You would have to get rid of the knapsack too if you want to deceive the sorcerers, but I doubt you want to be without your magical powders. For that matter, you will have to get rid of me too, for my stature is more obvious than any garments- even my own."

Thom saw the truth in that and would have nodded his agreement, but his head was still swimming from when Dorthos had moved it about during his examination.

"We should rest here for a time and eat that bread we took," suggested the pixie. "You need some time to recover."

Thom surrendered the last of the bread willingly and only grudgingly took a morsel of it back. This time he was able to eat some, the ache of his jaw of no consequence when compared to his pounding head.

It was Dorthos who picked their next destination. He chose to head for Camelot Castle, reasoning that the wizards and pixies had retreated to the king's side.

It took a few hours to cross to the western end of the city because they kept to narrow roads and twisting alleys, but they made it. However, they found King Arthur's keep already under siege from sorcerers aided by an army of knights and centaurs. There was no way they would be able to get past them and to those barricaded inside.

Thom wondered if Adele was trapped inside there. If she was then she was safe— for now. His worries next turned to his king. The enemy was obviously after Arthur. He took some comfort from hearing enchantments being crafted on the ramparts. The retreating guild magicians must have come here to help protect the king.

He saw the griffins again. The eagle-lions were swooping over the castle and dropping large boulders on the defenders. Some of the magicians tried to strike back with magic, but the monsters were too swift.

It was obvious that neither Thom nor Dorthos would be able to get through, not with the two sides hurling magic at each other. Just then a windstorm enchantment was thrown from the castle, only to be met by a fireball from some sorcerer. The two enchantments crashed into each other and exploded, tearing up the grasses just beyond the castle wall.

"There is no way we can get to them, and I am uncertain I would want to," stated Dorthos.

"Can we somehow help them to fight off these invaders?"

Dorthos looked up at him with a grin. "I love your courage, Road Saver, but the two of us cannot break the siege. Your mind is too rattled to concentrate on any crafting and I am without a weapon beyond my belt knife. As heroic as it sounds, this is not our time to charge into the fray."

"What should we do then?" asked Thom. It was already late afternoon and the nearby fighting showed no sign of abating. "We can't linger this close to the castle and expect to go unnoticed much longer."

"Truth in that. We need to escape down one of the Roads," said Dorthos, helping Thom to his feet. "Once we you are recovered and I am fully armed, then we can return and drive off this scum. Come. Rowan Gate is not so far from here."

Reluctantly, Thom agreed, letting the pixie lead him away. Leaving somehow felt like abandoning his fellow magicians during their time of need, but he knew there wasn't anything he could do to help them now.

As they retreated, his thoughts returned to Adele. He wondered where she sheltered, whether at the castle or at the monastery. Wherever she was, he hoped she was well protected.

* * *

It took some time to reach Rowan Gate, for they were forced to hide twice as centaur patrols trotted by. For all their effort they were too late, for they were denied entrance to the Road of Leaves also. In the last light of the day, Thom spotted a large group of centaurs guarding the courtyard to Rowan Gate. From beyond the high wall that surrounded the courtyard, Thom could hear an open magician's box but no one was crafting any enchantment at the moment.

He told Dorthos what he heard, suggesting that he could destroy the exposed element cache with a well-aimed enchantment.

The pixie shook his head. "Your attack will expose our presence. Do you think you can outrun that herd of horse-men? Or stop the retaliation of any sorcerer who survives your blind attack?"

Thom knew that Dorthos was right, but the open magician's box still bothered him. "Why would anyone expose his presence? He is just begging to be attacked."

"So he is either an idiot or, more likely, this is a trap. How do you know that the owner of the cache is standing over it? What would happen if a wizard charged out of the Road of Leaves and suddenly heard the magical elements like you do? Would he not target his hastily-crafted enchantment at that very spot? And if the sorcerer is elsewhere with another magician's box, would he not be able to then kill the wizard before the attacker could craft a second enchantment?"

Thom's breath caught, although the thought of wasting such a precious supply of elements was beyond him. Dorthos was right. For one who couldn't do magic, the pixie had a better grasp of how to fight with the craft than Thom.

"Well, if we cannot escape down the Road of Leaves, where should we go?"

Camelot had four Roads: Clouds in the south, Leaves in the west, Short in the north, and Waters in the east. He was going to suggest they head for the harbor, but Dorthos answered his own question.

"We shall try the Short Roads when they open at dawn, but I doubt Sorcerer Dalrake has left it unguarded. The invasion of Camelot is too thorough, too planned. I think the attacks on the Roads were merely the vanguard of taking all of Arthur's domain."

"Maybe we should go to King's Harbor instead…"

Dorthos the Deranged shook his head emphatically. "That route is already closed to us. That is obvious from all the centaurs in the city."

"Might they have invaded from the Short Roads?"

"Doubtful. Moving so many centaurs across the exposed countryside would have been noticed. No, Dalrake used Merlin's magic against him. By keeping to the Roads, the centaurs and soldiers were hidden to all who weren't on that particular enchanted route."

Thom couldn't argue with the crazy man's wisdom.

* * *

They fled the general area of the Rowan Gate, but with night settling in and Thom's strength quickly waning, they decided to find a place to shelter for the night. They had passed numerous parties that had packed their belongings into handcarts and were trying to flee the city. People were abandoning their houses and shops in fear of what was happening, even though the fighting had not yet reached this part of the city.

Dorthos noted one cooper's shop with its door askew and looked in. The owners had apparently fled in haste, taking their most valuable goods and possessions with them, but you can't easily pack and flee with half-finished casks or the many heavy metal tools used in shaping, making, and repairing barrels.

"I think we will shelter here tonight," stated the pixie. "We will be less noticeable behind a closed door than out on the streets."

Thom was reluctant, for it seemed like trespassing, but he had no better idea. So they stayed there for the night, sleeping on the dirty floor behind a stack of finished barrels. Neither had any desire to take any of the leftover bedding in the back room, so they shared Thom's travel blanket and settled in as darkness fell in the city around them. Should any invaders break in, they would likely miss the pair sheltered among the wood. It made for a restless night, but Thom's pain would have robbed him of any slumber even if he were in the most comfortable of beds.

* * *

At dawn, they set off again, making their careful way northward. Thom walked with a throbbing headache, a painful side, and a limp, but he kept up with the pixie's shorter stride. By late morning, they came to the edge of the large square that fronted the city's outer wall and the twin towers that pierced it. Through each tower passed a paved road, well guarded by stout doors. These were the Double Gates, the entrance to the Short Roads, one magical route leading away from the city and the other path leading into it.

The gates should have been opened hours earlier, but they found them still shut and a herd of centaurs standing watch at that end of the square. A large crowd milled in the plaza, folks anxious to get out of the city, but the presence of armed centaurs kept them from getting too close to the gates.

"What now?" Thom asked. He wondered if the owners of the cooperage were among the crowd in front of them.

"Let us linger here at the edge of the square for a time and see if they open the gates later. There are many here who seem to think they will."

"Even if they do, will they let us pass through?" asked Thom. He feared that they would deny exit to the pixie.

"Let us see. I can pretend to be a human child if I must."

So they stayed there for a few hours, hoping the gates would open. At noon they did, but only for the road coming into Camelot.

The centaur guards pushed forward, to clear more area around that gate, and then it opened as a band of armored knights rode through, dozens of men behind two banners, one displaying the black crow of Dalrake and the other the two-headed eagle on blue of Prince Mordred, the bastard son of King Arthur. The men were hidden behind their helms, but Thom wondered if one of them was Mordred himself.

"It looks like the Short Roads now connect to Mordred's keep," said Dorthos, his voice low and sad.

The centaurs continued to push the crowds away as more men arrived through the magical road behind them. Foot soldiers were starting to march through. Hundreds of them.

Thom and Dorthos were watching from the mouth of an alley, so they weren't yet feeling the press of people.

"Another Road closed to us," noted the pixie.

"We should seek refuge at the Saint Barnabas Monastery," suggest Thom.

"I want to try the Road of Waters first. Maybe that route is clear for us now."

Thom wasn't sure about that, but since both the Road of Waters and the monastery were at the eastern end of the city, they didn't need to settle their difference yet.

"We should move on before the centaurs cause the crowds to stampede," said Dorthos. "I have no desire to be trampled."

Thom agreed but, before they could slip down the alley behind them, they were spotted.

A sharp-eyed centaur shouted out and pointed at them. Whether it was Thom's dark blue robes or the garishly-garbed pixie that caught his eye didn't matter. The horse-man shouted out to his companions and six of them charged across the crowded square, forcing people to scamper out of the way. They raced toward the alley where the two were hunkered.

It took a moment for Thom to realize that it was indeed them that had attracted the centaurs. He looked around for Arthur's warriors but realized they were none. "Are they coming for us?"

"We must run!" replied Dorthos, yanking on his sleeve and indicating the narrow alley.

So Thom and Dorthos ran. The young man's limp made them about the same speed.

Before they reached the end of the alley, he heard the clatter of hooves entering its mouth behind them. The centaurs were too fast. He felt panic rise in his throat, threatening to cut off his breath.

The horse-men would have caught them within a block, if not for Dorthos' quick thinking. As they left the alley and were running down an abandoned street, the pixie was looking up at the roofs to either side. He suddenly swerved, running up to a closed mercantile and found the door locked. He then grabbed a chair on its porch and, with all of his force, threw it into the shop's unshuttered window, shattering the expensive glass panes.

"We need to get to the roofs," Dorthos told him as he cleared out the shards still clinging in the frame. "Centaurs dislike heights. That is the only way we can escape."

Even as Dorthos was climbing inside, a centaur arrow slammed into the window's frame near Thom's head. He hurried to follow the pixie, using his staff to knock out the last piece of glass hanging in the way.

Dorthos looked around the darkened store and then ran for the back room, pushing past the stacks and bins of goods. Thom kept close behind him, following him up a stairway.

They were almost to the upper floor, when the shop's heavyset owner appeared at the top of the stairs and demanded to know who they were.

The pixie ignored him and raced past. Thom muttered an apology as he also ran by, having to push the man to avoid his attempt to restrain him. He was glad the man had no weapon in his hands.

Dorthos ran into the bedroom, jumping on the unmade bed to reach the window behind it. There was no glass in this window, so the pixie just unlatched the wooden shutters and threw them open, scrambling up the window sill and out onto the tiled roof beyond.

As Thom stepped onto the bed to follow, the owner yelled at him, again demanding to know what was going on.

Thom paused, not wanting the man to come to harm. "We are being chased by centaurs. You should hide to avoid their fury or at least go down and open the door so that they don't have to crash through. They want us, not you."

The man just scowled at Thom.

He hesitated, wanting to make things right. "When I can, I will send you coins for the broken window. You have my word on it, the word of Journeyman Thomas."

The man wasn't appeased and tried grabbing him again. Thom batted away the man's reach with his staff, trying not to injure him. The owner lost his balance while dodging the staff and fell backward, allowing Thom the moment he need to escape out the window too.

As he exited, he heard the front door crash inward. Even as Dorthos yelled for him to follow, he paused to urge the man to seek safety. "You need to hide, sir, for they are coming after us. Go into your closet before they see you."

"Thomas!" Dorthos was more emphatic in his call.

The shopkeeper was still watching when Thom turned to cross the roof in pursuit of the pixie. He hoped the shopkeeper listened.

Dorthos climbed to the peak of the roof and then started running. Thom watched him leap over the gap to the next roof, landing on his feet. The little man looked back and motioned for him to follow.

Taking a deep breath, Thom ran too, though not as surefooted. Right at the edge he jumped and made it, but his landing was not as graceful. He tumbled, almost losing his grip on his staff, and then started sliding down the other roof. He clawed at the tiles, but there wasn't anything to grip, then he saw a chimney below and stretched out his staff to help catch it. He was able to stop his plunge to the ground, but it cost him bloodied fingers and new pain to his wounded side and arm.

"Up to your feet, Thomas. We need to keep going. The centaurs will not follow us onto the rooftops but they can still reach us here with their great bows."

NINE

Overheard Death

They jumped three more times and then scrambled down a rain-spout into an alley that connected to a different street. For now, they had escaped the centaurs.

Before going any farther, Thom took off his robe and shoved it into the backpack. His clothes were threadbare and too short on him, but less conspicuous. That wasn't anything he could do to disguise his knapsack, but magicians weren't the only ones carrying a bag over their shoulder.

As for Dorthos' bright clothes, there was nothing that could be done about them now. Maybe if they came across a shop that sold children's clothing he could suggest a change, thought Thom, but he suspected the pixie would be offended by the idea. Besides, he had something more important to convince Dorthos to accept.

"I think we should go the monastery," said Thom again.

"I think not," argued Dorthos. "Most of the religious frown on magic and that is part of my very nature."

"Not the Father Abbot. He will offer us refuge."

"Do you think he will hide me if some sorcerer threatens the monastery? If it came to a stranger pixie or his beloved brethren, who do you think he would choose? Me?"

Thom wanted to argue that the abbot would, but he wasn't certain of it. His pause confirmed the pixie's suspicions.

Dorthos grunted, but then surprisingly nodded. "I will go with you to the monastery, since we have nowhere else to hide, but I do not promise that I will stay there. If nothing else, I will see you to its dubious safety."

Thom nodded back, knowing better than to keep arguing his point. At least the pixie was willing to try.

* * *

As they hurried down nearly-empty streets, they passed some families pulling handcarts filled with their most-treasured possessions heading toward the Short Roads. Maybe the centaurs would let them flee the city, but Thom doubted it. He suspected everyone was now trapped inside Camelot until the sorcerers had the city fully in their hands.

A block further away, they encountered a body sprawled halfway through the doorway to a butcher's shop. A large arrow protruded from the dead man's back and blood stained his clothes and the ground. Although there were other people on the street, no one showed any concern for the dead man. Thom noticed that they avoided looking, as if not staring would change the unpleasant truth- that their neighbor had been murdered.

41

The two decided to take the next alley just to get off this exposed street. They turned between an open carpenter's shop and a mercantile that had its windows shuttered. As they walked by the carpenter's open back door, Thom could hear a worker sawing and smelled the fresh sawdust. It seemed odd to hear something so normal on such a chaotic day. Either the shopkeeper was ignorant of the invasion or had decided to keep working in spite of the turmoil elsewhere in the city. Thom thought the carpenter was being foolish, for they had seen smoke rising from a building fire a few blocks over. While this street was peaceful right now, that could change quickly.

They were soon past the carpenter's shop, hurrying down a wide and relatively clean alley. Because this was a better section of the city, they passed numerous gardens behind high walls. Trees and plants thrived inside the enchantment of Camelot, even if animals did not. Thom could smell ripening fruit and fragrant flowers. A pair of Scarlet Bees buzzed past. In this secluded corner of the city it seemed like nothing was amiss. At least it did if you couldn't hear the sounds of the magical battle still happening around the castle.

They nearly walked out in plain sight of another centaur patrol, but spotted it farther up the road before the horse-men saw them. Hastily, they ran back down the wide alley before the patrol made it this far. They were nearly back to the carpenter's shop when they heard hooves on the cobblestones of that street. They both stopped and looked around from some shelter, but the alley was too clean.

"What now?" asked Thom, ready to take off his knapsack and start an enchantment.

"No magic," replied Dorthos, as if having read Thom's thoughts. Instead, he pointed at the walled yards on one side of the alley. "We need to hide in one of these gardens."

Thom didn't argue. He ran to the nearest wooden gate and tried to open it. It was barred for the inside.

"Boost me over, Thomas, then I'll give you hand up. Be quick about it."

He gave the short man a step up and then tossed his staff over the wall and jumped to grab the top of the gate himself. Dorthos' strong grip helped pull him up.

They dropped into a lush and overgrown garden. A large house was partially visible through the foliage, but it was either empty or its occupants were in hiding, for no one ever came out to confront the two trespassers. Journeyman and pixie moved hastily under the nearest trees and then listened for any pursuit. None came.

For now, they had escaped the centaurs.

Dorthos sat down in the shade of a plum tree, leaning his back against the garden wall.

Thom winced when he tried to do the same, grabbing at the back of his head. He had almost forgotten his injuries in all their running around, but the large lump now reminded him of his tumble at the guild house. He tried leaning back again, but this time more carefully, letting his knapsack cushion his back and keep his head away from the hard stone wall.

They decided to spend the rest of the day sitting in the shade of that plum tree, resting until sunset. They ate some of the ripe fruit, for the moisture as much as for nourishment. Thom asked Dorthos to help him find this place again later so that he could repay the owner for what they took. Dorthos nodded, apparently understanding his need to be diligent in his honesty; Thom didn't want to slip back into the habits of his thieving childhood.

* * *

The killings began in the early afternoon.

Thom didn't notice the noise at first since wounded magical beings are not as loud as the crafting of an enchantment, but there were so many. He stared in that direction, although he couldn't see anything from this far away. He hesitated in telling Dorthos, for they were killing his people, but the pixie noticed the change in his demeanor.

"What is happening?" asked Deranged Dorthos.

Thom didn't want to answer; he remembered that the man's wife had been murdered.

"Tell me," he ordered in a harsh whisper.

"I hear the rhythms of wounded beings. People wounded grievously and then silenced." He didn't want to say it, but the sudden silence came from death.

Dorthos needed no further explanation. "They are killing my people for their magic."

Thom expected the pixie to jump to his feet and start running back to Clas Myrddin. Instead, Dorthos bit into a plum. Thom thought him insanely callous until he saw tears running down his cheeks like the plum juice dripping off his chin. Yet he sat there and finished the plum, saying nothing and looking at nothing. He seemed so deadened to the news.

Thom noticed the pixie digging into the soil beside him, then he spat the plum pit into his weathered hand and carefully placed it into the hole. Without looking down, he swept the dirt back over the seed and patted it in place.

Thom looked up from the plum pit burial when a sudden noise came out of the pixie, an agonizing groan.

Dorthos sobbed and did not stop until an hour after the killing ended.

Thom cried as well, finding magic abhorrent and wondering why he ever wanted to practice this cruel art.

TEN

The Monastery

They waited until evening's cloak spread over the city before moving on. It was now the second night since the fall of Clas Myrddin and the invasion of the city. The magical fighting had stopped a few hours after the pixie killing, though Thom doubted they were related. The magic surrounding the city was regaining its rhythm, as if it were slowly healing, and that was likely directly connected to the killings. The pixies had been sacrificed to stabilize the magic. Once again, Thom saw how ugly his chosen craft could be.

Now, as the sunset settled the city into shadows, the silence deepened. Thom's inner ear discerned only the faint hum-beat of the enchantment that enveloped the city and nothing more. Why weren't they fighting anymore? He wondered if one side had won and, if so, which side.

When he asked his companion, Dorthos grunted his doubts and shook his head. "It is a lull. We go to the monastery as planned."

At least the pixie was talking to him now. For hours, Dorthos hadn't replied to anything he said. The pixie cared deeply for his people and took their deaths as a personal offense, almost as if he *was* their leader. Maybe the man really believed the stories he told about being a prince to his people. He certainly seemed to feel for them as if they were his responsibility.

Thom wanted to comfort him, but he didn't know what to say. He remembered losing his mother so long ago and the death of his master only a few weeks ago, but he didn't know what it was like to learn of dozens of your people getting slaughtered just to gain their innate magic. He whispered a prayer, asking God to do something to bring comfort where he couldn't, then led the way out from under the night-shadow of the plum tree and went up to the garden wall. There was a gate, but the locking latch defeated his attempt to open it. Rather than fight with it, he decided it would be easier to just climb the wall again.

Dorthos let him make the decisions and readily let Thom give him a boost up. As he helped him scramble over, Thom thought the scrapping sounds were very loud. Even when he tossed his staff over, it seemed loud as it clattered on the cobblestones. He did his best to be quiet himself, as he jumped up and grabbed the edge, but it wasn't easy to stifle a cry of pain as his slipped over the hard stones. Once down, he retrieved his staff and then followed the pixie down the alley. At the far end, they stopped to stare at a glowing sky. Part of the city was truly on fire now. Thom wondered why no magician had gone to douse the flames with a water enchantment, and decided that the battle at the castle wasn't decided after all. The sorcerers and wizards were still entwined in their battle, even if no one was crafting any magic at the moment, so neither side had time for the city. Dorthos must have guessed right, that it was just a lull in the fighting.

Thom led onward, picking their route across a silent city.

* * *

The night provided cover, but it also concealed the invaders. The centaurs were easier to avoid at night, their hooves loud on the cobblestones, but the human patrols were much quieter and as the night wore on there seemed to be more of them. Nonetheless, Thom was able to keep them unnoticed as they made their way toward the monastery, but it required a lot of skulking in alleys and hunkering behind crates. Somehow, he succeeded in getting them to the eastern edge of Camelot city, but it had taken a long time. The night was now old.

When he finally saw the gates of Saint Barnabas, his feeling of success fled. The gates were closed and they were numerous people huddled around the square it faced, most likely refugees waiting for the monastery to open at dawn. Thom considered what to do. It would be too obvious if they walked up to those large doors and banged on them until someone answered. The city was too silent and they had dodged a centaur patrol just a few streets away from here. If he made a commotion, the others awaiting entrance would also stir and add their voices. It would be too much. He decided to see if he could find a more obscure entrance.

He led Dorthos around the large compound, keeping to the night shadows as much as he could even though the moon was just a quarter of its size. He found a postern gate and tried gaining entrance there, but no one responded to his rapping and the walls were too tall to climb. He dared not yell or pound, so he withdrew in frustration.

In the end, he and Dorthos had to hide in a cluttered alley for the night and wait the last two hours for dawn's arrival and hopefully the opening of the main gate. Neither of them truly slept, but they rested.

No patrol ever came down that lane but they did hear a griffin's cry overhead once. They kept perfectly still to prevent detection and the lion-eagle passed unaware, the next scream came from farther away, to the southeast. A bit later, Thom heard a new surge of magic, coming from the area of the harbor if he judged rightly. Then he heard two enchantments collide and explode. It was in the same direction as the griffin had flown. He told Dorthos about the magic.

"Maybe a magician is trying to escape down the Road of Waters," he said. "I hope he makes it."

Thom heard two more enchantments quickly made and then exploding as they clashed. Then it became silent again. He heard no more magic that night, beyond the gently hum of the city's enveloping enchantment that was always there in the background of his hearing. Whatever had happened at the harbor, it was done now.

* * *

When the monastery's gates opened after sunrise mass, the two hustled across the plaza and joined the other newcomers that walked past the welcoming monk. Thom felt almost pushed through the gates by the resumed magical battle that was happening at the other end of the city. Even at this distance, his inner ear could hear the clashes of elements and he strained to discern the rhythms of their powerful enchantments. Because of the noise, he wanted to get inside and tell others; if nothing else, the abbot should be warned.

He was so focused on the distant battle, that he took little notice of the many people who were already inside, sheltering in the forecourt. Instead, he absently stepped around them as he led Dorthos toward the tall chapel that stood at the other end of the courtyard.

They did not stop until they were up the stone steps and inside the dim chapel. Only then did Thom leave off trying to hear the distant magic and focused on his surroundings again. He stopped at the back of the towering hall and surveyed it. The chapel was also crowded, and not with resident monks or nuns from the convent. The long hall was full of city folk standing quietly in prayer, their few possessions at their feet.

"We are not the only ones to seek refuge here," whispered Dorthos in a voice so low that Thom barely heard it.

He had planned to take the pixie directly to Abbot Justin, but reconsidered when he saw the crowds. The Father Abbot was probably too busy for them. He decided to find his friend Francis first and ask him to get them in to see the abbot.

Although now eager to locate Francis, he took the time to show proper respect. Thom crossed himself in the name of the Father, Son, and Holy Spirit, then knelt to offer a brief prayer. It couldn't hurt to ask for divine help, though he doubted God was much concerned with a former thief. Dorthos stood next to him, head bowed but did none of the other rituals. Thom wondered if pixies worshiped God in a different way, but he felt it presumptuous to ask so he said nothing about it.

After praying, Thom led Dorthos out the side door. He had decided to look for Francis in the scriptorium, for that was where his friend usually worked. He passed the gurgling fountain where he and Francis had talked only a day... no... two days ago. From some reason, Thom wondered where its water came from; he assumed one of Camelot's twenty-three springs fed it. But where did those springs exist? They must move along with the city, but how did that work? The thought was only fleeting, though, for his focus was on finding his friend.

A slim, middle-aged monk was walking through the courtyard too, carrying a hoe and a shovel. When he saw them, he motioned for them to go back. "This area is not open to those seeking refuge. I must ask you to return to the chapel or to the forecourt by the front gates."

"Forgive our trespass, brother," replied Thom, "but we are looking for Brother Francis. I know that he is usually to be found in the scriptorium, assisting Brother Colwyn with the books and scrolls."

"Outsiders should keep to the chapel and the forecourt," insisted the monk, now frowning at them. His eyes kept going to the garishly-dressed Dorthos and Thom wasn't sure if the monk disapproved more of the pixie's race or his attire.

"It is urgent, brother," continued Thom, trying to keep the frustration out of his voice. Maybe the monk would have been more respectful if he had been wearing his magician's robe, but Thom had kept to his normal clothes out of caution. "We have much news about the invasion of the city and the taking of the Magicians' Guild house."

"That should be told to the Father Abbot, not to a simple monk like Francis."

"We were hoping that Francis could help us get word to Abbot Justin, knowing that the Father Abbot is an important and busy man."

The monk nodded. "The Father Abbot is indeed busy."

"Then you will let us go on to the scriptorium?" suggested Thom.

The monk folded his arms. "These grounds are holy; outsiders shouldn't be here. It is bad enough that noblemen have taken over the guest house. No, you must keep to the chapel and the forecourt."

"Oh, for the love of God, then go fetch Francis for us," blurted out Dorthos. "War has come to the city and you worry about a delay in your gardening. Go tell Francis that we wait for him in the chapel and be quick about it."

"I have no time to search out Brother Francis," argued the monk, looking at Thom instead of the pixie. "I am already late to my assigned chores."

"Then let us pass," said Thom. "We promise to go straight to the scriptorium. I have been there often and have even helped the brethren in reading and sorting through some of the newest acquisitions. I know the way."

The brother stared at Thom, then at Dorthos, and then back at Thom. His frown deepened, but he motioned toward the monastery's library. "Go then, but no side trips. We cannot have outsiders wandering the grounds; there *are* limits to the compassion we offer. Our godly duties cannot be interrupted."

Thom thanked him and hurried on with Dorthos, before the monk could reconsider.

* * *

They made it to the scriptorium without any other problems. Thom entered the quiet refuge and turned right, leading Dorthos down one of the rows. He looked for Francis, but instead he found only the librarian. Brother Colwyn first noticed the pixie and gave a questioning look, but then smiled when he noticed it was Thom with him. "I almost failed to recognize you, journeyman, without your magician's robe. So Francis found you! Did he tell you to wait here while he reported to the Father Abbot?"

That confused Thom. "What do you mean? I'm here looking for Francis."

The librarian's smile wilted. "He went out in the chaos to find you. He insisted on it. You have not seen him?"

"No. Dorthos is the one who helped me escape the guild house. We've been all over the city, trying to find a way out but there is none, so we came here. Are you saying that Francis went looking for me?"

"Oh, this is not good. Where is Brother Francis, if not with you? The Father Abbot will not like this."

Thom nodded. "He should be told. I think he will also want to hear our tale, for we saw the taking of Clas Myrddin, the siege starting on the king's castle, and more."

"Maybe we should all go to the abbot and talk with him," suggested Dorthos.

Brother Colwyn frowned at the pixie's suggestion. "Outsiders are not allowed to wander the monastery grounds… and do not try finding him on your own. Legends might claim that your kind are able to disappear, but there is no chance that you could vanish in such eye-straining attire, pixie. No, you two will have to wait here while I find Abbot Justin."

He led them to an almost-barren study at the rear of the scriptorium and asked them to remain there until he returned.

Before the librarian could close the door, Thom asked one more thing of him. "Brother Colwyn, do you know if any lady from the castle is sheltering here at Saint Barnabas?"

"There may be some women sheltering at the convent— there are numerous noblemen at the monastery's guest house after all— but she wouldn't be on this side of the wall unless she was among the commoners sheltering in the forecourt and chapel."

Colwyn glanced at Dorthos one more time, absently shaking his head at something, then quickly left.

ELEVEN

Mousehome's Door

During their time alone, Thom decided he ought to get into his journeyman's robe again. He removed it from his knapsack then tried to smooth the worst of its many wrinkles and to fold the cloth over the rip in the side. Finding that futile, he still slipped it over his head, doing it slowly because of all the injuries. The robe settled over his stained clothes; it wasn't much of an improvement but it felt right.

As he dressed, Dorthos was pacing the room, seeming anxious to get moving again. Thom understand his companion's restlessness. He must feel like a mouse trapped in a deadly maze. Thom wanted to help the pixie escape the city but he didn't know how he could do so. He didn't even have any encouraging words to share, so he just sat on a stool and watched as the pixie paced.

When the door opened again, Colwyn led Abbot Justin inside. He carefully closed the door behind them.

The abbot stepped forward and grasped Thom's hand in a strong handshake. "Welcome, journeyman. I am glad you are safe; I only wish that Brother Francis stood here too. But, God willing, he will soon. Francis is a tough one; I have seen him come through worse."

He turned to Dorthos. "You are also welcome, sir pixie. Please introduce yourself."

The small man bowed. "I call myself Prince Dorthos. Some others call me Dorthos the Deranged."

Justin nodded. Thom couldn't tell what the abbot thought of such an introduction.

"Well Dorthos, you will soon be reunited with some of your brethren who have also found refuge here."

Dorthos raised an eyebrow in surprise. "I am glad to hear that, but I am puzzled. Most religious houses fear those of us who are magical. They act as if our very being was an affront to God."

Justin sighed. "I must admit that some of my brethren are superstitious like that, but most here are not. I want Saint Barnabas Monastery to be as welcoming as our namesake, who risked embracing a terrible persecutor who claimed to have changed. There is much less risk embracing magical beings, except for maybe a mermaid…"

The abbot blushed at his own joke.

Dorthos chuckled. "Indeed. It would be best to leave them to their mermen."

"In truth, even merfolk are welcome here though I doubt they would travel this far from water." The abbot turned his focus back to Thom. "I want to hear what you have experienced these last few days, but please keep it short. Camelot is falling around us and just as I am expecting visitors. Dalrake's timing could prove disastrous."

Thom sensed the abbot wasn't upset because the war had ruined some garden party. Whoever the visitors were, it was no social call. He wondered if it had anything to do with the League of Barnabas. But now wasn't the time to ask; the abbot was looking at him in expectation of his report. So he shared what had happened over the last two days, trying his best to keep it concise. Dorthos added a few comments, but left most of the talking to Thom.

The abbot shook his head when the tale ended. "It is dire for the city and the kingdom. I would like to linger and hear more details, but I cannot. There are so many others demanding my attention, from noblemen seeking refuge to the commoners crowding our courtyard." He turned to the librarian who was still with them. "Brother Colwyn, please escort them to Mousehome, for I cannot think of any other place to shelter them. I do not think either will expose our secret. After all, Thomas has known of the league for some time now and has said nothing to the Guild."

When Colwyn gave a nod of acceptance, the abbot turned back to Thom. "You are about to enter the league's shelter. Do you swear to keep our secrets? I cannot have the Guild or the sorcerers learning of our existence too soon. They would surely seek our destruction if they learned about us."

"I will tell no one of your secrets. I may not be a member, but I deeply care for some who are."

Justin smiled. "That you do."

"Do you know if Lady Adele and Journeywoman Vivien are at the monastery?"

"Vivien is either at Mousehome or at the convent. I am uncertain about Lady Adele, for she is only here for lessons and spends the rest of her time at the king's castle. Too much is still in confusion and the invaders have not even entered our part of the city yet."

Thom nodded understanding, becoming more worried about her. Was she trapped inside a castle under attack? Had she been caught out in the city during the invasion? He whispered a prayer for Adele's safety. It wasn't much, but he thought it might be more likely heard when said on such sanctified grounds.

The abbot moved toward the door, but paused with his hand on the latch. "Colwyn, make certain that their injuries are tended. Thomas' head especially needs some attention. And I would suggest the journeyman go in his street clothes; we don't want to double the offense. If you can disguise that staff in any way, please do so. Maybe wrap that jewel in cloth or add it to a bundle of sticks to carry. Something to make it less obviously a magician's staff."

"Yes, Father Abbot," said Colwyn.

Thom struggled to pull off the robe he had just put on, catching his breath as sore muscles tightened. Dorthos helped him stuff it away in his pack.

The abbot nodded his approval and opened the door and strode away. Colwyn caught the door before it could swing shut. "Come along. I might as well get the two of you to Mousehome now. There is a gardener's shack behind the scriptorium where we should be able to find some stakes to bundle around your staff. Many at the monastery do not know about the league so we will need to be circumspect as we cross the grounds." He frowned at Dorthos. "I wish I had a robe to cover those garish clothes, but we have nothing so small."

"That is for the best, for I will not pretend to be a monk. No one would believe it anyways, for my form is too comely to be draped in ebony curtains."

The librarian monk chose not to reply. Instead, he held the door open and motioned the two down a poorly lit hallway. He pushed past them in the narrow way and led them to a side door. Motioning for quiet, he opened it a little and look out, but then softly shut it again.

"We will need to wait here a few minutes until the way is clear," he whispered.

"Where is this Mousehome?" asked Thom, having caught the abbot's strange reference. "Is it close?"

"You will find out soon enough," said Colwyn. "Mousehome is the Father Abbot's nickname for the league's corner here at the monastery. The Father Abbot must trust the two of you greatly to allow you entry there."

"Are you in this League of Barnabas?" asked Dorthos bluntly.

Brother Colwyn smiled. "I am, though I have no skill in magic. There are a handful of brethren who have joined, for we believe strongly in the Father Abbot's vision of a league to defend the land and its people."

"You are not troubled by magic?" asked Thom, knowing how much it bothered his friend Francis.

The monk tilted his head slightly to the right as he considered Thom's question. A small smile touched his lips. "It troubles me, but so does war. It seems that magicians and warriors are both tempted to cruelty and abuse. I think those are hazards in either profession. But there can also be good, such as defending the weak and righting wrongs."

Colwyn went to the door and peeked out again. "The others are well-and-gone. Come with me and do your best to remain inconspicuous." He frowned at Dorthos' height and bright garb. "Try to stay out of sight."

* * *

The monk librarian led them away from the scriptorium. They followed a trellised walkway that was shaded by bloom-ladened vines, the fragrant air abuzz with Scarlet Bees gathering pollen. Nearby was a row of beehives and Thom remembered Francis mentioning that the monastery was known for its beeswax candles and honey. He wondered where his friend was now. He hoped Francis would safely return soon.

They stopped at a gardener's shed, where Colwyn gathered a bundle of garden stakes. He helped Thomas hide his staff within the bundle and then the librarian offered to carry it since the magician was rather weak from his injuries. The difference in woods was obvious, but from a distance it would seem that the librarian was carrying an assortment of woods.

Colwyn led them by a shortcut through a dormitory, since all the monks were away, and then had them wait hidden behind a low wall until a trio of brethren passed by with small handcarts ladened with freshly-pulled tubers and carrots. Once those men were out of sight, Colwyn led them through another courtyard where Royal Blue chickens pecked at corn someone must have tossed out for them earlier. They were a proud brood, strutting in the sunlight so that their blue-black feathers shone.

The only magical thing about Royal Blues that Thom knew about was their extraordinary taste; the very thought of it made his mouth water. But he doubted he would get a taste of their delectable meat while here; monks weren't prone to waste a good bird for a fine meal, especially one of the few animals that could stand living inside an enchantment all of its life. They likely wanted them for their eggs only.

Even though his stomach embarrassingly grumbled, food was not utmost in his thoughts. As they walked, he was looking for any glimpse of his former companions like Journeywoman Vivien or his friend Francis. Most of all, he wanted to find Adele and know that she was safe. But the rest of the way they saw no others, though Thom could hear a blacksmith hammering nearby.

They passed behind a granary and around a cold kiln, then among a collection of sheds and storehouses. They were at the back of Saint Barnabas, where the monastery's wall came closest to the city's walls. Without even looking, Thom could tell that Camelot's enveloping magic came down very close to here, meeting the ground beyond the city's encircling ramparts which lay just a short city block beyond the monastery's outer wall.

Suddenly they came to a solid wooden fence that spanned between two windowless storehouses, blocking their path. Above the fence towered mighty evergreens, making the eight-foot-tall fence seem small in comparison. Colwyn walked up and rapped his knuckles on the boards. A spyhole opened and someone checked who was there, then part of the barricade swung in to reveal a well-armed warrior. The man motioned for them to enter quickly. The guard's attire was nondescript except for a bright blue armband that stood out even among the shadows on this side of the wall. He said nothing, but closed the gate quietly yet firmly as soon as they passed through.

Beyond, they entered a place of shadows and tree-filtered green light, following a narrow arbor walk that curved to the right. Tall conifers grew to either side of the arbor, the damp soil at their base was thick with succulent mushrooms. Beyond the boughs on the right was a raspberry thicket rich with fruit. Looking to the left, Thom saw a similar bramble forming an interwoven hedge to the left, but this one was blackberries. Above Thom's head, the arbor itself was covered by the twisting vines of some plant that appreciated this dim corner of the monastery.

Another warrior passed them on the path, apparently having gone ahead to alert someone of their arrival and now returning to the gate. He said nothing as he passed but did give Brother Colwyn a nod of acknowledgment.

The path ended at tree-shaded fountain where another monk stood, arms crossed. He offered no smile of greeting, just a stern gaze that seemed to Thom like it stripped him of clothes and skin to examine his very bones and sinews. A hard look.

"What have you brought me today, Colwyn?"

"Brother Alun, meet Dorthos of the Clan Brythoni pixies and Journeyman Thomas of the Magicians' Guild."

This new monk seemed most concerned about Thom. "He isn't of the league?"

Colwyn shook his head. "But the Father Abbot is the one who wanted them sent here."

"Fine, but I'll not let him into the hole. He's not one of us."

"Do as you think best," replied Colwyn, then turning to Thom and Dorthos. "Brother Alun oversees Mousehome for the league. He'll see to it that your wounds are tended and your other needs are met. Now, I need to get back to my work."

The librarian undid the bundle of sticks, handing Thom his staff and setting the rest in a neat stack in one the planters on the edge of the courtyard. Then Colwyn wished them well and left.

As soon as the librarian had departed, Alun turned his steely glare on the pixie. "Are you color blind?"

The short man set hands on hips. "Have you ever tried wearing anything besides black? I hear other orders enjoy wild colors like brown or even white."

Alum missed the sarcasm. "Our color helps signify our religious order. All Benedictines wear black."

"But it is such a dreary color. You should suggest to your abbot something more cheerful, maybe in a shade similar to my yellow shirt."

Alum scowled. "I think not."

Dorthos shrugged his indifference. "Remain dreary then. Will you be entertaining us with your banter until the abbot sends for us? Or will you see to my companion's injuries?" When the monk wasn't quick enough to move, Dorthos motioned toward Thom's head. "He thumped some cobblestones rather hard and I know the Father Abbot is expecting to see his injuries cared for…"

Alum hmphed. "Well then, come on. To the mercenary's medic with you."

The monk led them down another shady path to a storehouse where a small group of warriors were tossing dice near the doorway. These all wore the bright blue armbands too. Seeing the brother, one quickly pocketed the dice, while the others hid the coins that had been set for a winner's pile.

Alum was not fooled. "I will talk to your leader about your gambling. Now, see to some food for these two and then tell your medic to attend to the magician's injuries. The Father Abbot orders it."

With that the monk turned and strode briskly away, as if he wanted to leave before their sins could pollute him.

One of the men led them inside to a small room crowded with simple trestle tables and rough benches. Thom and Dorthos sat down and soon had bowls of vegetable stew in front of them, along with fresh bread and honey. Each got a chipped mug of watered wine too. They ate quickly, not having had a decent meal in days. The men returned to their dice game, leaving them to eat undisturbed.

It was not until Thom had finished eating that two men came over, one of them carrying a bowl of water, a wash cloth, and some clean strips of cloth, while the other held a jar of some kind of pungent cream.

"Brother Lemon Face told us to tend your wounds. What's wrong with you, kid?"

"Can't ya see the lump on his head, Grip?"

"I see it, oaf, but I want to hear 'em talk. Want to make sure there's no slur."

"Nothing is cracked up there," said Thom, gentling touching the swollen spot. "Dorthos looked at it yesterday. It is just very tender."

Grip leaned over Thom's head to look closer. "I'll still slather it with some of Marcus' Miracle Mud."

And before Thom could jerk away, the man had smeared some of the smelly ointment into his hair. He winced and fought hard not to move, even though Grip had a surprisingly gentle touch.

"Now where else are you cut or bruised? No false pride now, lad. We all got our share of beatings as youth, didn't we, Horace?"

"That be truth. Who beat ya? Father, master, lord? Or was it some woman? They can be meaner than any man..."

"It was nothing like that," explained Thom. "I ran into the middle of a magical battle and was tossed across the cobblestones when two enchantments exploded nearby."

Grip whistled in appreciation.

"Sounds like something our captain would try," said Horace. "Ya should hear his tales from the Road of Leaves. He was one of those who rescued the queen and was rewarded quite a pocket full of change, he was."

That caught Thom's attention. Who was their captain and why did he claim to be one of the rescuers? Thom knew everyone in that small party, and the only soldier in the group, besides the pixie warriors and clumsy Geoffrey, had been..."

"So it is true, Apprentice Thomas has joined us... no, excuse me... Journeyman Thomas."

The deep voice caused Thom to turn his head too quickly, making his vision spin a bit. When his watering eyes cleared enough, he recognized who had spoken— the captain of this motley band of warriors. None other than Marcus the Mercenary stood in the doorway. The large man was wearing a heavily padded outfit and his hair was damp with sweat.

"Marcus? What are you doing here?"

He sat down next to Thom. "I took a break from my training class when I heard that you had arrived."

"No, I mean what are you doing in Camelot, at the monastery of all places." Thom could think of many words to describe Marcus, but devout was not one of them.

The big fellow chuckled. "Your master arranged it, along with your friend Brother Francis. They knew that the league needed a weapons master. My former employer was not about to take me back. Not after what happened on the Road. Right after the king's banquet, Wizard Levitanus took me to see Francis who then brought me to meet Abbot Justin. They were all rather convincing, so here I am. I'm sorry that I missed all the fun on the Road of Waters, but I was off recruiting the rest of my crew."

Thom was surprised to hear that his master and the monk had done anything together, for they seemed in enmity. He was even more surprised that Francis had talked Marcus into joining the League of Barnabas. Francis, who swore off magic, was doing more to help the league than almost anyone else. His smile faded as he wondered where the monk was. "Have you heard anything about Francis? They told me that he went out into the city to find me."

"I will ask around," said Marcus. "If nothing has been heard, I'll send one of my men to search for him. But you shouldn't worry about Brother Francis too much; that man is very capable of surviving. Instead, you should get some rest."

Just the suggestion caused Thom to yawn, but he still protested that he could help in the search.

Marcus laughed as he stood, resting a hand lightly on Thom's shoulder. "You are done for today, young man. Finish bandaging him, Grip, and then find him a sleeping mat in one of the quieter rooms."

Thom didn't have the strength to argue further.

"Now, introduce me to your companion," said Marcus. "I have heard rumors about a pixie who dresses as bright as the sun, but thought it just ale talk."

Before Thom could say anything, Dorthos spoke up, "I am Prince Dorthos."

"Well, prince, let me take you to meet with some of your loyal subjects who also found refuge here at the monastery. Don't worry, it isn't far from here and my men will see to Thomas' needs."

So Marcus led Dorthos away while his two men finished caring for Thom's injuries. Too late, Thom remembered to ask about Adele. The mercenaries knew who she was but didn't know if she was at the monastery.

"Marcos would know," said Grip. "Not much misses his keen eyes, especially not a pretty lass."

"We can never get close to any of the women," complained Horace. "The sisters keep us away like we're plague infested."

Grip laughed, "They protect you, Horace. Just imagine what would happen if you were left alone with that fiery red-headed one."

Horace sighed, "Ya got that right. She'd kill me if ever I robbed her of a kiss, but what a woman!"

As the two men laughed, Thom decided to ask no more. If they started leering about Adele, he might become angered enough to challenge them and he was in no shape to fight. Better to let them dwell on Vivien.

Once done tending to Thom's wounds, Grip and Horace took him deeper into the building, past a small kitchen where a cook was working on a noon day meal, to a small room with one tightly-shuttered window that gave off only a sliver of light. Packs were neatly lined up along one wall, apparently belonging to the men who reported to Marcus. Yet all across the floor sleeping pads were strewn about.

"Pick any mat," said Horace, making a sweeping motion over the room as if he were the owner of it all.

"We aren't choosy about where we sleep," said Grip, "and don't worry, none of the other fellows will be coming in here for hours yet."

Thom pick one that looked fairly clean and sat down. He took off his knapsack and set it down within arm's reach and placed his staff leaning on top of it. He then laid down and fell asleep not long after the door closed. But even exhaustion couldn't smother his concerns for Adele and Francis and his dreams were full of shadowy men who kept holding him back from reaching them.

TWELVE

Spying on Visitors

Thom awoke near sunset, startled by a collision of enchantments. He sat up, grabbing for his knapsack and fumbling to get out his magician's box of elements, but stopped when he realized that no one was attacking him personally. The sound was still reverberating in his inner ear, but he now realized the explosion had happened far away- probably at the other end of the city. Around him snored a half-dozen mercenaries, deaf to what had just happened. It must have been a huge clash of magic, for he could hear an echo of it murmuring through the enchantment that was the dome over the whole city. He swallowed as he wondered how close the magicians had come to shredding the very enchantment that enclosed everyone. He listened tensely, but the city's enchantment quieted down to a steadier hum.

Although he was still tired, he couldn't fall back to sleep after that scare, so he rose to his feet, took his knapsack and staff, and carefully made his way out of the room. He found his way to the room full of tables and looked around for anyone he knew. He saw Grip, the man who had bandaged him, so he went over to where the man sat with two others over empty bowls and half-empty mugs.

"Here he is now," said Grip when he spotted Thomas.

"He looks like a dead man walking," one of his companions replied. "If this is an example of your best doctoring, then keep your mitts off me, Grip."

"You'd look bad too, Howler, if a sorcerer had skittered you across a courtyard like a rock skipped across a pond."

Thom felt sore almost everywhere but he hadn't realized that it showed so obviously.

Howler shook his head, "No offense, lad, but I've lost my appetite after seeing your face. Why don't you take my seat. I need to be leaving soon anyway." He turned to the other man in their group. "You ready, Josh? I want to get some extra things from the supply man before we leave, since the city will be a crazed mess tonight." He shook his head again. "Marcus has his reasons for sending us out there, but I sure do hope we find this monk quickly."

Josh grunted his doubts as he swung his leg over the bench. "It will take us most of the night, if we're lucky. Big city. Just hope no one has robbed him for his robes, because without 'em he'll just be another balding man among the city's thousands.

"Truth in that. Let's get our things and get out the postern before sunset."

The two were gone before Thom realized that they were probably talking about searching for Francis. He almost went after them, but knew he was in no shape to help.

"Let me get ya some food," said Grip. "Just sit down like Howler suggested and don't let his remarks about your face upset ya. The bruises will fade soon enough, the scrapes will heal, and ya can wash the poultice out of your hair in another day or so."

Thom felt his face and it was tender all over, but he simply hadn't noticed it against the greater pain from other areas. He hoped he could make his appearance at least a little less appalling before Adele saw him... would she see him anytime soon? He frowned as he wondered about where she might be sheltering.

"Eat some of this," ordered Grip, handing him a steaming bowl of more vegetable stew. "It's overdone but filling. And don't be worrying about Howler's weak stomach." He also handed over a mug of watered ale. "You'll heal up soon enough, journeyman. Your looks will be back, and even if they didn't, you could always use your magic to woo a pretty lady."

Thom didn't even try to explain that magic didn't work that way nor that he was forbidden to craft anything. Instead he concentrated on eating, for he needed the nourishment. Grip was soon drawn away by the conversation at another table, but Thom didn't mind.

After his meal, Thom wandered outside. The sun was close to setting and the tall evergreens in this corner of the monastery created long shadows over the area. It didn't take him long to discover the boundaries of this enclave within the brethren's larger compound. The tall wooden fence enclosed six small buildings, the fountain, and another two courtyards. As he walked past one closed door, he heard the muffled sounds of battle. For a brief moment, he thought the city's invasions had reached the monastery and he shifted his staff to his left hand and set his right hand on the sword that he still wore from his battles on the Road of Leaves. He moved closer, silently debating if he should set aside his staff to open the door's latch when the door was yanked open from inside. Startled, Thom jumped back and pulled out his sword.

"Sword instead of magician's box?" asked the man standing in the opened door, his features hidden by the bright light behind him. The clashing of metal was much louder now.

Thom relaxed a bit as he recognized Marcus' voice but he was still confused about the fighting going on behind the man.

Marcus stepped out and closed the door. "Are you any better with a blade now? If not, then you chose wrongly, Thomas. Have you come to me for training? If so, maybe the abbot will let you spar with the others, because I think you could use the training. Your stance is too close and you hold your weapon awkwardly."

Thom smiled a little as he put his sword away. "I don't think I'm up to mock fights with your men."

The mercenary chuckled. "My men don't practice indoors. That would be too confining for them. No, in there I train those we don't want noticed by any who might be trying to listen over the fences: the women, the magicians, and the monks."

Thom stepped closer, almost grabbing the man's shirt in a sudden urge for answers. "Is Adele inside?"

"Not this late. The women go back to the convent well before nightfall.

Even that fiery instructor, Vivien, has to obey the rules, as much as she hates it."

"But Adele is here? She's safe?"

Marcus tilted his head in interest. "So that one's truly caught your eye, eh? You have good taste, Thomas. Yes, she's here. She left the castle early on the day of the invasion and was caught out in the city, but she made it safely here." He paused a moment and looked up at the darkening sky. "I don't know how long this place will remain safe. Will the sorcerers respect the sanctity of a monastery? Do they have any idea what the abbot is plotting here with his league?"

Thom relaxed in spite of Marcus' troubling questions. He knew tomorrow might be full of more terrors but at least for now Adele was safe. He considered what Marcus had asked. "I wouldn't look to the sorcerers for any mercy. If they learn of this, they will end it."

Marcus looked back at the journeyman. "The abbot told me of your experiences during the taking of the guild house. Do you think the magicians will try to retake their keep or leave it in the rebel's hands?"

Thom pondered. "I honestly don't know. I saw them flee Clas Myrddin in defeat, but I can't see them abandoning their home or the enchanted city they worked so hard to build."

Just then the clash of enchantments reached a new crescendo. Even Marcus noticed, for the exploding magic lit up the sky over the western end of the city.

"Can you tell what's happening?" asked the mercenary.

Thom shook his head. "The enchantments are coming so fast and then colliding with others... I would judge it to be at the Camelot castle, but I'm not sure who is winning. I cannot tell who is crafting what..."

They both turned as they heard someone hurrying toward them. One of the mercenaries came into view. "Captain, that group has arrived. They came in the front gate just before it closed at sunset. We missed them at first as they mixed with the hundreds of others seeking refuge. Maybe they used some kind of invisibility magic."

Marcus cursed. "Where are they now, Killian?"

"They are approaching our yard with the abbot."

"They made it to the abbot without any of you seeing them? That isn't good. What if they had been sorcerers?"

"I told the men the same thing, captain. But how can we fight against magic?"

Thom broke in, "You need someone who can hear it."

Marcus looked at him and nodded. "Come with me Thomas. I would guess that they are heading down the Hole. I want you to observe them as they pass by. Do nothing to draw attention to yourself, but watch and listen carefully."

With no further explanation, Marcus sped off to greet the newcomers, with Thom and Killian running after him. The guard captain's limp was obvious but didn't slow him at all, unlike Thom's newly acquired sore leg.

They made it the Mousehome compound's gate before the newcomers. Hastily, Marcus ordered Killian and Thom to stand off to the side, in the shadows. "You are on duty as guards, should any ask," he said to both of them, then focused on Thomas. "Watch as much as you can but most importantly you are to listen. I want to know if they are using magic as they come in."

Thom nodded agreement, not fully understanding but trusting the man.

He stood behind the line of conifers on the left side of the arbor walk, the fresh smell of pine filling the air as the higher branches directly overhead waved in a breeze that wasn't strong enough to weave through the collection of buildings that were Mousehome. It was a calming whisper. For a moment, it did not feel like war was happening only blocks away.

The gate opened and a group of five entered: the abbot and four who were hooded in black robes of mastery. A guard closed the gate behind them. Each of the four were enshrouded in enchantments of disguise, a subtle magic that Thom now recognized quickly after hearing it so often on the Road of Waters, when his master had disguised himself as a mere journeyman. The thought of Levitanus caused a sudden ache in him. If only he were here...

Marcus greeted the newcomers and then lead them along the arbor walk to a building Thom hadn't seen anyone entering yet. After a series of knocks, the door opened and Marcus lead the abbot and the visiting magicians inside.

Killian stirred now that the newcomers were out-of-sight, but Thom kept concentrating. He could still hear their enchantments. They seemed to pause inside for a few minutes and then began to descend. Into a root cellar? A basement? Curious, Thom stepped closer because it became harder to hear as they descended and then abruptly they ended their enchantments. He could no longer track them, at least not without sending an enchantment after them and that would reveal his interest.

"Were they using magic on me?" asked Marcus. He had come out of the building and around to Thom's side while the other had been staring at the building.

"Not exactly. They were using magic as a disguise, blurring or altering their appearance. But I heard nothing for me to suspect anything beyond that." He stopped staring at the building and looked around. Killian was no longer about. "Who are they?"

"The chief magicians of the League of Barnabas. I understand that they traveled here to talk about the league's future, unaware that Dalrake was planning to seize the city. They arrived at King's Haven shortly after the sorcerers began their invasion and were forced to act. It was kill or be killed from what I hear. The secret conference they had planned is ruined, but they still came here to talk with the Father Abbot."

"Do you know any of them? Why the need to hide their identities?"

"From what the abbot told me, the master magicians want to keep the league a secret as well as hide their identities. It is feared that when the wizards and sorcerers finally learn of this rival band, they will drop their squabbling and seek the league's destruction."

Thom could see how the wizards and sorcerers might fear the league; they wouldn't like anyone giving a voice to magical beings. He wished that the guild would be more like the league in that way, but it seemed that so many of the wizards craved for the others' innate magic far more than ever desiring to know them as people.

He said nothing of this to Marcus, for it would feel disloyal toward his guild even though it was true. Instead, he simply asked, "Why did you suspect that they might use an enchantment against you? You're in their service, after all."

"Too many years spent serving crafty traders is the main cause of my doubts, but I've also had other dealings with magicians." He paused to look again at the building in front of them. "I trust Abbot Justin but not these unknown others. No insult toward you, but most of your kind are rather cagey and prone to half-truths."

"Well, they aren't using any enchantments now. That stopped soon after they entered the building."

Marcus nodded. "To be expected, considering how the Hole is built."

"What do you mean by that?"

He grimaced. "I've already revealed too much, considering that you aren't in the league."

Thom didn't press him on it, but wondered if it was some kind of magically-muffled room used for training the league's magicians. He strained, trying to hear any telltale whisper of an enchantment at work, but his inner ear caught nothing. Maybe the background hum of the city's dome masked it or maybe being underground dampened the sound. Thom was too ignorant to know, but he heard no evidence of any magic inside or under the building.

"Will they be here long?" he asked the former mercenary.

Marcus took a deep breath, his eyes sweeping the horizon to the west. "I would think not. The city is in chaos and that unrest will soon reach this section of the city. I would say that if they stay later than midnight, they will be forced to join the fighting."

"Haven't they already? Didn't they retake King's Haven when they landed there?"

Marcus nodded. "The abbot told me it was them, but he said the sorcerers will assume it was guild magicians who fought there, for the four made certain that no one survived to say otherwise. But if the league's magicians want to escape by way of the Road of Waters, they will need to take a river galley and those only sail at night. They will need to catch a ship tonight or likely get stranded in the city."

"What about the rest of us? Will the abbot also want us to flee down the Road of Waters?"

"I doubt there are many galleys at the harbor. Most likely, almost all fled as soon as they heard about the fighting. There will no room for the likes of us, Thomas. I'm just a strong arm and you... you aren't even part of the league."

Thom wondered what he should do. Now that Dorthos was safe and his own wounds tended, maybe he should go back out into the city and do what he could to stop these invaders. He wasn't certain what one inexperienced journeyman could do, but he ought to try.

Marcus seemed to assume that fear caused Thom's silence. "Don't misunderstand me. You're allowed to stay here, but I don't know how long the monastery will remain safe. I doubt the sorcerers have much respect for religious orders, but my men and I will do our best to defend the monastery."

"So you think the sorcerers are winning?"

"One of my men counted over three thousand warriors marching out of the Short Roads, all under the banners of Mordred and Dalrake. Add to that number the hundreds of centaurs and soldiers who arrived by ship and the many sorcerers who descended from the Road of Clouds and I fear the king's force is greatly outnumbered. Unless Merlin has some great magical feat to chase them all out of here, I don't see the king easily winning his own city back."

"Is there nothing we can do to help turn this battle in the king's favor? Should we go out there now and do what we can to harass their ranks?"

Marcus held up a hand. "Patience. You can't go anywhere tonight, for the abbot has ordered the gates secured and I'm not about to disobey him, not after you've seen the arrival of our visitors. If a sorcerer were to capture you and learn about them… well, it would bring utter devastation on the brothers and sisters who live here, not to mention the slaughtering of all those seeking refuge in the forecourt. Besides, I don't think you would want that either.

"Let's see what comes of the meeting they're having. The time to fight is coming soon, but maybe they will arrive at a better way to do so, a way that might bring victory to the king while still keeping the League of Barnabas a secret."

Thom was about to express his doubts about that but a huge explosion distracted him. He stared to the west, hearing the magic explode loudly in his inner ear. It was so strong that it sent ripples through the city's enchanted dome, causing a light show to flicker across the sky.

"What was that?" asked Marcus, for he saw it too.

THIRTEEN

Four Master Magicians

The journeyman magician didn't answer immediately. Instead, he listened intently to the city's enchantment as it whined a little, it's rhythmic beat sputtering, recovering, then getting out of rhythm again. He waited, breath held, until he heard the enchantment return to its usual pattern.

"Well, what happened?"

"That last attack was so large that its backlash brushed against the city's magic. If that had been any worse, everything would have gone up in a conflagration."

Marcus growled. "I'll not die from a distance. Let me see my killer; let me spit in his face as he sinks a sword into me. This wizardry is wrong to kill from afar. Why ever did I agree to work inside a magic-encircled city?"

Thom was only half-listening to the man next to him. His concentration was on the magical battlefield at the other end of the city. The fighting had paused as all watched Camelot's enchantment stutter and then stabilize. Yet soon they started throwing enchantments at each other again. Only some of elements were recognizable to him. But then again, he was just an apprentice that had been promoted to journeymen too early.

"They are still fighting," he told Marcus, "but they are keeping the magic closer to the ground."

"It promises to be a long night," the mercenary remarked. "I'm staying here to keep watch while they are inside, but you can go back to the makeshift barracks. Get some more sleep and regain your strength."

Thom ignored the suggestion, distracted by what was happening at Camelot castle. He began describing to Marcus what he was hearing with his inner ear. Although he couldn't tell which side was doing what, it was obvious that the fighting had intensified.

After listening to Thom share for an hour about the raging warfare, Marcus remarked, "Maybe I should go inside and warn the others."

"Surely, they can hear it as well," argued Thom. "The ground wouldn't dull the sound that much."

"They won't be able to hear anything if they are inside the Hole, not from what they've told me about the place. That is why Journeywoman Vivien takes her students down there for their lessons. It dampens the magical sounds somehow."

That made Thom curious. What would create a place where magic couldn't be heard at all?

Just then one of Marcus' men ran up and whispered into his ear. Marcus nodded and motioned for the man to get back to what ever he had been doing.

"We are about to get more visitors, two of them known to you."

"Has Francis made it back?" asked Thom with sudden hope.

Marcus shook his head. "I told you that the gates are all barred for the night. If the monk has returned then he'll be hunkered down in a nearby street waiting for dawn when the gates will reopen."

There was a commotion around the corner of the nearest building. Thom heard two women arguing.

Marcus continued, "No, these four are from the convent, so they only needed to pass through the small gate that connects it to the monastery. I have two men on watch there but they know better than to try stopping these four."

Around the corner strode Vivien and a nun. They were the two arguing.

"Your frock may not be gray, but you are still a mere apprentice. I am the teacher here, Sister Harmony, so cease your squabbling. It is unbecoming of your office."

"Don't try to shame me, Vivien. You are my teacher in magic only. In all else, I am your assigned chaperon and I say it is unseemly for us to be among the men after sunset. Most unseemly."

"Practically sinful," echoed another nun who was a step behind them.

"But this is a matter of magic. The enchantment covering the city was almost destroyed. We almost died."

"I am still breathing," argued Sister Harmony, "as is everyone else we've seen in this most-inappropriate jaunt across the monastery's grounds, so your supposed destruction did not happen. This is no time for hysterics."

The two came to a stop in front of Thom and Marcus but said nothing to them. Instead, the red-headed Vivien turned on the two nuns and set her hands on her hips. "Hysterics? How dare you accuse me of such. I have been in battle. I have endured the raging storms on the Road of Waters. I…"

Sister Harmony stepped close, almost nose to nose with the journeywoman. "I too have been on battlefields, tending wounded and caring for those widowed and orphaned. I have seen hysterics and you are starting to fall under its influence. There is nothing so urgent as you seem to think. The city is not falling at this hour, is it? This can wait a few more hours."

"Come, let us return to the convent," urged the other nun. "We can seek out the Father Abbot in the morning, but now we should be away from these men, especially the uncouth warriors here at Mousehome."

Vivien's jaw tightened, but she didn't reply. Instead, she turned away from the two and looked at Marcus. "I understand the abbot has gone down into the Hole. May I go in to talk with him?"

"None are to pass," said Marcus. "He is not to be disturbed. But as soon as he comes out, I'll tell him what has been happening over at Camelot castle. I assume that is what has you so concerned, isn't it? Well, Thomas has already told me about it."

Vivien seemed to notice Thom for the first time. "Ah, you are here. Well good. Yes, Thomas can serve as the Father Abbot's ears, though he does not understand magic as well as I do."

"See? The Lord has already provided for the abbot," said Sister Harmony.

"Come along then. We must flee back to the convent before more learn of our wanton charge into the men's camp."

Another voice spoke up, one that made Thom's heart leap. "Thomas? Is that you?"

Behind the three squabblers came the fourth person in their party: Adele. Surprisingly, she was dressed in the gray robe of a magician's apprentice and had the typical knapsack over her shoulder.

Thom let out a yell of joy and moved toward her. He would have run, but he was still too weak for that. Soon, he had Adele in his arms as tears of relief filled his eyes. Unrestrained, he gave her a long and passionate kiss.

"How dare you!" yelled the one nun as she started raining blows on Thom's back.

Despite his injuries, Thom kept on hugging his beloved. It was so good to see her alive and well.

"Restrain your man, Marcus!" ordered Sister Harmony as she loosened a wicked-looking truncheon that had been hanging at her side.

Marcus chuckled. "He's not mine. Apparently, he belongs to Adele."

Harmony closed the distance and took a strong swing at Thom's back. His knapsack took the brunt of the assault, but not enough of it.

With a yell of pain, he let go of Adele and turned on his two frocked attackers. He stayed between these mad nuns and Adele, holding his staff out as a defense.

"Stop," shouted Adele, trying to spare Thom.

"Enough of this," said Marcus, stepping into the fray. He grabbed Harmony's right arm to keep her from swinging. "Thomas and Adele are old friends, so let them have their kisses and hugs. Must you nuns always be so prudish?"

"Now who is being hysterical?" said Vivien. "Put away your club, Sister Harmony. Unclench your fists, Sister Myrna. Thomas is a magician of the guild, or didn't you hear what Marcus had said about him reporting on the magical war?"

"I heard it plain enough," replied Harmony, "but his behavior is still boorish. This is a place sanctified to the Lord, not some lovers' path. He should learn some restraint."

"As should you, sister," said Vivien and proceeded to lecture the nuns on how magicians also have a code of conduct.

Now that blows had stopped, Thom ignored them. He turned to Adele and focused solely on her. "I am so thankful that you aren't trapped in the castle with the others."

She frowned, her eyes drawn to his blood-encrusted, larded hair. "What happened to you?" She reached up but stopped before touching.

"I was caught in the middle of a magical battle. It will heal and hopefully not leave too many scars." He suddenly felt concerned that his appearance might disgust her. "I pray that I won't look too much worse once I heal."

"Oh, Thomas. You'll always be handsome to me." Her soft yet firm hand took hold of his chin and turned his head so that she could look more closely at his bump. "Are you certain that your wounds have been well tended? That looks so….so messy."

He smiled. "They call it Marcus' Miracle Mud. I'm told it will speed up the healing."

"Did Francis rescue you?"

"No, it was Dorthos who helped me out of Clas Myrddin. We crisscrossed the city, trying to find an escape route for the pixie, but ended up here at last. We never saw Francis."

He looked again at her unusual attire; it wasn't the kind of garment worn among nobility. "Have you renounced your position as a queen's lady?"

"No, but whenever I am here for training, I wear an apprentice robe." She nodded toward the two nuns still watching them. "The sisters are also students, but they hold their vows to God as greater than their vows to the League of Barnabas so they remain in their habits. Vivien grumbled about that at first, but she finally relented and gave in to their logic."

While the two were talking, the others had finally calmed down and had come to some kind of agreement. A calm Sister Harmony came over and suggested that Thom and Adele separate. She was polite but it still was more of a command than request.

The two complied.

"I know you want to consult with the abbot," said Marcus, "but I don't think he will appreciate such a large audience when he and his visitors come out."

"Visitors?" asked Vivien. "They are finally here? The league's masters? Were they the ones who were fighting at King's Harbor? I wondered what was happening when there was a sudden burst of enchantments south of us so many hours after the sorcerers had captured the area."

"I'm not telling you anything more," said Marcus, crossing his arms.

Behind him, Thom heard multiple magicians' boxes opening and the sudden crafting of enchantments. He was about to warn Marcus, but Vivien spoke first.

"Too late. The abbot and his guests are up from the Hole and one of them is spying on us now, making sure it is safe to come out." She pointed at a small purple-glowing orb that suddenly appeared above them. Thom knew the enchantment as Eagle's Spying. The orb swept closer and then sailed off to look over more of the area.

Marcus cursed, mumbling something about getting an earful from the abbot.

The door opened and Abbot Justin came out alone. "What is the meaning of this, Marcus? Why are these people here?"

"They all came with warnings for you. The battle in the city took a bad turn…"

"We apologize for intruding, Father Abbot," interrupted Sister Harmony. "We will withdraw to the convent and leave you to your other business."

Justin held up a hand in restraint. "Not yet. Since you are all here you should at least tell me what brought you. What foul thing has happened now?"

"They nearly shattered the magic encasing the city," said Vivien. "Everyone almost died an hour ago."

The abbot looked up quickly at the invisible dome, but there was nothing to see now.

Vivien continued, "Even now, the battle at the castle is more intense, but at least they are keeping their clashing enchantments close to the ground. Even sorcerers are not completely reckless."

"Can you tell which side is pressing the attack?" he asked.

Vivien shook her head. "I recognize most of the enchantments but at this distance I cannot tell who crafts what."

Behind the abbot, the door opened again and four people in black robes came out. Thom could see nothing of their features and probably never would, for he could tell that magic surrounded them.

"We heard what they reported, Justin," one of them said in almost a whisper. "It is true. The city's enchantment still has echoes in it of the near calamity."

Something about the speaker's voice teased at Thom but he couldn't place it.

"Should we flee?" asked the abbot.

"No, at least not the four of us. Although we are not that sentimental toward Camelot and the Roads, we have no desire to see its sudden destruction. The cost in lives would be too great. We will stay and fight."

"You will expose our secret?"

"Maybe not. Two of us are in good standing with the guild. It will raise no suspicions if those two are seen in the city."

"The league is still small," argued Justin. "How can we turn Dalrake's forces if the king and Merlin cannot?"

"We will find a way. We must, or see the kingdom fall into anarchy. The lords of the land will never accept Mordred on his father's throne."

One of the other hooded magicians spoke up. "We cannot do anything tonight, not after fighting all day to regain the harbor. Can you find us beds for the night, Justin?"

"The guest house is already full of nobles who have sought refuge here. Do you want to go among them?"

"I will," said one the masters. Thom heard him drop his magical disguise as he reached up to lower his hood.

Vivien caught her breath, obviously recognizing the gray-haired master, but Thom didn't know who he was.

"Very well," said the abbot.

Another master dropped both hood and disguise, revealing a striking woman whose white hair almost glowed in the moonlight. "And I will go with the women back to the convent."

She looked at a suddenly-stiff Vivien. "I think I will need to have a long talk with the journeywoman, for now she feels even more slighted by the fact that I didn't choose her as a student."

Thom remembered that he wasn't the only one without a master; Vivien had lost hers as well and no wizardess had stepped forward to take her on. Even though he disliked Vivien's often haughty manner, he felt for her. If this wizardess had taken her on, Vivien could have joined the league and still maintained her status in the guild.

"You have no need to explain yourself to me, Wizardess Bronwen," said Vivien coolly.

"But I do. You may not believe all that I tell you, but I kept you ignorant for your own good. We will talk about it on our way to the convent."

Wizardess Bronwen walked over and took Vivien by the elbow, steering her back up the path. The red-head didn't resist. With her other hand Bronwen motioned for Adele and the sisters to follow.

"The two of us will stay here with Marcus' men," said the still-hooded master who had first spoken. The fourth wizard nodded in agreement. Both of them had kept up their disguises.

"It is rough bedding," warned Marcus. "We sleep on thin mats over rough planks with just a blanket for covering."

"Both of us have slept in worse places," replied the one, who then turned his attention to the abbot. "Where is the young journeyman staying? He is not of the league now, is he?"

"This is Thomas of York," said Abbot Justin as an introduction. "He was the Wizard Levitanus' final student and is still in the guild, though I consider him a friend of the League of Barnabas."

"You reveal much to one who has not sworn allegiance."

"I will not expose the league," assured Thomas. "I care too much for many in it."

There was a long pause, then the speaker nodded. "Very well. We will take his word on it, unless he proves otherwise."

"I planned to have him stay with Marcus' men too," explained Justin, "but that wouldn't be best now…"

"He can come with me to the guest house," said the wizard who had already revealed himself. "He can pose as my student."

The abbot nodded at that solution, apparently not too vexed by the small lie.

* * *

One of Marcus' men was ordered to guide Thom and the wizard to the guest house. The guard led them through gardens and then around a jumble of buildings to another corner of the complex, until he stopped in a cobbled courtyard and indicated a building set apart from the others by a chest-high wall.

"There's your place, sirs," he said, pointing at the separated building that had light shining through most of its downstairs windows. He gave them an awkward bow and then hurried off.

The wizard turned to Thom. "Well, I probably should introduce myself before we go in, especially if you are supposed to be my student. I am Wizard Osric. We have something in common, Thomas. I too was once a student of Levitanus."

That surprised him. Osric looked about as old and his late mentor. Fit and trim, but definitely into his sixth decade of life if not seventh. How old was Levitanus when he died if this white-haired man had once been his student? "Levitanus taught you?"

Osric smiled. "I know it is hard to believe that a white-hair could once have been a young apprentice, but I was. Actually, I was one of his first two students. But now is not the time for reminiscing. Let us get inside and find some beds for the night. Who knows when we will get another chance, for this battle for Camelot is not going well."

Thom wanted to ask him about so many things, about what the master magicians were planning to do tomorrow to stop Dalrake, about being Levitanus' student, about whether he would take on Thomas as a real student and not just a pretend one. But Thom didn't say anything. Osric was right; now was not the time.

He followed the wizard toward the guest house, hearing the sounds of singing inside and heated conversation. But as he walked, he remembered that the council had mentioned three previous students, two of which already had apprentices and one who was unable to take one on at this time. So that question died. Osric was a pretend mentor for just one night.

They had reached the front door. Thom collected his fractured thoughts and tried his best to act the subservient student, for they were about to enter the presence of a large party of nobles.

Osric didn't knock, he simply opened the door and strode inside.

FOURTEEN

Among Nobles

Thom followed close behind, squinting against the sudden brightness of multiple oil lamps and chandeliers. The increased noise was a bit disorienting, but he soon had them sorted. To one end of the main room a quartet was playing on their instruments. Nearby, a group of men sat at a table playing a card game. Another group lounged on the wooden floor in front of the fireplace. Osric ignored them all, for they were just retainers and soldiers. He marched into the smaller room beyond where a dozen better-dressed men had their heads together over the remains of their dinner, talking intensely.

It took them a moment to notice the two magicians in their midst, but once they did the conversation stopped.

Into that silence, Osric walked. He stopped so close that the seated men had to look up. "Who ranks here?"

The silence continued for a moment longer, then one well-dressed, younger man stood up. "I do. I am Lord Lionel. What brings you here wizard? Has Merlin finally sent reinforcements to help us break the siege?"

"My activities are not your concern, Lord Lionel. At least not here. Take me to your room for some privacy."

The noblemen frowned, probably not liking that he was being ordered about, but he eventually nodded. He picked up a half-full glass of wine and walked toward the staircase. The wizard followed, motioning for Thom to join them.

Lord Lionel led them up to the third floor to a large corner bedroom.

Thom was the last in and he closed the door behind him then stood near the door, uncertain what was expected of him.

The young nobleman went to a divan that sat in front of a cold fireplace and sat down, stretching out his long legs and taking a sip of wine. "Well, magician, you have your privacy now. What is the great Merlin up to? Can I lead these men out to counterattack that vile Mordred now? We haven't dared to do so before because we had no one to protect us from any magical blows that might rain down on us."

Instead of replying to the prideful man, Osric walked farther into the room and surveyed it, nodding approval to something.

"Well, speak up, magician! How many of you have come to work for us? Surely not just the two of you."

Osric didn't respond, but instead swung his knapsack onto the bed, pulled out his magician's box and was quickly crafting an enchantment.

Thom was surprised, recognizing many of the elements as their sounds mixed together.

The young nobleman sprang to his feet, maybe not fully understanding what was happening but becoming concerned nonetheless. "See here, old man. Get your rubbish off my bed and answer my questions."

Osric finished his crafting and suddenly his left hand was crackling with power, a Hand of Lightning enchantment. Thom got gooseflesh from the bad memories of facing that awful magic while on the Road of Waters.

Osric walked toward the young nobleman, speaking to him in a calm voice. "You are confused, Lord Lionel. I am not in your hire. I am here at the monastery to get some rest before I have to get back to fighting sorcerers. I will be taking over this bedroom for tonight, so you will remove your belongings immediately. Do you understand me?"

For emphasis, he sent a small tendril of lightning to snake past the man's face close enough to make the noblemen twitch away from the heat. The lightning ended just before it hit the wall.

Exquisite control, thought Thom.

Lionel noticeably swallowed. "You... you have no right to be kicking me out. I am the abbot's guest..."

"As am I. Gather your things and find somewhere else to sleep. I'm sure there's some other bedroom that will be acceptable to your needs."

The nobleman glared at the wizard but the sight of lightning playing from finger to finger was just too intimidating. He gruffly grabbed his clothes from the wardrobe, picked up an extra pair of boots, and headed for the door.

"Thomas, could you please see the lord out?"

Thom nodded, hurrying to open the door before Lionel got there.

"One more thing, my lord. Be glad this was a private lesson on humility. I could have just as easily done this to you in front of all the others. You should thank me for my restraint."

The man paused, his jaw set and Thom was sure he was about to spout out something very defiant. But instead, he said, "Thank you. You did show restraint."

"I hope the lesson is learned and there will be no need to repeat it, for any lesson I must teach a second time is much more painful. Any student of mine will attest to that" Osric's eyes darted to Thom and then back to the nobleman. "Now, I care not what you tell the others about what happened. You can tell them I stole your room or you can tell them you volunteered it to me. I will not contradict either story."

"Thank you again, master wizard. Please enjoy the use of my old room. I will tell one the servants to bring up refreshments for you and the journeyman. Will he be needing a room also?"

"Food would be appreciated, but the journeyman can use the divan when it is his turn to sleep. You may go now, Lord Lionel, and have a good night. Tomorrow we will talk about how we can fight against Dalrake and Mordred."

Thom shut the door behind the nobleman and then just stared at Osric as the man let the enchantment dissipate. The wizard went back to the bed and tidied up his magical supplies. Thom had never seen a magician so frank, so blunt. The man was even more combative than Vivien.

"Thomas, no questions tonight about what just happened because I am just too tired for a lengthy explanation. I know the young man's pride has been badly bruised, but this way saved me hours of trying to reason with someone who probably would have forced me to use magic anyway. Now, can you set a Whisper of Warning on the door after they deliver the food?"

"Um... well... I..."

"You are ignorant of such a simple enchantment?" His voice reflected incredulity that Levitanus had left such a gap in his knowledge.

"No, sir," Thom replied quickly, "but I have been forbidden by the council to practice any magic."

"I declare that ruling to be suspended by these unprecedented times. As the ranking wizard here, I have such a right to do so. Should the council complain, I'll hammer all five of them on their dim heads. Now, can you set a Whisper of Warning?"

Thom nodded, "Yes, sir."

"Good. Do so, but after the food arrives. I do not expect any trouble tonight, but it is always best to be prepared. The enchantment will provide us with ample warning should anyone try to break in. Set the outer edge to be just outside the door so that we will know if anyone is lurking out there; I would rather not have to deal with an ambush when we go down for breakfast."

* * *

The next morning, Thom and the wizard went downstairs together, leaving nothing behind in the room they had confiscated for the night. Most of the nobles seemed to have already gathered in the smaller room, still eating their breakfasts or getting fitted into their armor with the help of two overworked squires.

There were two male servants who were taking care of the food and cleaning up the emptied plates. Thom guessed them to be employed by the monastery to attend to any guests staying at the house. But other than those two, everyone else was either a noble or attached to a noble as squire or soldier or other servant. Thom felt isolated as he followed Osric into the dining area and sat down. The other conversations seemed to die away and Thom felt dozens of eyes on him. It didn't seem to perturb the wizard at all, who ordered breakfast for both of them and then pulled out a small book from some pocket in his voluminous robe and began to read. Thom just sat there, trying not to stare at all the men around him who were giving the wizard furtive glances.

It was awkward.

He finally focused on the woodgrain of the tabletop, following its wandering pattern with his eyes while his inner ear listened in on the magical battle still happening around the king's keep.

When the food arrived, Osric shifted his book to the other hand and kept reading while he ate. Thom ate as well, wishing he could question the wizard but knowing that was inappropriate for a student, especially with so many ready to overhear.

Finally, after finishing most of the food, Osric slipped the book back into his robe pocket and looked over to one side. "Lord Lionel, would you please assemble your fellow noblemen for conference? I think it is time for us to talk about the retaking of Camelot."

The man nodded and rose to gather the few who weren't already there. Two other lords stood to assist him.

"Do you think the king's bastard will run off like a beaten cur because you order him to?"

Thom looked at a group of nobles who are still lounging nearby. The one who had spoken was staring hard at Osric, waiting on a response.

The wizard said nothing.

"See? His schemes are as solid as a morning mist," the man said to his table-mates, making sure it was loud enough for all others to hear. "We are less than a hundred blades here, and that is counting squires and common soldiers. How can we make a difference against so many? I am no log for this wizard to throw onto Dalrake's fire. If I am to burn up, I want it to happen in a way that will save the realm."

Thom didn't quite understand what the nobleman meant about being a log, but he caught the gist of his emotions. This fellow was full of suspicions and doubts, especially toward any plans offered by a magician.

Lionel returned with the remaining lords and told Osric that they were now ready to talk. Thom was surprised by the man's politeness.

"Thank you, Lord Lionel," said the wizard. He stood, nodding at Thom to do likewise, and then walked to the nearest end of the room so that he could see everyone at the same time. Thom stood at his side. Uncertain of what was expected of him, he decided to just observe for how the nobles reacted to whatever the master magician was about to tell them.

"I am Osric, a master of magic and a servant of our king. You may not know me, but you know the color of my robe. I want to talk about war and forcing these invaders out of the city, but I only want to talk with those who are brave enough to fight for king and country. Some of you are only here because you think there is no other option open to you. On that you are wrong. I and others broke through the attempt to isolate Camelot. Even now, King's Harbor is free of the invaders, which means that the Road of Waters is open for any of you who want to escape Camelot. I know the boats only run at night, but now would be the time to get down there to buy passage out of here. So if you are one of those eager to run, go now. I do not want to waste my words on any cowards."

He paused, looking over the room.

No one stirred.

"Maybe you are scheming to linger in this meeting and then slink away afterward to avoid public embarrassment, but I will remind you of this: those river galleys are small. They cannot fit all the refugees who will flood the harbor as soon as word gets out that the Road of Waters is open. You should run to get there and secure places for you and your entourage, or else some fat trader will buy all the remaining berths and you will be left behind. Go now or you may miss that last galley out."

He paused again, waiting.

Many men shifted in their seats. Some of those leaning against the walls also stirred. Then a pair of them suddenly moved toward the front door. Others protested, telling them to stay. As they paused in their retreat to mutter excuses, another one suddenly dashed from the room, not even bothering to go back upstairs for his things. That caused the other two to also hurry away, calling for their soldiers and retainers to join them.

Osric waited for them to leave before starting again. "No more hiding behind monk robes, gentlemen. It is time. Magicians go to fight, as do loyal centaurs and pixies. Even common men of the city have joined our ranks. Will the nobles do their part too? Will you bring your arms to King Arthur's aid?"

"You are not my liege lord, wizard. Why should I follow your lead?" The nobleman who spoke did not look angry or frightened. Thom thought his gaze seemed thoughtful.

"My fellow magicians and I liberated King's Haven with the help of loyal centaurs and sailors. Has anyone here shown any greater initiative for the king's sake? Anyone? I thought not. Join us because at least we are marching forward to engage the enemy."

The man nodded. "Who commands?"

Osric smiled. "You'll like this even less, my lord. The centaurs all follow the lead of Laodamia, a lead mare among their tribes. She coordinates with us, the four masters who lead the magicians."

"Then I think we should take a similar stance. We will appoint one to lead us and coordinate with the four of you too."

"Fair enough," replied Osric, "but do not take long to reach your decision. We must move swiftly on the sorcerers and Mordred."

The wizard then turned to Thom, "Come along, journeyman. We cannot dawdle here either."

As Osric and Thom began to walk out of the guest house, Lord Lionel came after them. "Where do we find you once we have settled on our war leader?"

"Send word to the chapel. There are guards there who will know where I am."

With that, wizard and journeyman strode off into the morning sunlight. It felt good to Thom walking beside a strong magician. Even though he knew this was just temporary, it felt right. Every student needs a mentor.

* * *

FIFTEEN

Among Old Companions

Once back in Mousehome, Osric went off to find the other masters. Thom lingered on one the arbor walks, uncertain where to go or what to do.

That is where Vivien found him. "There you are. Come with me, Thomas, for I want to get this over with."

The nun who followed her like a shadow said nothing, just gave Thom a hard look.

"What do you want with me, Vivien?"

"I have been ordered to test you, which I think is a waste of time. Everyone knows you are a journeyman in name only, that you were promoted from apprentice as a reward for rescuing the king and queen, that it had little to do with your skill or knowledge."

Her attitude stirred his pride. He wanted to show her that he knew at least some magic and so he almost took her challenge, but then remembered the orders he was under. The council members had carefully studied his cache of elements and would know if any had been used. To use them would mean banishment from the guild. "I cannot work with elements. The council forbade it."

She set hands on hips and raised one eyebrow. "The situation has changed. We are at war now and the masters need to know your skill level before we go off to battle…"

"But the council…," began Thom.

"Has been overridden by the masters on hand. I was told that Wizard Osric informed you of this last night. Now, come along. I want to get this over with so that I can get back to my students, for they certainly are not ready to use magic during the insanity of battle."

When he still hesitated, Vivien added, "Are you frightened to reveal your own ignorance? Well, it will be no surprise to me."

"What is the journeywoman baiting you into doing?" asked a new voice.

Thom looked behind him and saw Francis and Marcus walking toward them. "Francis!"

"I told you that we would find him, journeyman," said Marcus.

"I made *my own* way back," remarked the monk just before he was crushed by a hug from his young friend.

"Where have you been?" asked Thom. "Are you well?"

"I am well enough, though heartsick over the evils being done in the city. You heard the killings?"

Thom nodded.

"I would almost take up a magician's box again, if it meant I could scour the realm of sorcerers and stop their callous killing of magical beings," said Francis. He looked at Vivien. "So, what is it that you are wanting from Thomas?"

"The master magicians of the league want him tested. They want me to determine his skill level to help prepare for the fighting we will start soon."

"Test him now? Is that wise?" asked Francis.

"I would have thought that they already understood his shortcomings, but it is what they have ordered."

"You will be surprised at what you learn," predicted Francis. "I wonder which one of them is wanting to expose Thomas like this."

"One of the four masters or all of them. Wizardess Bronwen did not explain herself when she gave the order."

"Bronwen? The Keeper of Camelot? So she is part of the league?" Francis seemed thoughtful. "You must have been miffed at that secret, journeywoman, since she refused to take you on as a student. Have you learned the identity of any of the others?"

"Wizard Osric," said Thom.

"And one of the other two is a former sorcerer but he renounced that path," said Vivien. "The Father Abbot told me that much a few days ago."

"Truly?" Francis frowned. "So two are still concealing their identity but you know one was once a sorcerer. I fear that I may know who the other one is, especially considering that Osiric is part of this."

"Who is he?" asked Vivien.

Francis shook his head. "It is but a hunch on my part. I will need more than that before I blurt out any names. Besides, it is not my secret to reveal." He paused in thought. "If the secretive master is who I fear he is, then many will be very upset. He is wise to keep his identity well hidden. But I will say this, it appears the abbot was better at recruiting than I ever realized."

Vivien frowned. "Now I am even more intrigued. I thought the presence of a former sorcerer would be the most upsetting news. Who is this other mystery magician whose identity would stir up such a hornet's nest? I will get the answer from you yet, Brother Francis."

Francis gave her a friendly smile but shook his head in denial. "Will you be taking Thomas down the Hole for his testing?"

"Where else?"

"Well then, get to it, but keep in mind his injuries for he looks like someone drug him behind a horse from here to the Ipswich and back. Do not exhaust him in trying to prove your bigotries, for we will have need of him soon. I don't think we have much time left."

"Before what? The fall of Camelot? An attack on the monastery? A call to battle from the league's leaders?" asked Vivien. "What is it that you see around the corner, monk?"

"I'm no seer or prophet. I just have a feeling… it is almost as if I can smell change and sense the approaching wind of a great storm…" Francis shook his head. "Maybe I spent too many hours hunkering behind alley debris these last two days. Obviously, change is coming. The city is at war… and yet I think there is something greater involved here." He looked up at the sky and the invisible enchantment that covered the city. "Maybe this will be the end of Arthur's reign and even the end of the Ways of Camelot."

He looked again at those around him. "No matter what is ahead, may God protect us, for threats seem everywhere."

"Amen," agreed Sister Harmony.

"Enough chatter," stated Vivien. "Come along, Thomas. Let's get this testing done so that I can give an accurate report to the masters."

She led him to the building that stood over the Hole. Harmony, Francis, and Marcus came with them. There was a guard at the door, but he let them go inside without a challenge.

Thom found himself in a bare room with a trapdoor at its center. Vivien opened it and started down the wooden ladder. He would have followed right after, but Harmony pushed ahead of him. It seemed like the nun wanted to protect Vivien from getting too near any man. Thom wondered what the journeywoman thought of such prudery. But Thom said nothing; he merely waited his turn.

The ladder ended in a dirt-floored hole with rough wooden walls. The room held two worn benches pressed against opposite walls and a pair of oil lamps in wall sconces, but nothing else. A monk stood watch there, though Thom had no idea what a monk could do that the guard above couldn't. He didn't seem to be particularly burly. Vivien didn't wait for Francis and Marcus to get down, but set off down an unlit tunnel. Thom and the others followed.

The timber-reinforced passage ran quite a distance, straight and true. Ahead, Thom could see the glow of a well-lit room, but the tunnel itself had no lights in it. Nonetheless, it was an easy trek on level and smooth ground. As he walked down it, Thom's thoughts wandered back to Adele. He was so thankful that she was here and safe.

He wasn't really paying attention to his surroundings. But then he suddenly stumbled. It wasn't any treacherous ground that tangled his feet though; it was the sudden silence in his inner ear. He could no longer hear the magical battle. He couldn't even hear the city's enchantment.

He just stood there, staring up at the ceiling of the tunnel, as Francis caught up with him.

"What is it?" asked Thom. "Is this some type of magic?"

"No. We are now outside of Camelot's enchantment," said Francis calmly in explanation.

"How can this be?" asked Thom. It seemed like he had gone partially deaf after having heard the background rhythms of magic for months now. It was disconcerting.

He took a few steps back and the sounds returned. The others had all stopped for him, but none of them seemed alarmed. Even in the darkness of the tunnel, Thom could tell that they were familiar with this phenomenon. He walked back to where the red-head and the nun waited and was startled again by the sudden silence.

Vivien smiled sadly. "Are you surprised that they lied to you once again? Camelot is no floating city. It sits in one place, like any other settlement; only the magical Roads shift."

Francis spoke. "We are outside of Merlin's enchantments. I think this is your first time free of it since we entered the Road of Leaves so many days ago. I find it a relief, don't you?"

"I find it unsettling, now that I'm aware of magic's pulse," said Sister Harmony. "It is almost like my heart stopped beating."

"Most of the realm is like this, Harmony," stated Vivien, "so you need to become comfortable with it."

Thom ignored them as he strained to hear. He could now make out the steady, complex rhythms of the magic-encircled city above and behind them. But the sounds were faint, as if far away.

"It is somehow muffled to help hide Camelot's location," said Vivien, anticipating his question. "That is part of the enchantment's weaving, though do not ask me to explain which elements they used to create it. I have been the student of a wizardess for decades and I still do not understand how the enchantments are interwoven and maintained. Everywhere else, magic repulses other magic, but the Ways of Camelot somehow bring them together. My mistress taught me much, but not this. Maybe she never understood it either."

Once more, Thom stepped backward in the tunnel to pass under the enchantment then stepped forward again. The line where it changed was very obvious when he concentrated on it.

"As I understand it from the abbot, your friend Brother Francis suggested digging the tunnel," said Vivien, with a nod toward the monk. "For someone so offended by magic, he certainly knows far too much about it. I admit that I would never have thought of digging under Camelot's enchantment."

Thom wouldn't have thought of it either. He looked at the shadowy figure that was his friend and wondered what other secrets the monk held back from him. He knew that he had good reason to do so, including the confidentiality promised to others, but still it hurt to be reminded that his friend kept secrets from him.

"Now, keep moving," ordered Vivien. "I want to get the testing done quickly, before something worse befalls the city."

They came out in a narrow room with a wooden floor that echoed with hollow thuds with each footfall, a room empty of people or things. It was a very plain room, with rough wooden walls to match the floor. As soon as he entered, Thom's ears and eyes were drawn to a pair of lanterns hanging from the ceiling. Both burned by magic, steady and smokeless. The magic was a subtle thing, barely a whisper to his inner ear. He looked questioningly at Vivien.

She answered his obvious question. "One of the league masters set those up, for it is no simple enchantment; it needs no regular attention, but slowly burns through a mixture of elements like a normal oil lamp burns through its fuel, yet I think these will last for months if not years. Their existence down here tells me that at least one of the four masters has been here before this current visit of theirs."

Thom wondered how many magicians were part of the League of Barnabas. Did they have other hideaways like the monastery? He would likely never know, since he planned to stay with the guild. He brought his thoughts back from such ruminations, and concentrated on the room in front of him. It seemed rather bare, a disappointing end to such an elaborate tunneling. It seemed too small for a training room, especially after all the effort taken to dig under the city walls. "This is it? This is not much of a refuge. Is this where you hold your classes, Vivien? It seems rather small and plain."

"You don't judge a shop by its front porch, do you? We stand at the entrance to the league's hideaway," replied Vivien, rapping her knuckles on the far wall in four quick taps.

A door appeared, swinging inward to reveal a much bigger room, one well-lit and with people in it. Thom could hear their muted conversation and smell the breakfast they were eating. His stomach grumbled in hunger, for he hadn't eaten much at the guest house.

"Welcome to the heart of Mousehome, Thomas. This is the Hole where we magicians scurry to practice our craft unnoticed," said Vivien as she motioned for him to enter. "As you surmised, the Father Abbot has me train the apprentice magicians for the League of Barnabas down here, out of the guild's hearing."

Thom entered what turned out to be a common room of sorts, also lit by magical lanterns suspended from the ceiling rafters. A half-dozen trestle tables filled the place, each with a set of benches. Half the tables were occupied with an assortment of monks, eating quietly at what must have been a late breakfast for them. He also saw two rougher-looking men who reminded him of the mercenaries and soldiers he had met in his travels- two of Marcus' men he guessed. They were the ones talking, for monks avoided any conversation while eating. Marcus pushed past to join his men, getting loud greetings as he approached.

Thom almost missed the five people in the corner, for they were nearly as silent as the monks and they were much smaller. Two pixie couples sat at the far table, finishing their meal. Their facial and arm tattoos were black in color, proclaiming the four to be part of Clan Pitheni. With them sat Dorthos. It didn't seem to matter that he was of another tribe, the Brythoni; they appeared to have accepted him readily.

"I hope he finds solace among his own," stated Vivien. When Thom gave her a puzzled look, she added, "Did you think you were the only one who heard the pixie massacre? It was a shameful act."

She cleared her throat and then pointed Thom to the nearest empty table. "Go sit down, while I prepare an examination room."

Before Thom obeyed her, he took out his robe and put it back on. It was an insignificant gesture, he knew, but he wanted the visible reminder of his current rank in the guild. He might have only an apprentice's level of understanding, but his acknowledged rank was journeyman, no matter what Vivien's testing showed.

SIXTEEN

Training Apprentices

When Vivien returned, she said nothing about Thom's dark blue robe. They entered a long passageway that had numerous doors off of it. The journeywoman's constant escort, Sister Harmony, joined them. Surprisingly, Francis followed behind. Thom would have thought the monk would avoid this, since he had such a dislike of magic. Vivien led them to the deepest room in Mousehome's Hole. A single magical lantern hung from the ceiling, casting large shadows behind them as they entered. It was a barren room with a shaft in its ceiling in the far corner. A ladder climbed up that opening.

"The Father Abbot ordered me to reveal this to you. This is Mousehome's back door," stated Vivien. She gave Francis a flat look. "You needn't have followed, monk. I wouldn't have shirked my duty to show him."

Francis gave her a brief smile, but said nothing.

Vivien continued, "If you were to climb that ladder and open the hatch at the top, you would find yourself in a small cave on the highlands that lay outside Camelot's enchantment."

"What does it look like from outside?"

Vivien shrugged. "I have not climbed out. Have you, brother?"

Francis gave her another smile. "Indeed, I have. From this side, the city's enchantment is hard to hear and even harder to see."

Thom nodded, for he had heard similar things about the Roads.

"It is rough country up there, with little in the way of natural shelter or food," added Francis. "I would say none should flee in that direction unless things are dire and no other way exists. It would take many days of hard travel to reach any settlement because you would be on foot."

"Do all the others know of this exit?" Thom asked, thinking mainly of Adele.

"All who train or guard have been shown," Vivien answered, motioning for them to leave. "Now I have another task to attend to. Come along."

They went back up the passageway to another door. There Vivien paused to tell him she had to get her students' instruction started first. "I fear that I have little time left to train them, so I will not neglect their lessons just to appease the masters' desire to have you tested. I will have you watch, Thomas, and maybe help with some instruction."

"I will wait in the common room," stated Francis, moving on toward the main room.

Vivien continued in her lecture of Thom. "Each student already has a magician's box with the typical Beginner's Handful of elements, but I have already been exposing them to the second tier of apprentice enchantments."

"You've moved on to the Double Handful?" asked Thom, mentioning the next five elements usually introduced to an apprentice. It was how Levitanus had trained him and most likely that was how Vivien was trained too. As Thom understood it, the Double Handful were usually introduced two years into an apprentice's training, so Vivien was definitely rushing things.

"They know some enchantments using the second five, but not all. No, their training is specialized toward enchantments that can be used in battle. It means neglecting some things and mastering others that are usually left for later."

Thom frowned, not sure if he liked such a concentration. Was the league trying to create magic fighters?

"It is only an introduction for them, so that they can recognize certain rhythms in case particular enchantments are used against them. I would say it is rather prudent of the masters, considering that both the sorcerers and the wizards will likely hunt us once they learn of the league."

Thom shook his head at the risk involved. "And you do this with a group of students? Even at Clas Myrddin, they limit classroom training to advanced apprentices and yours are only months into it, if even that."

Vivien raised an eyebrow at his comment. "I am well aware what is taught at the keep. Unlike you, I was a student there once, and I have taught a handful of classes too."

"Journeywoman Vivien is careful in her training of us," stated Sister Harmony, speaking up in her defense.

Thom gave her a surprised look, having forgotten that she was also a student. She might not be in apprentice gray, but she did have a small knapsack on her back that apparently contained a magician's box with at least five elements in it. He doubted the querulous sister was easy to instruct.

"Watch and see how their training progresses," suggested Vivien.

So Thom follow the journeywoman and the nun to another room where Harmony immediately joined the four others seated at the large table. Among the students was Adele, still in her gray robe.

She and Thom shared a smile but there was no chance to talk, for Vivien motioned for Thom to stand to the side as she proceeded with the day's lesson.

Listening in, Thom learned the names of all the students. The ones he hadn't been introduced to were Sister Myrna and Brothers Michael and Canon. Usually, magician apprentices were children or youths, not adults and most certainly not old ones like Canon. The monk's thin hair was gray-touched and his skin weathered and wrinkled. But his eyes sparkled with curiosity as he watched and listened to Vivien's example, the creation of Wizard Lights.

They were in an almost-bare side room off the larger training room, gathered around a large table. Vivien had placed her magician's box, mixing bowl, and pestle on the worn wood. She pulled out vials of powdered Azure Fireflies, powdered Meadow Dragon wings, and dried and crushed Glow Berries, explaining briefly how each element was made and what properties it would add to the magic she was about to craft. She carefully set the glass vials on the table and shut the box to silence all the competing rhythms.

Thom's old master had often done the very same thing during his training, for those other sounds could easily distract a new student.

Vivien mixed the elements in her bowl and then discreetly added her spittle. She then formed small balls out of the resulting paste, balls that started to glow as she worked them. She handed one to each of her students, letting them hold the soft lights and examine them more closely. Wizard Lights were safe to touch; they might cause your skin to tingle, but they certainly wouldn't burn anyone.

Thom just looked on, having made Wizard Lights often enough over the years. He watched as the bluish glow highlighted Adele's look of surprise and joy. She sensed him watching and looked up, smiling at him. "I can now see why you were willing to spend so many years studying this craft. It is a wonder."

He nodded, smiling back at her. "Crafting magic still fascinates me, even after spending a decade as an apprentice." But then he remembered some of the darker secrets of the craft and his smile faded. More complex enchantments required the killing of beings to gain their innate magical abilities. He dared not mention it to her for he didn't want to rob her of the joy at handling an enchantment. He did his best to strengthen his smile. "Can you hear the various elements as they meld their beats into one rhythm?"

Her focus was back on the glowing sphere. "Yes. I am starting to, but I am so new at listening to things with my inner ear."

He was about to reply, when Vivien interrupted.

"Thomas, can you work with Brothers Canon and Michael?" she asked. "Test them on identifying the unique rhythms while I work with the women?"

"Did the masters order this as well? I still belong to the guild, so please don't ask me to do more than they have actually approved," he replied.

"I will make the enchantments; you need only test them on identifying elements and rhythms. I doubt the council ordered you not teach anyone, for they would never have even thought of the possibility."

She was right on that. A journeyman never taught unless ordered to do so by his master, and then it was only when the wizard had two students, a journeyman and an apprentice. The council certainly couldn't have anticipated that he would teach without actually doing any magic. The splitting of hairs made him pause.

"Well?" Vivien's tone sounded impatient.

He looked at the men and Canon caught his eye. The old man was looking up from the light he held, expectant. The elderly monk obviously had innate skill; it seemed unfair that he had been denied teaching just because no master had chosen him as a child. Canon deserved a chance to learn.

Vivien was right; the council hadn't forbidden him to *teach* about magic. If he didn't handle the elements himself, he could still claim to have followed their orders... at least for now. He wasn't certain what Vivien would be demanding of him during her upcoming test.

He reached a decision. He might as well do something worthwhile. "Of course, I will work with them. It will be my privilege."

Canon smiled. Brother Michael was still entranced by the Wizard Light he was holding and had missed the exchange.

Eric Loren

SEVENTEEN

Testing

For the two hours, Thom did his best to instruct the men. He had Canon and Michael pick out particular beats in the enchantment rhythms, tapping out the pace with their index finger on the table's edge. That was how Levitanus had taught Thom many years ago, so he used that technique with the monks. He was a bit surprised when he noticed Vivien doing the same. Apparently, there was more similarity in apprentice training than Thom realized.

Mixed elements didn't sound the same as isolated ones; the tempo often changed. It was important for a magician to recognize those changes, for it helped him to know if an enchantment had been crafted correctly.

A Wizard Light was a fairly simple enchantment where the elements had no odd reactions to each other, but it was still like picking out the sound of a single instrument when a whole band was playing. So Thom was pleasantly surprised when the two monks succeeded in picking out all three elements by the end of their session. They seemed zealous to learn.

Their training ended abruptly, with Vivien standing up and announcing, "Enough." She let go of her focus on the lights and they all vanished. "You have all worked hard and it grows late. You have earned a respite. Eat something, for this can drain your strength as much as a sparring session with Marcus. You have an hour, then return here and work together to compose a list of elements that you can recognize by their sound. Adele, you and Sister Myrna eat quickly and then take your turn at watch in the tunnel. Brother Peter has been on listening watch long enough. Go now."

As the five students left, Vivien motioned for Thom to remain. Sister Harmony looked ready to remain too, but Vivien would have none of it and ordered the woman out of the room. Once the others were gone, she closed the door and confronted him.

"We might as well get this over with now. I have been asked to test your skill level, even though I have told the Father Abbot and Wizardess Branwen that you are a journeyman in name only."

Thom didn't reply to her challenging tone. Instead, he waited.

"I have your test set up in the next room, so come along."

He followed her down the hallway to a much-smaller room with a small table and two chairs. The magical lantern hanging from the ceiling was partially shuttered, making the room rather dim. She motioned for him to sit down and took the chair across from him. On the table between them was a piece of dark cloth.

Vivien placed her knapsack on the floor and took out her magician box, mixing bowl, and pestle. Thom wondered if he should be taking out his own equipment but she shook her head in the negative when he slung his pack off his back, so he just set it on the floor between his legs.

Once her things were laid out in front of her, she grabbed the cloth and held it out. "Cover your eyes. The first test will be on recognizing the sounds of elements."

He complied, blindfolding himself. He heard her slide her magician's box before him and open its lid. The sounds of the enclosed elements filled his inner ear.

"Pick out the vial of Phoenix tongue," she ordered, "and do it without fumbling."

Thom looked down although he could see nothing. He tilted his head, trying to pick out the sound of that particular element. It took a moment but he was able to isolate it. He then had to blindly guide his fingers to that glass vial among the many in her cache. He almost pulled the wrong one but corrected himself and pulled out the right vial.

She took it from his fingers and returned it to the box.

"Slow," was her only remark before ordering him to find the vial of powdered Azure fireflies.

Thomas found that one too and with a bit more speed.

She snatched the vial away, but before putting it back she unstoppered it and poured some of its contents out. Thom heard that much, though he didn't know if she had just dumped the precious powder on the table or into her mixing bowl.

"Find me Griffin claw," was her only remark.

She had him pull out powders of pegasi mane, Copper Dandelion seed, and Rowan root. Not all were added to her bowl, but some were. She was slowly mixing them into an enchantment that he didn't recognize, although he knew all of its ingredients. That developing magic became louder as she prepared it, making it harder for Thom to hear the elements she was demanding from him.

Vivien went beyond apprentice-level powders, but Thom was still able to find them. Finally, she stumped him when she told him to pull out powdered roc feather.

He hesitated, trying to remember if he had ever heard that particular element.

"Faster. Hand me the vial of dragon blood."

He moved his hand over the magician's box but had no idea what one to pull out. He suspected guessing on the wrong one would be worse than admitting his ignorance; he knew his master wouldn't have tolerated a guess. "I haven't learned the sound of that element yet," he confessed.

"Finally. Well then, find me rainbow dew instead."

He did recognize that element and actually was able to pick out its unique beat easily.

His sure response seemed to upset Vivien, for she sped up her demands now and these were for rarer powders, some with more subtle sounds.

He knew less than half of them.

When he missed three in a row, she called a sudden end to her test and ordered him to remove his blindfold.

A harsh light accosted his eyes as he took off the covering cloth. Whatever she had mixed in her bowl was now glowing in a garish yellowish light. The sound of the mixture was jarring, a rhythm that seemed to falter then speed up and then stumble again. He didn't ask what it was, not wanting to admit more of his ignorance. It seemed a simple enchantment, but he had never seen such a combination of ingredients. He wasn't certain if she has added any mundane elements, but such ingredients often affected the sound of magical elements.

"You, of course, recognize this *enchantment*," she stated, giving the word an odd emphasis, as she pointed a thin finger at the glaring light in her mixing bowl.

"I don't," Thom confessed.

"How could you not?" she asked, now sounding angry. "It is used during the initial testing of all journeymen."

"You know that my master never formally started my training for the next level," he replied, puzzled by her anger. He had been promoted rather suddenly after saving the queen from kidnappers and then he had been sent off on another journey before his training could start.

"Am I wearing motley? Don't mistake me for a fool. Your element knowledge is that of a veteran journeyman, not an apprentice."

"I don't understand what you mean." The stench from the burning enchantment was starting to aggravate Thom's breathing and he suppressed a cough. Why was she suddenly so angry?

The light spurting and flaring in her mixing bowl gave her features an extra harshness as she glared at him. "You know too much, Thomas."

He was unsure how to respond. She was wrong; it was his ignorance that had endangered him so many times over the last few months.

She gave him no time to explain anything. Instead, she threw another question at him. "Tell me, how would you mix a Twist of Air enchantment?"

He answered her, explaining the order that the powders were put into the bowl and the ratio of each.

She followed that question with twenty more, about enchantments at all levels. He readily admitted ignorance of all master-level magic and doubted she knew many of them either, since wizards guarded such secrets carefully. However, he did know a few of the journeyman-level enchantments, having learned them during his recent Road journeys. Many more were apprentice-level and those he knew well enough. Yet, in spite of that, she was able to stump him more quickly this time.

Vivien seemed a bit more satisfied now that more of his ignorance was showing, but she made no more snide remarks. Instead, she started questioning him about harvesting magical plants and animals, and how to render them down into their useful magical elements.

Thom had done this since his first week as Levitanus' student, for his old master had mostly made his own elements instead of buying them from suppliers. He answered her questions with renewed confidence. He had spent too many days knee-deep in a moor or shivering in a winter storm to not know how to gather particular berries or snare a specific magical animal. Some of the harvesting trips he had gone on had lasted weeks as he and Levitanus wandered the wilds looking for some rare plant or hard-to-find bird.

When she moved onto rarer animals, he was still able to answer, for although he had never worked with the corpse of a griffin, unicorn, or basilisk, his master had explained what parts were most useful from each animal. She quickly realized that he had no first-hand experience with any of these beasts and seemed to take some satisfaction when he erred a few times while repeating his master's long-ago instructions.

Finally, she finished her questioning and just stood there for a time, staring at him with her arms crossed.

The fire in her mixing bowl had died down to a mere ember, its magical elements only a faint whisper now. The relative darkness made her seem brooding.

After a few minutes, the silence became too oppressive for Thom. "What is wrong now?"

"You are not who you claim to be, Thomas of York."

Startled, he shook his head. "I am no shape-shifter, if that is what you're implying. You would know if I were using magic."

"But neither are you merely a boy fresh out of his apprenticeship. You know too much. What I do not understand is why you have stopped feigning ignorance. Why reveal yourself to me?"

Thom was confused. What was she talking about? "I am the same person who I have always been. You know me, Vivien. We sailed the Road of Waters together. What are you trying to imply? That I am a wizard in hiding? If so, then you've lost your senses."

"You are not a master, but you certainly *are* a veteran journeyman. How many years ago did your master promote you? I am not surprised that he kept it a secret, since you are so young." She leaned closer. Even though she was quite a bit shorter, he almost pulled back from her. "You and your master were playing a dangerous game, Thomas. The guild has rules against such things. And now you must be feeling very alone, worried that a new master will discover your knowledge and expose you to the guild. They will banish you for certain. Maybe even kill you, just to make sure you don't join up with Dalrake's sorcerers. I doubt the league will want to keep you either, not if you are so deceptive."

Thom had had enough. "Why are you speaking such insanity? Is this some jest? You know very well that I've never been trained as a journeyman. The others at the guild house would laugh behind my back because of it; they all knew that I was a journeyman in name only."

"I will advise the Father Abbot *not* to let you join. The league has no place for someone as deceptive as you."

Thom was becoming angry. "What deception? You are talking nonsense."

Her eyes seemed to shine with a blazing anger. "You lied to me."

EIGHTEEN

A True Journeyman

Vivien didn't explain herself. Instead, she grabbed the abandoned blindfold and used it to wipe out the goop still in her bowl, then packed her items away in her knapsack. Without saying another word to Thom, she walked out of the room.

For a moment, he just sat there. Confused. Why did she think he was a liar? What had he done or said?

He heard Vivien in the hallway, talking to Sister Harmony, asking her where the abbot was.

Suddenly concerned that he might be banished from the only sanctuary he knew of in Camelot, Thom hurried after her. When he came out, he saw the two women just passing through the door to the common room. He ran after them.

When he barged through, he found them talking to Francis, so he hurried over.

"No, I will not send for the abbot," the monk was saying to Vivien. "As Sister Harmony will tell you, Abbot Justin cannot be interrupted during some of his duties. He is the spiritual leader of this monastery; he cannot drop everything just because some journeywoman magician has a sudden concern."

"I am no fluttery female, Brother Francis. My concern is for all of our safety. There is an impostor in our midst." She hadn't yet noticed Thom coming up behind her.

Francis glanced quickly at Thom and then back at her. "You are accusing Thomas of being an impostor?"

She noticed the glance and whirled around to confront Thom. "Yes. He is an impostor." She said it loudly, so everyone else in the crowded room overheard, including Adele.

"I am not," protested Thom. He wanted to say more, but he still didn't understand why she thought him to be a fraud.

Francis looked from Thom to Vivien and then back. "Has this anything to do with Thomas' past training?"

"His claims of ignorance are a mere act. He…"

"Enough," stated Francis firmly, raising his hand to forestall her. "The three of us must talk. Now." He looked around. "And alone."

Francis motioned for Vivien and Thomas to go back to where they had come from.

Vivien crossed her arms. "Why shouldn't the others hear this? I have no secrets."

Francis' eyes narrowed. "We all have our share of secrets, follies, and sins. Don't think yourself immune. Frankly, I wouldn't mind if you shouted out the guild's secrets to everyone who will listen. However, when I left the guild, I swore to uphold their confidences. I'll not break that vow today. Come, both of you. We must talk of guild business. Sister Harmony, I must ask you to remain here and trust that I can serve as temporary chaperon."

The nun frowned but gave him a slight nod of the head.

Francis squeezed between Thom and Vivien and headed down the hallway that led deeper in Mousehome. Vivien frowned at his back, gave one more glare toward Thom, and then marched after the monk. Thom followed.

Francis led them to the same room where the class had been held. The monk closed the door firmly and then confronted them. "Vivien, you tested Thomas and found him skilled beyond a typical apprentice newly raised to journeyman. Is that right?"

"Yes." Her arms were crossed and her back to the far wall.

"You think that he is far more than what he claims. That he is really a senior journeyman who pretends at his naivety."

"Yes," she repeated.

Thom started protesting, but Francis cut him off. "She is right, Thomas. You know too much. I realized that while we were on the Road of Leaves."

Thom was shocked. Francis also thought he was a fraud? "You never said anything."

Francis shrugged. "I have no desire to meddle in the guild's affairs. Your master trained you to a journeyman's level, that became obvious to me during our trials on the Road. Did Levitanus never tell you what he was doing?"

Thom shook his head no. He began to wonder if there was any truth to what they were saying. He thought back to his years of training by Levitanus but couldn't recall the wizard ever telling him that his training had passed beyond that of an apprentice.

"You still insist on pretending ignorance?" asked Vivien, clearly not believing him.

"I think he is ignorant," said Francis. "I think his master did this without telling Thomas."

"But why?" asked Vivien.

Thom was wondering the same thing.

"That I do not know. Why did Levitanus train Thomas in relative isolation? The wizard was one of the three Founders of Camelot and the Roads. By those rights, he sat on the council, yet he never took his apprentice to the guild house. Your mistress was also on the council; did she keep you away from Clas Myrddin? Didn't anyone question why Levitanus kept his student hidden?"

"Some wondered," admitted Vivien. "I heard some say he was overly protective after the loss of his last two students."

The apprentice that Levitanus was teaching before Thom had been killed by the senior journeyman also under Levitanus' tutelage. The crime was only discovered later, when that journeyman, Gweir, openly turned to the Dark Arts. Thom was sure that Gweir also killed Levitanus, though the man had claimed innocence of that crime just before Thom watched him fall into a raging Road of Waters.

"The wizards are overfond of intrigue," muttered Francis with a pitying look at Thom. "It makes me wonder why Levitanus decided to send Thomas to Camelot at the exact moment that Dalrake was planning his attack. Did he know something was amiss? Was he expecting Thomas to notice and report back to him?"

"You think he was sent as bait?" asked Vivien. "If so, then they failed to catch their plumpest prize. Dalrake escaped both the Road of Leaves and the Road of Waters."

"My master wouldn't have done any of that to me," protested Thom. "I lived with the man for over a decade; I knew him better than anyone. Levitanus was too fond of me to do something so callous."

"You may be right," said Francis, "but he certainly schemed to train you beyond your acknowledged level in the guild. You are truly a journeyman magician, Thomas, and I suspect that you have been for years now."

Thom wasn't so sure about that.

"I do not think there is anything to alert the Father Abbot about," remarked the monk with a firm look at Vivien. "Thom's unusual pace of training is not the abbot's concern. He knows that Thom is a journeyman and didn't your testing prove that to be true?"

Vivien raised one fine eyebrow at the monk but gave a slight nod.

"It's a pity that you blurted out your suspicions to everyone. Are you willing to apologize to Thomas in front of them?"

Thom liked that idea but he saw Vivien put her hands on her hips in defiance.

"Apologize? I said nothing worth apologizing for."

That angered Thom more. "You called me an impostor."

"Well, there is that," she admitted, "but you deserved the charge for pretending to be a mere apprentice."

"I wasn't pretending anything!"

Francis raised his hand. "Vivien, your pride is getting the best of you. A strong woman should know humility too."

She opened her mouth to protest then thought better of it. She glanced at Thom again. "Maybe I was too quick to judge. I will explain my mistake to the others."

"Good, for I am tired of talking about the guild and its scheming ways," stated Francis, opening the door. "As for Wizardess Bronwen and the others, tell them the truth of what you found, that Thomas has reached a solid journeyman-level in his training. Leave off any judgment of his late mentor. They can come to their own conclusions about that."

He paused until Vivien nodded her agreement, then walked out. Thom hurried after him, having no desire to linger in that room with Vivien.

Francis had taken only two steps into the hallway when Adele rushed up, looking for them.

"Come quickly! Something is happening in the city. Maybe the sorcerers are making their final assault on the castle."

NINETEEN

Noise and Silence

Thom and the others ran after Adele, through the common room and down the tunnel. As soon as he crossed under the city's enchantment, he heard the difference that had worried her. Enchantments were being crafted just minutes apart and many were exploding in a cacophony of harsh sounds. He gritted his teeth at what his inner ear was hearing, but he kept running so that he wouldn't get trampled by all those running behind him.

At the end of the tunnel, Sister Myrna waited. She had been on watch with Adele. She backed up to the tunnel's wall as the crowd joined her: Adele, Vivien, Thom, Francis, Sister Harmony, Brothers Michael and Canon, Mercenary Marcus, and two of Marcus' men.

"What is happening?" asked Marcus in a demanding tone. "Is the monastery under attack?"

"No," answered Francis, "but the battle at the castle has heated up. Either the sorcerers have breached the wall and are taking it, or the wizards have started their reprisal."

A particularly loud explosion happened; those who could hear it winced in unison.

"What now?" asked Marcus, deaf to such things.

"That must have lit up the sky," said Vivien, more to the others than to him. "Fire and Air enchantments clash terribly when they meet."

Marcus ordered one of his men to go up and warn the guard on watch upstairs, adding, "And then go on to warn the men guarding the outer walls. I want to know if anything is stirring in the city anywhere near the monastery." He sent the other one back into Mousehome to get one of his companions.

Those gathered at the mouth of the tunnel began to talk, excited and worried, but Francis interrupted. "Quiet. Everyone. Those who can hear, need to concentrate on the elemental sounds. Try to decipher what is happening. You can tell much by the enchantments being crafted, if you listen carefully."

Silence fell, while those who had an ear for magic did their best to listen.

Thom concentrated on the distant battle. It was hard to distinguish what enchantments were being crafted at this distance, but he could certainly hear whenever any enchantments collided and exploded. Each time that happened was a jarring screech or wail to his inner ear, ending in a boom like thunder as the magic shredded. While listening, he could tell the clashes were moving, that maybe the battling sides were changing locations. At first it sounded as if the clashes were coming closer, then as if the battle was getting farther away. He wondered what that meant, but he didn't want to speak and disturbed the others trying to listen.

Then, suddenly, the magic battle ended. For a moment, Thom wasn't certain about that, for the earlier explosions had made his inner ear ache. He tilted his head, puzzled. He was about to say something, but others blurted out before he did.

"Did it stop?" asked Harmony.

"Is it over?" asked Adele. "Which side won?"

"It may just be a pause to regroup," said Vivien.

Thom strained, but could only hear the encompassing enchantment of the city and, faintly, something from Sky Tower, where it pierced through to anchor the Road of Clouds. It couldn't be over. Days of battling couldn't have ended so quickly.

Just then, the man who Marcus had sent back into Mousehome returned with another guard. The head mercenary turned to Francis. "What can you tell me? Should I send them out to investigate?"

Francis focused his attention on Marcus. "The fight has moved away from the castle. I'm not certain but it seems like they have gone toward the Road of Leaves, to Rowan Gate. Maybe the wizards are driving the sorcerers out of Camelot."

"That would be good," replied Marcus. He turned to his men and gave them succinct orders to spy out what was happening at Camelot Castle and at the Rowan Gate.

"The battle may have moved onto the Road of Leaves," said Francis. "If so, I would advise your men not to follow. The surrounding enchantment is much smaller there and far easier to damage. It isn't pleasant to experience, as you well know, Marcus."

Marcus remembered; he told his men not to enter the Road. The two burly men then hurried to do his bidding.

Thom watched them climb. Not until they had closed the trapdoor behind them, did anyone in the group talk again.

"I recognized a few of the enchantments, but it is hard at this distance," said Vivien. "What disturbs me more is that the city's enchantment is reacting. Did one of them mis-throw a fireball or deflect a whirlwind into that enchantment? That worries me far more. If Camelot's encompassing magic is destroyed, all of us inside will die in the conflagration."

"The whole city?" asked Myrna.

"Would they be so foolish?" asked Adele.

Thom hoped not. He tried to catch the arrhythmic sounds that Vivien had, but heard no changes in the enchantment's steady beat. Whatever she had heard, the city's surrounding magic seemed to have calmed from it.

"I heard that too," said Francis. "Someone became reckless as they got near to Rowan Gate, most likely one of the pursuers was trying too hard to stop those who were fleeing. I pray no one else does anything so dangerous once they passed through to the Road."

"Does this mean the war is over?" asked Adele. "Have the sorcerers fled the city?"

"It seems so," said Francis, "but we should wait for Marcus' men to report what they find. As Vivien said, this might be a lull in the battle. Nonetheless, word should be sent to the Father Abbot about what we already know. He has the four masters, but we don't know what they've told him. Brother Canon, will you go with me? It would be easier with two of us looking for him, for he could be anywhere in the compound."

"I will join you" agreed the old monk. He and Francis climbed out of the Hole.

Everyone else just stood there, as if caught in honey. It took a moment for Thom to realize that he felt relieved, even a bit giddy. The invasion was over and this time it wasn't his responsibility to bring victory. Except for his failed attempt to join those fleeing Clas Myrddin, he had stayed away from any fighting.

And now it was over.

"Can we leave the Hole now?" asked Harmony. "I would like to see the monastery and convent cleared of all those refugees and our lives returned to normal."

"Have you no compassion on those who have sought shelter here?" asked Myrna in a reproachful tone.

"Of course I do, sister," bit back Harmony. "But there are too many crammed into the forecourts and in the guest house. This has resolved so suddenly that everyone can now go home and eat their evening meal in their own home. That would be so much better. Then we can come to them to offer food where needed or shelter to those who have been truly displaced by the city fires. There is no reason for them to be on these grounds except for spiritual solace. Let the monastery and the convent return to being places of divine service as they were intended. We will not neglect the needy, but it can return to the ways we cared for them before all this commotion began."

Would they be going back to the lives they led before all this? Thom didn't necessarily look forward to going back to living among the guild house servants. It also meant everyone else would be returning to their former ways.

"Will you be going back to the castle?" he asked Adele. The thought of her being wooed by some nobleman made his stomach turn.

She gave him a surprised look. "I hadn't thought of it, but most likely I will. It will raise concerns if I stay away, for I am one of the queen's maidens even if she hasn't yet returned to Camelot. Yes. Yes, I should go back, since that will be expected of me, but I will still come here regularly for my lessons. What of you? Will you return to the Magicians' Guild house?"

Thom grimaced, but nodded. "I am still part of the Magicians' Guild, even if I have no master. They will expect me to return."

"You should stay here and join the league," said Adele. "The guild sees you as a burden, while here you can help Vivien with her teaching."

"He would be a helpful addition," stated Sister Myrna. "Then the classes could be properly segregated, men from women."

Thom found the idea tempting, but he also remembered the charges Vivien had leveled against him less than an hour ago. "I would be honored, but I have my commitments to the guild. Besides, the league may not want me now, not wanting to draw too much attention to itself. Abbot Justin might even reject any offer to join due to turmoil."

"Don't be foolish, boy," replied Harmony. "The Father Abbot will do no such thing. You are practically a part of the League of Barnabas now… though he will probably demand that you take monastic vows. That would help to justify your lingering here."

Thom swallowed hard. Become a monk? Vow to a lifetime of celibacy? He glanced quickly at Adele, then reddened and looked away just as fast. "I… I don't know if I could do that. He never mentioned any…"

Vivien's laugh cut him off. "Harmony is joking, Thomas. After all, I stay here and I haven't made any such vows. Must you always be so gullible?"

"I wasn't joking," replied Harmony with a stern look. "The boy should take holy vows. It would quell his passions and bring him closer to God."

"Taking monastic vows is a good thing," agreed Sister Myrna.

Brother Michael's eyes twinkled but he said nothing.

Marcus laughed heartily. "Walk back into the Hole with me, Journeyman. If you stay here, these women might just castrate you on the spot to decide this matter for you." He laughed again when Thom blushed, then he threw an arm around his shoulders. "Come on, for even the bravest man retreats when faced with overwhelming odds."

Thom let Marcus lead him away. He was too embarrassed to meet Adele's gaze as he passed by.

TWENTY

Abandoned

Thom spent some time with Marcus in the Hole. They ate a mid-day meal while waiting to hear what was happening in the city. Vivien passed through with Sister Harmony, Sister Myrna, and Adele, most likely to continue their lessons. When he noted the absence of Brother Michael, Marcus stated that he was probably on watch at the end of the tunnel.

"Since the invasion began, they have usually kept someone on watch at that end who can hear magic whenever other magicians are in the Hole. They worried that the monastery might be attacked while they are out of hearing." Marcus shrugged. "You probably understand all of that better than I do, all this talk about an inner ear and the rhythms of magic."

"But do you still need to fear that the monastery will be attacked? Isn't the war over?"

"I'll know as soon as my men return from spying out the city. I sent them out on the only two horses we have, so they should be able to report back within a few hours."

"Have the nobles from the guest house also gone out?"

"Some fled for the harbor early this morning and then another pair left recently, heading toward the castle. I'm not privy to their plans, but they have been working with one of the master magicians."

Thom nodded, "That would be Wizard Osric."

"So that's his name. What of the others? The last two kept their identities will hidden last night while they stayed in the barracks with my men. I wonder when they will show themselves."

Thom had wondered the same thing. If one of them had once been a sorcerer then hiding that truth was understandable. But why did the other wizard insist on remaining anonymous? Most likely, he would never find out, for if the invasion was over then the four would likely go back into hiding.

Marcus finished his meal and then stood. "I'm going outside to see what I can. Will you join me, journeyman?"

Thom nodded, for he had nothing else to do with his time.

The two walked back up the tunnel. Once again, Thom paused at the spot where it passed under the city's boundary and suddenly he could hear the magic being used again.

"Something amiss?" asked Marcus.

Thom shook his head. "The enchantment covering the city seems stable, though it seems quieter… weaker in the west. I hear no other magic. None at all."

"Was it that way before?" asked Marcus as they started walking again.

"No. This city was the home of the Magicians' Guild. There was almost always something being crafted in the guild house. But now it is silent."

"Well, if they chased off the sorcerers then it won't be long before they return to the guild house and the magic starts up again. Will they use magic to rebuild the place?"

Thom had no idea and said so. He had never heard about building with enchantments except when creating something ethereal like the Roads or a shield.

They passed Brother Michael and climbed up out of the Hole. When he exited the building, Thom had to squint against the bright sunlight. It was a glorious day with a rich blue sky and a few white clouds that seemed to linger around the Road of Clouds as it soared over the city. A glorious day. A smile teased on his lips as he looked up. As his eyes adjusted to the bright day, he noticed a large bird flying over the city. It seemed to be enjoying the air currents as it circled here and there. But as it came closer to this end of the city, Thom realized how big it was... and that it was no mere bird.

He pointed it out to Marcus. "A griffin."

"Left behind when the sorcerers fled?" asked the mercenary.

"Most likely," he said after some thought. "The Road of Leaves wouldn't be the favored route of flying beasts. They came in by the Road of Clouds. I would think they would flee the same way, but it means landing on the Sky Tower and then walking their way up the stairs to get to the entrance."

"Maybe it's looking for a meal before leaving."

Thom frowned at that. He remembered when they had to fight one of those monsters. Griffins were vicious. He would hate to have one of those beasts swooping down on unsuspecting people in the city, but he couldn't think of anything he could do to stop it. For now, the beast was still far away from the monastery, so he could nothing to stop it even if he knew how.

They came to the wall that separated Mousehome from the rest of the monastery. At the gate, Marcus asked if there was anything new to report.

"No news, captain," replied the man on duty. "We will have a report from the outer walls within the hour if you want to check again a bit later."

"I think we'll go there now. Give us some armbands, will you?"

The guard handed over two bright blue cloths. Thom followed Marcus' lead and slipped it over his right arm.

"The Father Abbot has us wear these so that the monks know we are cleared to be walking around the place," explained Marcus as they exited the gate and started across the grounds. "Many of the brothers still dislike having us trampling across sacred grounds but they don't try to stop us anymore."

Marcus led him to the chapel and then through it to the forecourt. The area was even more crowded than the morning when Thom and Dorthos came in. It was obvious that some had spent days here already, for they had set up makeshift camps, clusters of bedding and small cook fires.

Many recognized Thom's journeyman's robe and some started yelling questions at him, asking when Merlin would drive off the invaders and if the centaurs would be corralled. He had no answers, so he simply ignored their pleas and kept his eyes focused on the mercenary he was following.

Marcus weaved his way across the courtyard until the came to the wall that protected the monastery. They found the gate closed even though it was mid-day.

A monk and a guard stood watch there.

"Why is it barred?" asked Marcus. "You know the Father Abbot detests that. He wants to welcome in as many as can press in here."

"We had no choice, captain. A herd of centaurs is marauding through the neighborhood. If we leave it open, they might charge in here and slaughter the masses."

Marcus nodded agreement. "How many in the band?"

"Over a half-dozen trotted across the courtyard outside only a few minutes ago, but there may have been more in the next street over."

"Did they try to break in?"

The guard shook his head. "They stopped and eyed the gate, but they went on without giving us any trouble. They seemed in a hurry to get somewhere, harassing any who crossed their path but not really hunting for victims."

Marcus turned to Thom. "Do you think they are heading back to King's Harbor?"

"They would if they are fleeing the city. The Road of Waters would take them to some of their favored refuges." But Thom wondered if that was what they were doing. Would they be willing to go back to what would be an exile on land inside an enchantment? Or would they want to trample more of the city first?

"Keep your eyes open, Wilton," ordered Marcus. "Watch the skies too. We spotted a griffin not long ago. You and the brother did well by closing the gates, but open them again once you are certain the centaurs have moved on."

With that, Marcus and Thom turned back toward the chapel. They were about halfway across the courtyard when a disturbance caused them to look behind them.

The gates opened to let two riders in- the men Marcus had sent out a few hours earlier.

Marcus waved to gain their attention and they aimed their horses toward him, walking them slowly across the crowded cobblestones. People made way, intimidated by the mounts.

"Lead the way to the stables," ordered Marcus, waving them past. "We'll talk while you take care of the horses."

The stable sat at one end of the courtyard and it was full. Obviously, most of the nobles were still here, or at least their horses were. Marcus' men passed down the row to a back stall that their mounts would be sharing. As they removed saddles and tack, they shared what they had found out in the city. But first they asked if Marcus wanted Thom listening.

"He is a friend of the league. He can hear what you have to say."

"Yes Captain," replied the thinner of the two men, but he still looked at Thom's robe suspiciously. "They have all fled, sir. All of them."

"Who is that, Bert?"

"The king. The wizards. All of them. They abandoned the castle and fled down the Road of Leaves."

"'Tis true, Marcus," replied the other scout, an older fellow with leathered skin, gray hair, and hard eyes. "The sorcerers have won. They hold Camelot now and they have guards posted around Rowan Gate to make sure the king's army doesn't try to push back into the city."

"How do you know this for certain? Did you see them running for the gate?"

"They had already fled by the time we got there," said the weatherworn scout. "We were able to ride into the castle and even enter the king's hall because Mordred and Dalrake had all their forces over at Rowan Gate. There was no one there to stop us except a few elderly servants who chose to remain behind. They told us what happened."

Marcus rubbed his face in frustration.

Thom closed his eyes in disbelief. How could the guild and King Arthur abandon the city? How?

"What are we going to do, captain?" asked Bert. "They'll be coming for us soon enough now that they have the city. Are we going to run for the Road of Waters?"

"That's not for me to decide. Do you have anything else to report?"

"Not much," replied the weatherworn one. "The usual collections of corpses scattered around the hill the castle sits on… those would be the invaders who fell during the battle. The servants had already gathered up any of the king's men who fell inside the castle grounds. We did see a pair of dead nobles and their fallen horses much closer to the monastery… maybe they came from the bunch of lords squatting in the abbot's guest house, but I wouldn't know for certain, captain. They were peppered with arrow wounds and we saw a few of the shafts that were too damaged for the killers to recover; they were those heavy centaur arrows but we never saw the patrol that killed those two. Oh, and we saw a small purple ball whoosh by us, going nearly as fast as a diving falcon. Some kind of magic I'd guess, but it didn't bother us."

"Eagle's Spying," murmured Thom, naming the enchantment, then said louder, "Did it pause to observe you? From what direction did it come and where did it go?"

The older scout hesitated to answer, looking to Marcus.

"Go ahead, Miles. Answer his questions."

"Well, it came from behind us as we were approaching the castle, so I'm not sure where it started. It shot past us, circled the castle a few times and then shot off toward Rowan Gate."

Thom nodded. "Most likely came from one of the league's masters. The magician links to the Eagle's Spying enchantment and then can see everything within a certain range of that orb. Kind of like sending your eyeball flying across the city to look at what's ahead."

"That sounds painful," muttered Miles, "and somehow wrong."

Bert crossed himself and whispered some prayer for protection.

Marcus grunted. "Don't judge a craft you don't understand, boys. That purple flying eye might help us live to see another day. We need to know what the sorcerers are up to if we want to help win the city back."

Thom despaired that it was too late for that; he just hoped that they could escape with their lives. The Road of Waters wouldn't be open until dark and sunset suddenly felt so far away.

TWENTY-ONE

Where to Go?

Thom and Marcus hurried from the stable, heading for the chapel with the hope of finding Abbot Justin. It took some time, but they eventually found him at the scriptorium with Colwyn and Francis. The report alarmed the abbot and he hurried off to consult with the league's master magicians, taking Marcus with him.

For a moment, the two monks and the journeyman simply stared at each other, then the librarian muttered, "He should be taken back to Mousehome, especially now. Our brethren might grumble but they will respect his blue armband, yet the commoners and nobles will not. They will only see the magician's robe and will either rage at him or beg protection. And at least a few might slither off to seek a reward from the invaders for revealing his presence. It would be best to get him hid in Mousehome as quickly as you can, Francis."

"But I don't want to hide," replied Thom.

Colwyn scowled. "Would you rather that we threw you over the wall and let centaurs use you as a pincushion? No bravado, young man. Your guild has fled and the sorcerers will be hunting down any stragglers."

"He has the truth on that," agreed Francis. "Dalrake would especially enjoy catching you after all you did to foil his earlier plans."

"And you should shed the journeyman robe," added Colwyn

"I shouldn't. The council ordered me to always wear it." Thom already felt guilty for the few times he had disobeyed and hid the garment over the last few days.

"The guild is no longer in Camelot," noted Colwyn.

"It would give them grounds to throw me out," argued Thom, crossing his arms in refusal.

"What if a wizard ordered you to remove them for the sake of the guild?" asked Francis. "Would you do so then?"

Thom gave him a puzzled look. His friend had never been a wizard and he had since denounced magic, so surely he didn't think his orders could override the guild's council.

Francis explained, "At least two of the league's masters are still in good-standing with the Guild. Maybe I can convince them to let you and Vivien hide your robes. You'll still be wearing that knapsack, but you'll be far less of a target."

Thom nodded agreement, but was still troubled. "Do you think we will be fleeing the city too?"

"If we stay, the sorcerers will find us," said Francis quietly. He sounded almost resigned to it happening.

Thom remembered that his friend had been despised by Dalrake for much longer than he had been.

"The Father Abbot will likely send the two of you away, since there is no gain in either of you staying," said Colwyn. "As for me, I cannot imagine leaving all of this behind." He swung his arms wide to indicate the whole scriptorium or maybe even the monastery beyond. "It is hard enough when I have to take the Short Walk four times a year."

"Short walk?" asked Thom.

"Leaving the city by way of the Short Roads."

Thom nodded, understanding the reference now. Staying too long inside an enchantment was dangerous for anyone who wasn't innately magical. The king's standing mandate was that all in the city had to spend some time outside of the encasing magic to keep sane; that much Thom knew, though not how the king's officials kept track of the people's compliance. This was the first time he had heard it called 'taking a Short Walk' but it made sense. "If only we could take that walk now. I fear that it will not be that easy to leave the city now. Is the Road of Waters truly open or will there be more centaur troubles on that route?"

Colwyn and Francis exchanged a look that Thom didn't quite grasp. Maybe they knew about other problems along the Road of Waters but they said nothing to him. He didn't press it, trusting that his friend would tell him if it was a threat they would be facing.

"I think we should go to Mousehome now, for the others need to hear of this" suggested Francis to Thom, then turned to his superior. "That is, if you will release me from my duties for the day."

Colwyn actually laughed. "What is this? A late conversion into a humble monk? Brother Francis, that robe ill fits you."

Francis smiled back, but it was a sad one. "Patience, brother. The Lord is reworking me, but he didn't have much to start with and so it takes longer."

"I'm almost tempted to send you back to the candleworks for the rest of the day just to teach you what it means to have patience and perseverance."

Francis feigned terror at the threat and Thom remembered his tale of being rather incompetent in working with hot bee's wax and tallow. But his mock fear didn't last and soon broke into a more genuine smile.

"That is better," stated Colwyn. "Do not let the enemy rob you of the Lord's peace, Francis. Now go on to Mousehome; we'll leave the candle making for some other day."

* * *

Within the hour the abbot was having a meeting in the common room down in the Hole. The four masters came with him, yet two of them were still hooded and masked by magic. Vivien and all her students were there, as well as Colwyn and Marcus. Dorthos and the rest of the pixies also joined them. The abbot insisted that Thom and Francis join them as well.

He began their meeting with soft-spoken prayer, confessing his fears for the safety of the many people in the city and then beseeching God for wisdom and guidance.

Thom joined in the amens, but wondered how much God would help. Maybe he would for someone as holy as the abbot, but not for an ex-thief turned into a half-trained magician.

After a moment of silence, Abbot Justin began. "By now you have all heard that King Arthur and the Guild have fled the city. We will need to do so as well or the sorcerers will learn about the league and will hunt us all down."

"Can't we fight them?" asked Thom. "That was what you originally planned. I should think that the king and the wizards are planning some counterstrike. They will not give up so easily and neither should we. Maybe we can keep Dalrake and Mordred occupied and make it easier for the king to return."

"We have no idea when the king will strike back," replied one of the hooded magicians. "It may be weeks from now or even months. I doubt the king can rally his knights and lords so quickly and it will take some time for Merlin to gather in the magicians who are spread out all over the realm. Do you really think we can hold Dalrake at bay for that long? No, we need to retreat for now, but that doesn't mean that some of us cannot return later."

Thom was frustrated but had to admit that the wizard was right.

"We will need to flee quickly," stated Marcus, "for I doubt they will remain hunkered around the Rowan Gate for much longer."

"By tonight we want the ships loaded and on the Road of Waters," stated the abbot, "which means we will not be taking much with us."

"Who will stay behind?" asked Brother Colwyn.

"You have already asked to remain and I will allow it Colwyn, but I think anyone of the league who uses magic must go. I want to stay as well, for the monastery is my responsibility, but Prince Dorthos reminded me that I know too much and cannot risk falling into the hands of the invaders."

Thom looked over and saw Dorthos nodding vigorously; he might be crazed but the pixie was also wise.

The abbot continued, "Marcus has chosen four warriors to remain to offer a token force, since it has been known that the monastery has added guards, but he and most of his men will also be leaving. I want them to protect us as we establish the league's new home."

Sister Harmony spoke up. "Father Abbot, will that new home include a convent?"

"We can discuss that later, once we reach the place where the new monastery will rise."

"You fear that some of those left behind might be tortured to reveal any secrets they hold," stated Marcus softly, "that is why you avoid sharing too much."

The abbot gave a quick glance toward the clustered masters before nodding agreement to what Marcus had said. "Yes, I fear that for those of us who will be traveling down the Road of Waters and for those staying behind. I have been told that Dalrake and his sorcerers are very thorough in their interrogations. I pray that all of us make it safely through the fall of Camelot, but wisdom tells me to plan for the worst."

"Then shouldn't we all be going?" asked Myrna. "The sheep left behind will weaken without a shepherd. Dogs can protect from some threats, but certainly cannot serve in the chapel."

Marcus chuckled, knowing that she was calling his men dogs, but apparently he took no offense in it.

Thom listened to all of this and it seemed unreal. Suddenly, they were talking about running away and there seemed no other option. Had Dalrake really won so easily, after failing on the Roads? How did the sorcerer turn his defeats into such a stunning victory?

"Sister Myrna, for a time we will be two flocks, one here in Camelot and one elsewhere, and I cannot be in both places. Brother Colwyn and the others remaining will see to the spiritual well-being of those here, just as Marcus' men will see to their physical well-being. Beyond that, we can only pray to the Lord for his protection."

But what of me? thought Thom. *Where am I needed?* He was glad that Adele and Francis would be leaving for safety, but should he be taking that same route? He wondered if he should be staying behind too, doing what he could to fight for the Guild and the kingdom.

TWENTY-TWO

Fleeing the City

Thom walked next to Francis. Right behind them came Ears, the monk's faithful mule. His journeyman's robe was stuffed into his pack, for Wizard Osric had done as Francis proposed and had released him from that council decree for now. They were just leaving the monastery as the sun lingered on the western horizon. He wished that Adele was at his side too, but she had left earlier in the day with the two nuns and Vivien. Most likely, the women were already on board one of the river galleys.

"Thank you again for your help," said his friend. "I think this is the first time I've taken a full load of books and scrolls *away* from the monastery."

Ears was loaded mainly with works that Francis and Librarian Colwyn had felt would be essential for the establishing of a new Saint Barnabas Monastery. They had packed quickly but not haphazardly, with very little debate between the two brothers on what should be sent out. During the packing Ears had been cooperative, standing just outside a side entrance to the scriptorium and contentedly munching on some fodder. Even now, he clomped along the empty streets without complaint. One last thing was tied onto the bundle: Thom's magician's staff. He had no idea how to use the thing and it was rather obvious even without its gem lit, so adding it to the load was an obvious choice.

Thom looked back at the animal. "Will you be able to take Ears on a boat?"

Francis shrugged. "He's been on the water before, so that will not be a problem. However, there may be no room for him."

"What then? Surely you won't let him loose in the city."

"There are other brothers who went to the harbor with the abbot's luggage, so I'll send Ears back with one of them. Brother Colwyn will care for him."

"Will we be going all the way to the end of the Road?" The Road of Waters emptied into the Thames; Thom had never been so far south.

"Most likely. The abbot wants to get outside of the enchantments. I cannot imagine that he'll want to linger along the waterway."

They fell back into silence, walking another empty block in mostly shadow as the sun dropped lower. Thom felt an urge to go faster, not wanting to be late to the harbor, but Francis kept a steady, seemingly unconcerned pace.

Another city block passed.

Suddenly, Thom heard numerous hoofbeats behind them. He looked back with sudden fear. "Centaurs!"

"Sounds like horses not centaurs," stated Francis, still calm.

Thom had no idea how he could tell the difference, but even if they were horses, their riders could be Mordred's men. "Are you not worried?"

Francis smiled. "Yes, but we can't flee so we might as well keep going. As for hiding… well, have you ever tried getting a mule to duck behind crates in an alley?" He finally looked back and the fast-approaching men were now in sight. "They've seen us. Just leave your sword in its scabbard and your magician's box stored. They will likely pass by without even stopping, for we are no threat to them. I think they are retreating to the harbor like all the rest of us."

Thom saw the wisdom in his friend's words, but it was hard not to react. The cantering horses sounded like twice as many because the paving stones and the buildings echoed their approach. Francis guided Ears to one side of the street, stopping at the mouth of an alley. Thom pressed close to them, giving the horsemen ample room. Thom recognized them as they passed- the nobles that had been staying at the monastery's guest house. The group paid them no heed and they passed too quickly for Thom to overhear any of their conversation. He told Francis who they were.

The monk nodded. "Even they realize there is no glory in fighting for Camelot now. Ballads may romanticize heroes destined for defeat, but these men have no desire to sacrifice their lives when their own king has fled."

"And I have no desire to remain behind because we arrive too late," said Thom. "Let's get going."

* * *

They reached the edge of King's Harbor just before sunset. Thom looked through the golden, peaceful light at a scene of anarchy. People swarmed the piers around the five galleys that were tied up there and, even from this distance, he could hear the shouting, the begging, and the crying out. He spotted the galley that had been commandeered by the nobles as the last two horses were led up the gangway. The sailors shoved off even before the animals could be settled, leaving behind a large crowd of people still clamoring for passage. He frowned and shook his head at the heartlessness that chose horses over people.

He saw another river galley push off from a pier to the left, and this boat's deck was crowded with commoners. Now there were two galleys in the harbor, angling toward the entry to the Road of Waters, which wouldn't open until full darkness. Soon, the other four boats would also head out. He and Francis had better hurry up.

"Father Abbot has his hands full," said Francis, indicating the nearest river galley where he had spotted Justin, "and more trouble is coming." He pointed to another street that emptied into the area.

Thom finally noticed a troop of centaurs. "Are they loyal to the league or to the sorcerers?"

"I can't tell at this distance but, even if they are allies, they won't be friendly. They will demand transport and rare is the captain who would refuse, for centaurs have remarkable memories, hold grudges for decades, and they are thick on the islands along the Road of Waters. I expect they will appropriate at least one galley. I just hope it isn't the boat my brethren have already started boarding."

As he and Francis followed the road down into the harbor's basin, Thom watched the centaurs arrive and scare everyone else off one of the piers. No one was so desperate to dare face those sharp hooves and mighty bows. Soon they had commandeered one vessel and anyone human on board that wasn't part of the crew was led off by the sailors, their possessions dumped on the planks nearby.

"Ah, they are going to be challenged after all," said Francis, pointing.

A group of very short people marched onto the pier even as the humans fled with their belongings. Those approaching were small enough to be mistaken for children by those no really paying attention. Among the group was one dressed in vibrant colors. Dorthos the Deranged strode with his fellow pixies.

"My error," corrected Francis. "They aren't fighting, so I think the centaurs are some of those who came here with the league's masters. And look, one of the masters is joining them."

In the fading light, Thom couldn't tell the color of the robe of the newcomer, whether brown or black or dark blue. He didn't see much more because the road they were following angled around a warehouse as it dropped toward the harbor. He didn't see the crowded piers again until they came out of the warehouse district and stepped onto the frontage road. Thom looked to the pier the centaurs had taken over but they were gone as was the river galley. He spotted it at the far end of the harbor, near the gateway through the city walls, ready to pass through the magical portal to the Royal Waywater beyond.

"Only three left," noted Francis, aiming toward the nearest galley.

As Thom followed, he wondered how they would get everyone onto a boat now. Even if they excluded the masses pressing in, he doubted there would be enough room for everyone from the monastery as well as the nobles, especially if the lords insisted on bringing their mounts.

The people milling about were growing anxious and angry. The only reason they let Francis and Thom pass was the monk's robe and the large mule right behind them- horses and mules were rare in the magical city and still intimidated most. As they stepped onto the wooden pier, they slowed down even more because the people were pressing together so tightly, so there wasn't much room to get out of their way even if the desperate wanted to. And it was loud.

"Where are we going?" asked Thom, yelling to be heard.

"I caught a glimpse of the abbot on that second galley. We go there." Francis gently but firmly pushed a woman out of his way. "Ware the mule! We don't want to trample anyone."

The woman gave him a hard stare but still pressed to the side to get out of their path.

Others saw them approaching and moved grudgingly to either side, and then they broke free to a clear area at the foot of the boarding plank. Some of Marcus' men guarded the approach along with a pair of burly sailors. The size of the men as well as their bared weapons kept the people back. The guards recognized Francis and let him and Thomas through.

The abbot shouted at them from the ship's rail, "You two barely made it. The mule will have to stay, Francis, for we are out of room. Help load the books on board and then we must be off. We have heard that sorcerers are riding in our direction and will be here within the hour."

A group of monks came over as well as some of the guards and soon they were unloading Ears under the direction of Francis. Thom joined in, carrying books and scrolls on board.

TWENTY-THREE

Harbor Aflame

As Thom walked up the gangway with a last stack of books, he realized that the sun had finally set. The lanterns on board were being lit, including the pair hanging near the pilot's position. He saw in the lantern light that Adele and Vivien were standing near the galley's captain, along with one of the hooded masters. Thom wondered if it was wise for Adele to continue wearing apprentice gray, but it was too late to protest. Besides, she was at the far end of the galley, while he was busy loading. He didn't even notice who he was handing the books to until that person spoke.

"Thank you, Thomas."

It was Justin himself, helping to store the precious cargo.

Surprised, he replied. "You are welcome, Father Abbot, but I can just as easily carry these the rest of the way."

The abbot smiled but didn't surrender the tomes back to him. "I enjoy the chance to do some work. I tried offering assistance to the sailors, but they ordered me back down from the top of the mast." The abbot turned as he ducked into a small cabin where they were storing those items that they didn't want to get wet during the trip.

The thought of the dignified man clambering up that high was almost impossible to imagine. Thom looked after him in puzzlement, not certain if the man was joking or not.

Francis came up, having handed his mule off to one of the bodyguards that had been securing the pier. Already the sailors were loosening the securing lines and getting ready to pull out into the harbor. He paused at the railing and looked back. "I hope to soon see Ears again, the Lord willing. I also hope to see many of those poor people who are still begging for passage out of Camelot. I wish there were thirty ships here and not just a half-dozen."

"Can't we fit more of them on board?"

Francis shook his head. "The captains won't allow their crafts to be overburdened, not when the Road of Waters is still so unsettled. Pack too many on board and the galley will surely capsize before you can reach the first Waywater."

Thom felt guilty that he was escaping and so many others weren't. "Should I surrender my spot to one of them?"

"Too late for that," said Francis, noting the quickly growing gap between them and the pier. "Besides, you're fleeing certain death, while most of them are not. The sorcerers will want your head for the trouble you caused them on the Roads. Most of the people will face hardship now but not death nor…"

113

Suddenly, Francis stopped talking and just pointed into the darkening sky.

Thom followed his direction and barely saw a small purple-glowing sphere soaring over the harbor. It had a very distinct click to its fast beat that his inner ear quickly caught once he knew where to focus. Someone had crafted an Eagle's Spying.

Francis pushed off the ship's rail. "I'll need to warn the Father Abbot," he muttered as he hurried off.

Thom did his best to follow the enchantment's course as it flew over the waters, but it was hard to see in the fading light, and as it got closer to the city's encompassing enchantment the sound also became harder to discern. He wondered how the magician controlling it was able to keep from getting queasy with the glowing ball skittered about erratically.

He heard the opening of a magician's box on one of the other ships as one of the masters started crafting some reaction to the magical spying. The enchantment's sound suddenly swelled and then a glaring white light appeared in the sky over the harbor. Thom shaded his eyes as he tried to see if the Eagle's Spying was still active, but he could neither see nor hear that other enchantment anymore. The white light continued to cast its harsh light on all in the harbor area.

As Thom looked around, he saw that the many still on shore were now cowering or running away. For some reason, he felt encouraged by the light and it took him a moment to understand why: the last time he had seen this particular enchantment, a White Sun, had been when Merlin had swept in and chased off Dalrake on the Road of Waters. The feeling cooled as he realized that such an appearance was doubtful. There was no rescue eminent. More likely, an attack was rapidly approaching.

He wondered why such a glaring enchantment had been chosen to combat the spying magic. The sudden blaze must have startled the spying sorcerer and shattered his concentration, causing the Eagle's Spying to disintegrate. And yet, there had to be more efficient ways to counteract the enchantment. Thom wondered if maybe the White Sun had been used to also startle everyone else at the harbor. The sailors did seem to be moving more franticly, working hard to get them away from shore. In all, six galleys were trying to flee for the Road of Waters. Already the first galley was slipping out of Camelot- Thom thought it was the one carrying the centaurs and pixies.

Those people on shore had also been startled to action by the glaring light, some cowering and others running away. Into that milling crowd came another patrol of centaurs, followed by a group of mounted men.

For a brief moment, Thom saw the sorcerers as they came into sight behind the human and centaur guards. Two of them jumped off their mounts and opened their magician's boxes, but then the White Sun enchantment sputtered out, letting night return to King's Harbor and it seemed far darker than before. Although he couldn't see them anymore, he could still hear the enchantments they were crafting. Behind him, he heard the master and Vivien react by opening their own caches of elements. Elsewhere around the harbor, Thom heard others doing the same, and then he heard more of the sorcerers crafting enchantments.

Thom swung off his backpack and was about to open his own magician's box, but Francis was suddenly there and putting a restraining hand on his shoulder.

"Not yet, my friend. They will target the sounds of magic. Begin crafting once the first round of enchantments have been completed, then carefully note where the sorcerers are and attack that area when the lull occurs."

"What should I craft?"

"Something that you can heft that far and that will at least distract them."

Thom nodded and decided that a Twist of Air would be the best enchantment, so he prepared what he needed without opening his box and revealing his location to the sorcerers. He sat down on the rough deck and then placed his mixing bowl, pestle, and magician's box in directly in front of his knees, keeping them close enough to grab should the boat get rocked in an attack. Then he waited.

The sorcerers completed one enchantment and then another, and two large Fireballs roared over the harbor to slam into the galley nearest the gate to the Road. There was no magician on that boat, for it was the one the nobles had commandeered, so there wasn't anyone able to stop it. Within minutes, the galley's rigging and one end of the deck were ablaze. The sailors tried to turn and row for shore, but it was obvious they had soon faltered at that, either abandoning ship or succumbing to the heat. The galley with the centaurs and pixies had to quickly alter their course to avoid the floating pyre.

Thom turned away from the wreckage as Vivien and the master released their magical responses, one a fireball and the other a shaft of lightning. Both roared over Thom's head, the lightning much faster than the fire.

"Start now," urged Francis. "The sorcerers will be moving to avoid those attacks and then they'll open their boxes to fight back. You want to time your attack to hit them as they are in the middle of crafting."

Thom filled his mixing bowl with the powdered magical elements of Snow Hummingbird feathers, Saber Leaf Dandelion seeds, and Midnight Petrel wings. To that he added the mundane elements of water and his own spittle to attune the magic to his bidding.

His last step was to smear some of the potion on his lips and hands so that he could guide the brewing breeze. A small whirlwind rose from the mixing bowl. He directed the swirling air with his hands and then blew it into motion, sending it to where he heard the cacophony of sounds from three open magicians' boxes. It was a greater distance than he had ever sent such an enchantment so it grew a bit wobbly and slow toward the end, but it finally reached the target. He caught at least one of the sorcerers in midst of crafting because a sudden burst of sound as the whirlwind swept up exposed elements from that unfinished enchantment. The whirlwind glowed and sparks flew, then it exploded.

Thom just stood there, staring at the surprising reaction.

"Come along, my friend," said Francis, pulling on his arm. "You must always move after an attack or they will too easily find you."

Thom realized the truth in that. He quickly grabbed his box, mixing bowl, and pestle, moving to another part of the galley with the monk. There wasn't much room on a ship to evade a counter-strike but he tried his best, wondering out loud if Adele and the others were doing likewise at the other end of the boat.

"They appear safe for now," replied Francis. "Vivien has set up a shield of Air Armor between them and the sorcerers, which protects her, Adele, and the nuns, along with the helmsman and the captain. The master has stepped outside her shield and is creating something larger that might end up shielding the whole vessel… what is that? I don't recognize some of those elements and it's very complex… almost like something I've heard in the enchantment around the Roads…" Francis stared hard at the hooded league master. "Who is that magician?"

Thom looked and listened, recognizing Vivien's enchantment to be the one the guild wizards had used during their escape from Clas Myrddin, though she set hers at more of an angle than theirs had been. That she knew how to craft such a powerful enchantment showed how advanced she had become as a journeywoman. He wondered how long she would be able to sustain it.

As for the league master, he was crafting something far too intricate for Thom to understand.

"That magic is something beyond most wizards," muttered Francis. "Is it him? Why would he choose to be on this river galley?"

Thom had no time to wonder about Francis' speculations. Just then, a spectacular explosion occurred on one of the other boats, apparently tearing a huge hole in its side, because the craft began sinking quickly, the harbor's water extinguishing flames as more and more of it sank. On their vessel, sailors were at the oars, rowing hard to get away from the shore, while the pilot worked hard to steer clear of burning boats and other flotsam.

Thom tried to ignore all the nearby noise: the screams and shouts and loud explosions; he needed to craft another Twist of Air and do what he could to fight the sorcerers. He tried to focus more with his inner ear, to catch when the sorcerers were as they continued to craft their magical attacks, but it was so hard to hear the rhythms of the elements with the din of battle shouting at him.

He listened for the sound of magical elements as he mixed, for he needed to find a target to aim at.

Where were they?

Finally, just as he was completing his crafting, he caught the whisper of a magical cache opening and it was far nearer than previous attacks. He stood up and released the Twist of Air, aimed toward a magician crouching on the pier they had just left. He concentrated, willing the miniature tornado to catch the sorcerer in mid-crafting, but he never saw if he succeeded because at that moment a different sorcerer struck.

Water fountained into the air, as if a huge invisible boulder had been dropped into the harbor, and suddenly a wave rose and crashed against the galley and it tilted to the side. Thom tumbled into Francis, his magician's cache racing down the suddenly-angled deck, his mixing bowl skittering after it and the pestle flying off somewhere.

"My box!"

The boat leaned even more to port and suddenly his staff slid away from him too. He and Francis were grasping for handholds to keep from being tossed into dark water. Somehow, they grabbed onto a sturdy rope and held on as the boat's starboard side lifted even higher into the night sky. For just a moment, Thom's feet dangled in the air and he looked down at the water rushing over the port rail, and then the galley rush back in the other direction as it righted itself.

He and Francis slammed onto the deck, their bodies whipping around with the inertia as the boat rocked back and then settled right-side up.

Thom pulled himself up, still holding onto the rope as the boat continued to rock. He looked desperately for his magician's box, but it was gone. Even worse, as he looked around he realized that the women had been swept overboard.

"Francis, help me! Adele and Vivien are gone."

He stumbled toward the port rail, the monk hurrying behind him, and they looked over the rail at the debris strewn waters. Numerous sailors were floundering there, some trying to swim back to the ship, while others were heading toward shore or merely holding onto anything that would support them. He couldn't make out any of the women in the murk.

"There," said Francis, spotting them. "It looks like all four are alive."

Thom finally saw them: Vivien, Adele, and even the two nuns who always insisted on staying near them as chaperons. The four were pushing a floating chunk of wood in front of them as they tried to swim back toward the river galley, using the wood plank to clear a way through the rest of the flotsam.

"We have other trouble," said Francis calmly. "It seems the league's wizard is injured and now one of those burning boats is floating toward us."

Thom look over and saw the master magician lying on the deck, with the abbot leaning over him. Beyond them, the captain was trying to turn the ship's rudder himself while yelling for any remaining oarsmen to help turn the ship away from the pending collision. Before they could prevent it, the burning vessel bumped into them. It wasn't a hard collision, but the knock sent embers and burning chunks of wood raining down on their boat.

"What now?" asked Thom, uncertain about what to do. Numerous fires had kindled across the craft, too many to extinguish quickly.

"We need to jump overboard," decided Francis. "This craft is in no shape to take on the Road of Waters, not in its condition. Even if there weren't sorcerers attacking, I doubt the captain could get it back to the piers. No, we need to start swimming before the next attack turns it into a pyre for all."

Thom looked back at the women already in the water and saw that they had already made the same decision. They were now pushing their log toward the shore. He nodded his agreement to Francis' plan.

"The wizard will need our help," noted Francis. "He cannot swim on his own. Even though I detest magic, I know the man is important to the Father Abbot and to the league. Come along, Thomas. Let us help lower him into the water and then we and the abbot will bring him to shore."

As the two of them made their way across the shattered deck, Thom noticed that fire was all around them, as boats and flotsam flamed high and as piers and warehouses burned. The water itself seemed aflame as it reflected so many fires.

Thom's magician's box was gone, but he noticed one still next to the fallen master. It was obvious to his inner ear because the lid lay open and the elements seemed loud in their symphony of sounds.

It was his only hope to fight back.

"Francis, I need to retrieve that box if we are to have any chance to defend ourselves."

The monk nodded and the two of them hurried across the deck to where the Father Abbot now kneeling next to the unconscious wizard and trying to revive him. There were some sailors still onboard and they were racing about to orders shouted at them by the captain. Thom and Francis dodged around them as they hurried to the stern of the vessel.

Just as Thom stepped over a snapped spar, he heard an intense enchantment drawing closer with great speed. He turned and saw a huge wave rumbling toward them and on the crest of the wave rode a rowboat with five men standing up in it, so steady was it on that churning pile of water. Thom yelled out warning and ran desperately for that cache of elements that was open and whispering to him.

He almost made it.

TWENTY-FOUR

Confined

Thom felt the spray of water on his back and knew the wave was about to slam into him. The abbot had stopped trying to wake up the wizard and was now gaping at whatever he saw behind and above Thom.

Desperate, Thom threw himself at the magician's box, but didn't make it.

He hit an invisible wall, first with his extended hands, then with his head and the rest of his body.

He collapsed in a wet heap, barely holding on to consciousness.

The wave never crashed into him, but Francis caught up. "Thom! Can you hear me?"

He heard a moan, then realized it was from himself. He struggled to sit up. As he did, he saw the wave lowering right next to the ship's railing. A sorcerer and a uniformed soldier jumped across and landed on the deck nearby. One of the three men remaining on the rowboat caught Thom's eye; it was Dalrake. With him was another soldier and a third sorcerer who was obviously the one maintaining the wave enchantment, for his concentration seemed elsewhere.

"Secure that cache, Wallace, and then bind up the wizard, the journeyman, the abbot, and that monk," shouted Dalrake over the roar of the unstopping wave. "I want all four of them alive."

Dalrake's gaze focused on Thom and Francis and raised an eyebrow in recognition. "I especially want to question those two."

Wallace replied that he would.

"Bring them to Clas Myrddin. I would rather leave the castle to Mordred, since he's coveted it for so many years." Dalrake then turned to the sorcerer next to him. "On to the next galley, Belden. Let's see what other prizes we might find."

Thom sensed that the shield that had blocked him was now gone, so he scampered for the magician's box. The soldier stopped him with a swift kick to the side. "None of that!"

Thom dropped, grabbing his side in agony.

The sorcerer walked past Thom so closely that his robe brushed him, but Thom was too pained to react.

"Away from the elements, Father."

The sorcerer quickly closed the box and tucked it under his arm. Thom heard glass break under the man's boots and realized that some of the vials had spilled on the deck during the near-capsizing. The sorcerer seemed unconcerned about the waste; instead, the man walked over to the still-unconscious wizard and probed him with a few tentative taps from his boot tip.

Apparently satisfied that the wizard was no threat, he looked about to spot any other threats. He ignored the cowed captain who still stood at the helm. All of the crew was avoiding them.

"Tie them up and be quick about it," he ordered the accompanying soldier.

"Even the knocked out one?"

"Especially him, and tie their hands behind their back. We have no time to search them thoroughly and who knows what they might have hidden in some pocket?"

Thom was forced to get up and kneel in a line with Francis and Abbot Justin. The soldier handed his sword to the sorcerer and then stepped behind them. He didn't know if the soldier already had lengths of rope on him or was able to cut some quickly, but there was not much delay before he had all of them tied. Then the soldier pushed the fallen wizard over and tied his hands as well.

The sorcerer forced the captain to turn back to the pier and then he did some kind of enchantment that gave the large boat a slight push in the right direction. Slowly they headed back toward the piers. Once they were tied again to the pier bollards, the sorcerer had the soldier march Thom, Francis, and the abbot down the gangway and then he forced one of the sailors to carry the still-unconscious wizard.

As Thom limped off, he gave a furtive glance around for Adele, but she was nowhere to be seen. He hoped she and Vivien were able to get away in the darkness.

* * *

The four of them sat in a dark and barren cell somewhere beneath Clas Myrddin. It would have been pitch black but their guards had left a lone lantern shining somewhere further down the hallway and that light seeped through the cracks around the locked door. The wizard was awake now, but had remained silent except for a brief whisper to the abbot that the others had been unable to catch. Both Thom and the wizard had lost their caches and their staffs, effectively keeping them from crafting any magic.

"We are in one of Merlin's holding pens," stated Francis to no one in particular. "This is where the guild keeps magical beings awaiting slaughter and rendering."

"Truly?" asked the abbot of his monk. "Are you comparing this to a slaughterhouse?"

"Father Abbot, they claim they only kill those deserving of death, but I noticed that they always seem to find violators when there's a need for certain... elements."

After a moment of silence, Francis continued, "They are not as blatant as the Butcher of Sherwood, a sorcerer who killed almost all the magical beings in that forest in one bloody month. No, the guild is more fastidious in their ways, claiming to be so much better than the sorcerers. Nonetheless, they somehow always find violators deserving of death from the very magical race whose elements are in short supply at that moment. Convenient that. I always felt it was like claiming that you only butchered the misbehaving cows."

"That is why we pray for a better way, brother."

Thom noticed that the abbot was careful not to mention Francis' name nor mention the league. He nodded to himself, seeing the wisdom in that. He hoped that they wouldn't learn his name either, for Dalrake had sworn to get revenge on him for what happened on the Road of Waters.

"Do you think they can hear us?" asked Thom in a whisper to Francis, who was nearest to him.

"They could with magic, but I hear no telltale rhythms of a listening enchantment. I doubt any guard is bothering to stand outside with his ear pressed against the door. Nonetheless, we should still practice discretion, if only so that it will be a habit when the questioning begins."

Thom nodded to himself, fearing an interrogation that would likely reveal who he was. "Are there enchantments that can force us to talk?"

"Magic can never destroy our God-given free will, but... magic can kill or cause great pain." The monk sounded weary and almost resigned to what was coming. "I have no doubt that Dalrake has followers who are skilled at torturing others for answers, whether the inquisitor uses magic or hot coals."

Silence settled in the cell for a while, then Francis cleared his throat and spoke again, loud enough for all to hear him clearly. "Journeyman, what do you know of the Three Founders?"

It was an odd question. His master was one of the three, although Thom had been ignorant of that fact until recently. He had no idea why Francis was asking about them now, but he answered clearly while keeping it short. "They are the three who united the magicians to build the enchantments that protect Camelot, including the Roads."

"What was it like being mentored by your master?" asked Francis in a lower voice, low enough that the other two could hear but most likely too softly for anyone outside their cell.

Thom frowned, wondering why his friend was pressing this now. He considered not answering, but he realized that his captors most likely knew his identity already, so he chose to compromise, answering in a cautious whisper, "At the time I never knew of his reputation. It was impressive enough going from street urchin to magician's apprentice. I had no idea he was as famed as he was. Frankly, most of those years he barely mentioned Camelot or its Roads, or even the guild."

"That is odd considering that you were day and night with one of the chief craftsmen of the kingdom's greatest enchantments. Did he sometimes leave to attend to those great enchantments?"

"He left me alone at times, but never really explained why." Thom considered their years at the wilderness cottage and how his master had a love for silence. Levitanus had often taken hikes alone. "He seemed to need his time by himself, but usually he came back with new magical plants for me to study and render into their elements so I just assumed his hunt for them had taken him afar. Maybe he used those times to take care of other matters without me knowing. It isn't the place of an apprentice to question his master."

"That is true," agreed Francis, "but you are no longer an apprentice. Even if your master were alive, you would no longer need to obey his commands without question. That is part of the privilege and responsibility of being of journeyman rank."

Thom had no response, uncertain what his friend might be trying to hint at.

The abbot scooted closer along the cell's wall. "Brother, what are your thoughts of escape?"

"It will not be easy, Father Abbot. They took all magical supplies, so neither of our companions can craft any enchantments. They also took all of our weapons." He turned his attention to Thom. "Journeyman, do you think any servants in the house would come to our aid?"

Thom remembered the fear of the serving staff. "I doubt it. The head cook threatened me with a clever for daring to escape through his kitchen when I fled the invasion. I cannot imagine any of them risking their lives for prisoners who are practically strangers to them… unless the master magician is close to some."

Thom heard nothing from the still-hidden master, but the abbot answered for him. "I think not. Like you, he wasn't one to visit Clas Myrddin often or to linger here when he did."

Francis spoke in a loud enough whisper that the man keeping to the other side of the cell could hear. "Why not tell the journeyman who you are, wizard? He will find out soon enough, so wouldn't it be better for him to hear it from you?"

The wizard said nothing and Thom wondered again who he might be. Was it someone he had met before at Clas Myrddin?

"Are you claiming to know his identity?" asked the abbot in a hushed tone.

"I don't know for a certainty, but I can deduce much from what has happened over these last few months. One name links so many events together, like a string binds the bangles around a maiden's wrist."

"Speak no names here," ordered the abbot firmly. "The sorcerers may still learn all of our secrets but there is no reason to make their task any easier. Besides, your guesses may be wrong. I've known you to be mistaken a few times over the years, dear brother."

"Names can be whispered quietly enough to not be overheard," replied Francis.

"But some names can evoke greater reactions than others," responded Justin in a whisper barely heard, "and I not only speak about the journeyman here. Some who are now loyal to our group have a past that would greatly anger you too, brother."

Thom wondered if the secretive wizard might not be a wizard at all, but a former sorcerer. If so, their captors would realize his betrayal soon. He looked over at the man, a blacker spot in an already dark room, and wondered. Who was he? Did he really think he could keep his identity secret without any magic to hide behind?

TWENTY-FIVE

Truth Exposed

Thom sat silently in the darkness for another hour, listening as Justin and Francis softly prayed. The two prayed for their fellow prisoners, for their brethren who were still out there, and for the people of Camelot who would be suffering under this invasion. As he listened, Thom's thoughts drifted to Adele. Had she survived the attack at the harbor? Was she safe? He silently added a short prayer for her, praying that she would find her way to Mousehome's back door and escape that way. It was a dangerous route, but it would be better than trying to hide in a fallen Camelot. "Please God, protect her."

For some reason, praying eased his worrying about Adele, but his thoughts were still troubled by other things. Who was the wizard across the cell from him? Why was he still hiding his identity? He wondered if that knowledge would infuriate the sorcerers, which lead his thoughts to something Vivien had said about one of the league's magicians having once been a sorcerer. Was it a sorcerer huddling over there? Was he hiding his face from their captors? If so, it seemed a futile task given the fact that he had no magic to enhance his masking.

A bit later, Thom heard a crowd outside, as guards escorted another group of captives to the next cell. He listened carefully, but was uncertain who the prisoners were. Using the noise to cover him, Thom whispered to Francis. "Who do you think that wizard is?"

Francis leaned closer. "I'm not sure, Thomas. I wonder if he's a supposed dead man, but why should I upset you with just a guess?"

A dead man? Did Francis think Dalrake was sure to execute the other? "Tell me who he is; I'll not blame you if you guessed wrong."

But before the monk could respond, there was a rattling at the door and then it burst open and bright lanterns blinded them. When Thom was finally able to see again through sheltered eyes, he saw two guards with lanterns and naked blades. Behind them stood two sorcerers, one of whom Thom recognized.

Dalrake.

"I would say this catch is better than the last, Horis. See those two over there? I want to personally break them." Dalrake was pointing at Thom and Francis.

"A journeyman?" asked the other sorcerer. "Why trouble yourself with a mere student?"

"He is the one who defeated Narissa on the Road of Leaves. He also fouled our plans on the Road of Waters and killed Gweir."

"He's that one? Doesn't look so fierce cowering from the light, does he?"

"Do not let the dark blue robe mislead you. He has shown more ability than half the wizards in the guild. Even without his cache, I would not turn my back on him if I were you."

"Understood. I will prepare him, but I will leave the final work in your capable hands. What of the monk?"

"Once again, an unassuming appearance misleads. That man is the Traitor, the one who killed his own master."

Sorcerer Horis nodded understanding. "What of the abbot? Do you really want to anger the church? It's one thing to torture or kill a mere monk who was once a magician, but to hold a leader of the church is not wise. Should we not just release him?"

"Not yet. Something is afoot that I do not yet fully understand. Some intrigue."

"He leads a monastery. What could he be plotting?"

Dalrake didn't answer as both men stared at the Father Abbot.

"And what of the wizard?" asked Horis, his focus moving on to the final person remaining in the cell. "Is he to be tortured and freed or should we simply kill him? Not much new to be learned among Merlin's followers."

"Ah, that depends on who he is." Dalrake touched the shoulder of the nearest guard. "Turn his head so that we can see who we've captured."

The guard, handed his lantern to Horis and then sheathed his sword. Unafraid, he swiftly pounced on the wizard and wrestled him around. The wizard tried to fight back, but the guard was too strong and the larger man quickly had him subdued. The guard tore back the man's hood and then forced his face around to expose it to the light.

Thom gasped.

"You!" proclaimed Dalrake. "This does explain so much."

Thomas just stared, shocked at who he saw. Across from him, exposed in the harsh light and still struggling against the guard's hold was his old master, Levitanus.

How could this be? He had been burned to death on the Isle of Mists. Thom had cried over his grave. He wasn't dead after all?

It must be some kind of trickery, but as much as Thom strained, he couldn't hear any telltale sounds of an enchantment.

"My brother mage, you still live. Why would you fake your own death? It seems so… melodramatic of you, Levitanus. So opposed to your nature." Dalrake chuckled, as if suddenly understanding a joke. "This is something I would not have expected of you. Merlin will be furious when he learns of this. Do you know how hard he and I worked to salvage the Roads and the city? Your sudden withdrawal from the enchantments almost shattered everything."

Thom stood and came toward his old master. He ignored Francis' pleas for him to remain calm. Anger and pain welled up inside of him. His eyes could only see one other person: the man who had been his teacher for so many years. "You deceived me!"

The other guard was quick to place himself between Thom and the sorcerers, but Thom didn't care. "I thought you cared about me. I thought you were my friend as well as my mentor. You let me think that you were dead."

Dalrake laughed again as he looked from wizard to journeyman. "Now I remember. Thomas of York was your student, Levitanus. So Merlin and I were not the only ones you deceived." He looked at the guard still holding the wizard. "Take him to the interrogation chamber. Bind him to a chair but leave him unharmed. I have many questions for him."

The guard pulled the wizard out of the room and down the hallway.

"Hold off on questioning the others, at least until I can learn more from my fellow Founder," said Dalrake to Horis, "and do not release the abbot. I think his role in all of this is still to be revealed."

"Yes, sir," replied the other sorcerer.

Dalrake turned to walk out but paused to face a still-shocked Thom who was being held back by the other guard. "You must feel betrayed, young Thomas. Abandoned by the guild, and lied to by your teacher. It must be terribly disappointing. I understand. They all lied to me as well. That was why I left Merlin and the guild."

Thom glared at the sorcerer but had no response. What could he say? He had indeed been abandoned and lied to.

"We will talk more of this, young man," promised Dalrake and then he strode out the cell, quickly followed by Horis and the last guard.

In the sudden return of darkness, Thom whirled to look to where he thought Francis still sat. "Did you know it was him?"

The monk didn't need to ask which 'him' he was referring to. "His name was on my tongue when the sorcerers barged in. It was still but a guess but, like Dalrake, I see how this truth clarifies many past mysteries."

"Why did he do it?" demanded Thom.

"You'll need to ask him how he justifies the deception of his death. That is, if we see him again."

"But how could he do this to me?" His anger was turning into great hurt.

Abbot Justin spoke up. "It grieved him deeply to deceive you, but he felt it was necessary for the good of the realm."

Thom pained confusion returned to anger. "Necessary? You knew who he was and it didn't endanger the kingdom. What would it matter to tell me? I have no influence in the land."

"The guild and the king needed to see you in genuine grief. For your own protection; you needed to think him dead. If certain people learned that he was still alive, they would have tortured you to find out where he was."

Francis replied before Thom could, "It seems all of his efforts were for naught. He is still found out. Not only that, but he is already in the hands of his enemy. In addition, his deception cost him the admiration and love of his student. What do you think, Father Abbot?"

"I will leave it to him to explain his actions. This is between Levitanus and Thomas."

Thom's feelings were a boiling mess of anger and disappointment. His master was alive? It still seemed unreal. Might it be some enchantment? But no, he heard no revealing rhythms of magic in use. Part of him wanted to run up and embrace his mentor and act as if the last few months of terror and misery were just a bad dream. Another part of him wanted to hit him hard in the gut and spit on him in contempt. But the man had been taken away just as he had been exposed. Thom could neither hug nor hit him. He was left with his absence once again.

Frustrated, he started pacing in the darkened cell.

For a time, the others said nothing, but then Francis whispered some harsh questions to his abbot, "What was his part in starting the League of Barnabas? Was it his idea or yours? Is this just another gambit by one of the Three? They do so love playing with our lives as if we were mere chess pieces."

Thom stopped pacing to hear the answer.

"It began as a dream we shared over twenty years ago. Yes, he had a part in it since the beginning, but it was no game for us, either then or now. It is a shared passion. A desire to see justice prevail."

"What was his part in my welcome to the order?" asked Francis softly.

"He encouraged it, hoping your disgust would lessen and you might become one of our first members. But the final decision was mine, Brother Francis, and I do not regret it. You have been a faithful servant to the Lord and our order, even while steadfastly resisting my attempts to lure you into the league."

"Even when I fled the guild, I failed to escape their long grasp." Francis sounded more sad than angry. "You must have thought my suggestions for the league rather inane, having such an eminent secret advisor as one of the Three."

"No, Francis. Your advice was irreplaceable. You were the one who pushed us to include the magical beings as part of the leadership. You were our conscience, always reminding me of the awful sacrifices made to create the greater enchantments. Even while hating magic, you helped to establish the League of Barnabas as much as he or I did. Even though I know it will pain you to hear this, I say it with utmost respect: the league is as much your legacy as ours."

"I hate all this plotting in the alleys," muttered Francis. "What other recruits did he bring in?"

"His students were an obvious source," answered the abbot, his shadowy form turning to look up at Thom, "though he was too hesitant in bringing in Thomas after the incident when one student killed the other. Levitanus had intended to recruit his previous apprentice, but then the journeyman killed him. That truly shook him to the core. The killing made him question almost everything about the guild and to flee Clas Myrddin and the city. For a time, he even avoided me. He wandered the realm, his grief overwhelming him. It wasn't until he found Thomas and took him in that Levitanus began to heal. You are truly precious to him, young man, and maybe that caused him to shelter you from too much. He tried to protect you from the schemes of the wizards and sorcerers. He worried that bringing you into the league would expose you too soon to the darker side of magic, to the battle we have in front of us."

"But he brought me up in a lie," argued Thom. "He taught me the craft as one apprenticed to the guild, not as one apprenticed to the league. We were far from Camelot and rarely visited by other magicians, so I see no reason why he couldn't have taught me differently. Why continue to pretend to be something he no longer believed in?"

"He can explain that to you, if he so chooses. I will just give you some questions to consider. Even though Dalrake renounced the guild long ago, why does he still help Merlin maintain the Roads? Although the wizards and sorcerers tussle for dominance and control, are they truly enemies? Why do so many magical beings cooperate with the sustaining of enchantments that costs their people many lives? Answer those three questions and you may have a better understanding of why the League of Barnabas is needed and why it had to be started in secrecy."

"Pardon my bluntness, Father Abbot, but I don't care to understand your league. Not anymore. Justify your actions to someone else. I'm tired of all the lies and secrets." With that he turned and walked to the other side of their cell and leaned heavily against the cold wall, hitting it once with his fist and feeling the rough stone bite back across his knuckles. That little pain was nothing compared to the hurt inside.

TWENTY-SIX

Unbelieved Reasons

They returned Levitanus two hours later when two human guards carried him in and dropped him in the middle of the cell. As soon as the door closed and darkness returned to their cell, Francis and the abbot hurried to his side. Thom watched their shadowy movements but kept away.

The wizard moaned as he lay there, so he was conscious.

"Can you speak? Are you hurt?" asked the abbot.

He muttered something too softly for Thom to overhear.

"Well next time avoid having magical battles on board a ship," replied Justin. "Did the sorcerers do anything to you just now?"

Again the response was barely above a whisper, too low for Thom to hear.

"Treating you like a newborn chick, is he? Dalrake will not be so tolerant in another day or so. He will want answers soon."

The wizard slowly rose, leaning on the other two for support until he could sit without help. Thom heard his shifting more than saw it. Thom could barely discern Levitanus in the dim lighting that seeped around the door, but he had a feeling that his old master was looking his way.

"Will he speak to me?" This time Thom heard the whisper.

The abbot also seemed to turn in his way. "Anger and hurt war inside him. I do not know if he will listen to you now."

"Speak only truth from this day forward," suggested Francis. "No more lies. No more misleading. No more hidden plans. Vulnerable honesty is the only way you can ever win him back to your side."

"I can hear all of you," stated Thom, not appreciating that they were talking about him, "but I have no interest in talking with *him*."

"Understood," replied Levitanus, "but I still apologize for hurting you so. It was a necessary deception, but I never meant for it to go so long. We thought the guild would disown you and then we would be able to quietly bring you into the league. None of us expected them to leave you dangling like that, forbidden to use magic yet still ordered to dress and act the part of a journeyman."

"You could have returned for me in secret," said Thom softly, his anger cooling into the chill of feeling betrayed and abandoned.

"He nearly did," replied the abbot. "The rest of the league's masters had to stand united to keep him away from Camelot. Their concern is shown to have been justified, for he was captured upon his return just as they feared. No, we kept him away from here and the recruiting of you was left in my hands. I am sorry that I failed to convince you, Thomas. If I would have brought you in, then you would have been sent to Levitanus to be reunited."

129

Thom thought back of the many times the abbot had attempted to convince him into joining the league. The man had tried, but that still didn't justify all the secrets and deceptions. Not only after Levitanus' supposed death, but throughout his adventures on the Roads. Another wave of anger came on him as he realized that the deception had occurred since the day he had been chosen as an apprentice. He had thought he was being trained to be a magician of the guild. But his master had already at that time started his plotting to create the league. "Over a decade of deception. I was with you every day but you couldn't bring yourself to telling me that I wasn't being trained for the guild. Was anything in my life true?"

"My fatherly love for you is true," whispered Levitanus. "I have affection for all of my past students, but you are the one whom I love like the son I never had."

"I don't want to hear that! Love doesn't lie! Love doesn't abandon." Thom would have stalked away, but there was nowhere to go in that stone prison. Instead, he stood rigid against the wall with arms crossed, hands clenched, and shook his head in denial.

Francis stood and walked toward him but not all the way. "You have wounded him gravely, wizard, with a weapon that cut far deeper than any sword. His soul bleeds from your abuse."

Levitanus sat there in silence, making no attempt to further defend his actions.

"He did what he thought best for the realm," said the abbot on his behalf. "He does not resist Merlin out of pride, like Dalrake. He did all this so he could break free of Merlin's endless and demanding enchantments because he knew that the Roads and the enchantment over Camelot cannot continue. The enchantments are too costly in lives. It is Merlin's folly and the rue of all magical beings. Does that not sound like a love for our land and its people?"

Thom chose not to answer. The abbot portrayed *him* as if he were practically a saint, some great hero sacrificing himself for others. He was no such thing. He was a coward, running and hiding instead of fighting for the change he claimed to believe in.

Just then the door opened again and harsh light filled the cell. Sorcerer Horis entered with another sorcerer and two guards, one of them holding the bright lantern. The sorcerer pointed at Thomas. "He is the one. Bring him to the questioning room."

TWENTY-SEVEN

Boiler's Grip

Thomas was escorted down the passageway to another room, where he was forced to remove his journeyman's robe but left on his long-sleeved undershirt and trousers, then they shoved him into a backless armchair. The guard bound his wrists to the chair arms, pushing up his shirtsleeves to well above the elbow. He then stepped behind Thom. Thom's robe was left crumbled on the stone floor.

Before Thom stood Sorcerer Horis, offering a friendly smile. The other sorcerer stood to the side, apparently here to observe what was coming.

"It is a shame that you have become entangled in all of this, young Thomas," said Horis in a friendly tone. "You are merely a student trying to master his craft, but others have ensnared you in their intricate schemes. Plots by Merlin and by Dalrake and even by Levitanus. Schemes of a king and his estranged son. Secrets of centaurs and pixies and other magical beings. Even hidden plans of an abbot. So many pulled their hidden strings, forcing you to dance to their music. I doubt you asked for such a life. Seems rather unfair, doesn't it?"

To himself, he admitted that the sorcerer was right. It had been unfair. But he made no reply. He was determined to say nothing to the man.

The silence didn't seem to disturb the sorcerer. Instead the man motioned to the room around them. "Do you know what the guild did here? This is one of their rendering rooms."

He stepped aside so that Thom had a clear view of the wall behind him. A stone catch basin sat at the base of the wall and iron shackles hung at different heights from the gray stone face. "Precious blood was gathered here from various beasts and beings. It is said the magicians who specialize at this are rather efficient, making sure nothing is wasted to splatter or cloth soaking."

He pointed to the other wall, where more empty shackles hung, waiting their next victim. "They collected other things over there, or maybe that is where the next victims waited their turn. In other rooms, there are cages for some of the more ferocious beasts and vats for boiling down certain things. There is a drying room and a grinding room for making of various powders. In all, it is quite an impressive operation for rendering the elements of our craft. The guild made sure their members were well supplied, at least with those elements needed in great supply. I hear they also bought powders from disreputable sellers with no questions asked on how they were obtained."

Horis brought the focus back to himself as he stepped closer to the tied-up Thomas. "Did you help with the killing and rendering?"

"Of course not," blurted out Thom, offended by the accusation.

Horis gave him a sad smile as he stepped back. "I thought as much. You are a mere journeyman, and barely that from what I've been told. They kept this a secret from you, just like they kept most of your deserved training from you. I'll admit to you that I have no admiration for how the guild treated you. I think they wasted your talents to have neglected you so. Wouldn't you agree?"

Thom didn't reply, though he did indeed agree.

"Did you know that we sorcerers have no great house like this?" He motioned around him to indicate all Clas Myrddin. "Dalrake has a formidable castle, but we have nothing like the guild's council or classrooms or its many rules. With us, your master trains you and then lets you live as you want. We are a freer people. Wouldn't you like that freedom, to practice your craft again?"

Although he very much wanted that, he didn't respond.

"No answer? That is disappointing. Will you be willing to tell me about what Levitanus is plotting? Why did he fake his own death?"

This time it was easier to say nothing because he had no idea why his old master chose to fake his death.

Horis sighed when Thom remained silent. "I had so hoped you would cooperate. It would have been much easier for both of us. In the end, you will tell me all that I want to know, so why not share it now and spare yourself the agony and damage."

He turned to the other sorcerer. "Make careful note, Belden, of what elements I use and how even the simplest of enchantments can be used to get answers from someone. Watch but make no comments, for I do not like to be disturbed at my work. Afterward, you can ask your questions. Understood?"

The other sorcerer nodded.

Satisfied, Horis moved to a plain table on which a magician's box sat, a mixing bowl and pestle waiting beside it. In addition, there was a pitcher- most likely of water- and some glass vials of dark liquid that Thom guessed to be blood, although he didn't know from what beast or being it may have come.

The sorcerer opened his cache and quickly picked out the elements he wanted and then closed the box. He worked efficiently, mixing powders and liquids into his bowl then adding his own spittle to attune it. When satisfied, he dipped one hand into it and then his other, almost like he was battering his hands for frying.

Thom sensed and heard the enchantment practically sizzling around the sorcerer's hands, but it was more defused than when Sorcerer Gweir had used the Hand of Lightning enchantment on the Road of Waters. Horis held up both hands and they were covered in a greenish goo that seemed to give off a slickly, weak glow. He kept his hands away from his own body, like someone who didn't want to get freshly washed hands dirty again or, more likely, as someone would carry a boiling pot to prevent any scalding.

"Have you experienced this enchantment before?" he asked in a still-friendly tone. Thom wasn't certain if he was asking himself or Sorcerer Belden. "It is called Boiler's Grip because it was originally meant as a way for a magician to get a hot meal while traveling through the wilds whenever he didn't have the means to make a fire. It is a fairly simple enchantment that any journeyman should be able to craft, or even an advanced apprentice. However, I understand the guild ceased teaching it because of me."

He stepped close and with his left index finger he lightly traced a line across Thom's exposed right arm. Although he was braced for something bad to happen, Thom still couldn't help letting out a grunt of pain. It felt like he had been seared with fire-heated iron. Looking down, he saw his skin was already red and angry blisters ran in a line where the sorcerer had merely brushed one finger.

"I simply found another practical use for an enchantment and they became incensed. Melodramatic of them to ban a useful enchantment just because I improvised, do you not think so?"

Thom held his tongue, trying not to show any reaction, but he was keenly aware that the sorcerer still had nine more fingers soaked in magic.

"I hope you will talk to me now. I am not asking for much; I only want to know why your master faked his death. Will you not tell me?"

"He's not my master anymore," Thom growled, his bitterness at Levitanus' deception still strong.

"Yes, I had heard that. So why do you endure this pain to protect him? He abandoned you. Just tell me about his schemes and this will be over."

He wanted to but he couldn't. Even if he felt no loyalty toward his old master, he knew that revealing his secrets would hurt all the others who were part of the league, from the abbot to Vivien. It might even hurt his beloved Adele, and Thom would endure anything to protect her from the wrath of sorcerers.

Horis lean closer and brushed his left middle finger across Thom's cheek. Thom tried to jerk away, but the guard suddenly grabbed his head and held it in place. The result was a staggered line of blisters across the side of his face that made his eyes tear and his cheek quiver in agony.

"Tell me."

When he still didn't answer, Horis ordered the guard to rip apart Thom's shirt to bare his shoulders and back. The soldier quickly cut the garment with his belt knife and then grabbed each section and pulled, leaving the shirt dangling to either side.

Horis set his ring finger and little finger on one shoulder, letting them burn in deeper, causing Thom to yell out in pain. Then he pressed his left thumb into the other shoulder, pushing even harder. Thom's yell turned into a scream of agony.

Just then another soldier barged in. Thom couldn't see him clearly through tear-filled eyes.

"About time," snapped Horis. "Where is my water basin?"

"I'm sorry, sir. I will get it now, but you should know that trouble has come to the city. Dalrake orders..."

"Get me my water first, then you can talk about other things," ordered the sorcerer.

The soldier persisted. "Rowan Gate has been overrun. Merlin and Arthur are back in the city, with many of the knights of the Round Table and a large contingent from the guild. I heard that even more have landed at King's Harbor, including centaurs and a pixie army. Dalrake orders all magicians to the council chamber immediately."

Horis cursed, then repeated his order for fresh water. "If I cannot wash off this residue, I will wipe it off on your face."

The soldier hurried away, not closing the door behind him.

Horis waited impatiently. Through his pain, Thom heard the sorcerer mutter, "Today's work is wasted. I will have to start all over and with something else. Belden, I will not be able to show you the other enchantments I like to use, but I will tell you about them later so that you can try them out. You might as well go see what Dalrake wants; let him know that I will be up as soon as I clean up down here."

"Very well," replied the other sorcerer, leaving the room without even a glance at the still-suffering Thomas.

Soon the soldier returned with a bowl of water that he carefully set on the table, along with a hand towel.

The sorcerer held up his right hand, which was still covered with the faintly-glowing slime. "I should grab your throat for disturbing my work. Do not interrupt an interrogation ever again. Do you understand?"

The soldier nodded. "Yes, sir."

Instead of grabbing the guard, Horis turned back to Thom. He slapped him hard on Thom's back and then smeared his hand to the side.

Thom screamed and almost blacked out.

The sorcerer didn't flinch at the noise. He strode over to the bowl and washed off any residue remaining, then headed out the door. His last words were an order to have Thom and his robe thrown back in the cell with the others. "Belden or I will have to start over in the morning."

TWENTY-EIGHT

Lost Fight

Thomas hit the floor hard when the soldiers tossed him back into the cell. He couldn't help but scream as it jostled his blistered back and shoulders.

As soon as the door closed, Francis was at his side. "What did they do to you?"

"Boiler's Grip," he muttered, carefully rolling on his side. He wanted to sit up, but his shoulders and back were in spasms of pain and with each shake he felt more pain.

The abbot came over too, as did his old master. The two stood over him, while Francis knelt at his side. It was the monk who helped him sit up.

"Horis has always favored that enchantment," said Levitanus. "It was his first perversion of magic."

Thom looked up at the dark outline that was his old mentor and shook his head. Levitanus probably knew almost all of the sorcerers by name. After all, decades ago the magicians had been united under the three Founders. The thought reminded him again that he had never really known the man, even after spending over a decade as his student.

"I wish I had some light to look at your burns," said Francis, "and also the supplies to make a decent salve to coat them."

Thom gripped his friend's forearm in thanks. "I know you would help if you could, but I think none are very deep. His torturing was interrupted before he could do any permanent damage. I might get a scar or two, but that will be all for now."

"What did he force you to tell?" asked Abbot Justin.

"He got nothing from me. As I said, he was interrupted. He was ordered to some sorcerers' council. If I heard true, the king and the wizards have retaken Rowan Gate."

Levitanus and Justin exchanged some kind of look, but Thom was uncertain what it was.

"The king returns," noted Francis. "That will distract the sorcerers for a time but it will not get us free. If anything, it will cause Dalrake to move faster to get his answers out of us. He won't have the time to toy with us as I think he would want to."

"I fear you are correct, Brother Francis," said Levitanus, "and he will focus his attention on you and Thomas. The abbot and I will likely be spared, at least at first, because of who we are and because he probably has some greater scheme planned for us. However, you are known companions of ours so he will torture the two of you to get his answers. I am sorry."

"Francis, is there some way we can escape?" asked Thom, trying to ignore his old teacher. "Could we surprise our guards or overpower the sorcerer?"

"We can surely try," said the monk. "Let us get behind the door and shove it back at them when they enter. Father Abbot, would you be willing to distract them when they enter? And you as well, wizard?"

"What do you have in mind?" asked Justin.

"The two of you will stand before the far wall, making yourselves as large as you can so that you'll cast a large shadow when they come in with their lanterns. They need to be fooled for a brief moment, thinking that Thomas and I are sheltering behind you. The plan is that we will attack in that moment of confusion."

Levitanus shook his head. "'Tis a plan as thin as an onion skin, but it is the only one we have. I will do what I can to help."

"As will I," said the abbot.

"Horis said he or Belden would be back in the morning," added Thom, "so we probably have a few hours to rest."

"We will need to be ready by dawn, in case they are early risers," replied Francis. "It is hard to tell time when you cannot see daylight, but I will stay up and track the night's progress. I will wake all of you when it is time."

Francis suggested that Thomas dress in his discarded robe, stating that it would offer some protection to his open wounds and a bit of warmth. Thom agreed, although he almost passed out from the pain as Francis helped him dress. Wiping at his tears, he sat down behind the door and tried to find a less-painful position to rest. Eventually, exhaustion pulled him into slumber in spite of the constant throbbing of his burns.

* * *

Francis woke them in what was likely the pre-dawn. Thom had no way to know for certain, but the sorcerers hadn't returned while he had been slumbering. According to Francis, no one had checked on them or offered any food or drink. They hadn't even brought a chamber pot, so the men had been forced to pick a cell corner to designate for relieving themselves.

Uncertain about when the guards might come in to check on them, they took their places in preparation. Thom and Francis stood behind the door, while Justin and Levitanus stood before the far wall.

After hours of waiting, Thom sagged against the cold wall behind the cell door. His shoulders and back were still throbbing. He was tired and wished he could just drop to the floor and sleep, but he knew he couldn't. Francis stood next to him, whispering encouragement at times, but he too seemed worn out by the wait. Levitanus and Justin had resorted to interlocking their arms to support one another as they stood in front of the far wall.

When the cell door finally opened, it was almost too sudden for Thom to react. He heard the latch being lifted. He barely got his hands up in time as the door was shoved open, toward them. He and Francis shoved it back, slamming it into whoever was opening it, then Francis grabbed the edge and pulled it back open. The two of them rushed around and stormed the staggered soldier. The three of them tumbled into the passage as the soldier grabbed at them. But before they could subdue the man, three other soldiers were on them, kicking and hitting and grabbing.

One moment, Thom was struggling with the soldier to get at his belt knife and the next he was pulled away by others. He tried to fight his way free, but to no avail. He was slammed against a wall and nearly lost consciousness at the sudden surge of pain as his wounds hit the cold stones. A sword point was set to his throat but he hardly noticed it.

"Let them live, men," ordered Sorcerer Belden from one side. He walked up to Francis and grabbed his ear. "Sorcerer Dalrake wants them for himself, so he would be angered if we killed them or even caused too much injury. Do not deny him his vengeance."

The sorcerer gave a hard yank to Francis' ear and then stepped away. "We came for these two and here they are. Take them to the room for more questioning. I want to be quick about it since they insist that I must take a turn at gate duty at midday."

Thom realized that Beldin was dressed as a mage-guard, with the red cape and the staff wrap, and he wondered why the sorcerers bothered to continue a role and uniform of the guild. At times he wondered if the sorcerers despised the guild or envied it.

Before leaving, Beldin turned to the two older men still in the cell. "I hear that Dalrake has asked Horis to prepare you two for your next questioning by him. You remember Horis, do you not, Levitanus? He certainly remembers you from when you had him cast out of the guild."

TWENTY-NINE

Butcher of Sherwood

Thom hung there, chained to the wall and once again stripped down to just his undergarment, as Belden took his turn on Francis. The sorcerer had already abused Thom for an hour and now he expected Thom to watch as Francis suffered. Belden didn't pretend to be kind or apologetic of his actions, like Horis had. Instead, the sorcerer set to his work with grim efficiency, though Thom still hadn't revealed anything. Both ankles hurt from having been shackled upside down during his torture and his back was covered by pussy welts caused by one of the enchantments used against him.

After Thom nearly lost consciousness, Belden had him switched with Francis, sending Thom to hang against the cold stone wall in slow agony and watch. He ordered the one remaining soldier to enforce his expectation that Thom remain conscious and watching, and the soldier took his duty seriously. When Thom's swollen eyes had sagged shut in exhaustion, a sharp jab in his side startled him back to awareness.

So far, the sorcerer had gained no useful information from either the monk or the journeyman, but he was persistent. Thom was determined to reveal nothing. It wasn't out of any loyalty to Levitanus or Justin. He remained silent for Adele's sake. If the League of Barnabas were exposed to the sorcerers, they would surely hunt down all who were a part of it and... Thom wondered what they would do. Most likely kill all of them. Whoever the sorcerers spared would likely be hunted down by the guild. He wanted none of that for his beloved.

At the moment, the sorcerer was crafting another enchantment to inflict on Francis. Thom was too dazed from his own abuse to recognize what elements the magician was using, though their sounds nagged at his memory even in his stupor.

The door opened and three people walked in. Thom looked over, noticing the colors for all three levels. The guard also looked, for once letting up on forcing Thom to watch the torture. Belden didn't look because he couldn't break his concentration in the middle of crafting magic. Francis just hung there, soaked in sweat and blood dribbling off his chin.

The newly-arrived master magician lowered his hood then motioned for the apprentice to close the door. Something about the hooded apprentice seemed familiar to Thom and he wished he could see the youth's face. Most likely his senses were playing tricks on him because he knew no sorcerer students. The short fellow in journeyman blue kept his hood up too as he quietly moved to stand against the wall. The apprentice came to stand next to the journeyman, both silently watching as Belden finished his latest enchantment.

"Hurry it up, Belden," said the watching sorcerer. "You dawdle over your crafting like a frightened apprentice."

The sorcerer grunted in acknowledgment but wouldn't allow the other to distract him.

"Why do you use Boiler's Grip to extract information? Has Horis been lecturing you about its effectiveness? If he has, do not believe him, for his attachment to that particular enchantment is just sentimental."

Thom now recognized what was being mixed and cringed for his friend. Horis had used the scalding magic on him only that one time, but the blisters were still oozing on his shoulders. He shivered for Francis.

Belden finished and lifted two gooey hands that gleamed green in the faint light. "I am tempted to slap you right now, Kane. Why are you interrupting my work?"

"Where are the other two prisoners? I was told to show them to these students."

"How should I know? If the cell is empty, then Horis has probably taken them somewhere to prepare them for Dalrake's questioning."

Kane nodded and turned back to the door, but the two students seemed to block his way. The apprentice shook his head in protest.

Thom thought it a strange act from students, to stand up to their master. He wondered if he had misunderstood, but then the sorcerer turned back to Belden, who was now walking toward Francis. Kane quickly came up behind him and suddenly Belden cried out and dropped to the ground, landing on top of his glowing hands and causing his body to shake in reaction.

The guard was distracted by the fallen sorcerer and that was to his rue, for Kane sprang at him and this time Thom saw the knife in his hand just before he drove it into the soldier's neck.

Sorcerer Kane had killed both, but Thom had no idea why.

"Help me pull the bodies into the corner," said the sorcerer to his companions. "We have no time to hide them but, if someone merely glances into this room, I want them to go unnoticed. Take the soldier's sword and knife, for we can use more weapons even if they are in shaky hands."

The three of them quickly had the dead sorcerer and soldier piled to the side.

As he straightened from the work, Kane pointed at Thom, "Release his chains and find him clothes. Give him the knife, since I doubt he's strong enough to keep the sword from dragging on the floor. And give him Beldin's staff because we have no time to search out his own."

The two students hurried over to do so.

Thom was shocked by the killings and was unsure why it had been done. Was it some feud among sorcerers?

As the two students started working on his bindings, Thom had another surprise. His eyesight was blurry and his left eye was almost shut from swelling but he suddenly realized that they were women and then noted the one had distinct red hair under her hood.

Vivien? Was she really a sorceress?

In his pain and exhaustion, he wasn't truly understanding what was occurring. He considered struggling against them, but decided to save what little strength he still had for when he was free of the chains. Could he fight off someone as fierce as Vivien and whoever was with her?

He was distracted as the killing sorcerer strode toward Francis. Suddenly, Thom feared the man would strike again and now kill the monk.

"What do you want with me, Butcher of Sherwood?" asked Francis looking up at the magician looming over him. His voice was loud yet hoarse from the abuse he had already suffered.

"I'm freeing you, Betrayer," answered the sorcerer, setting the captured sword on the nearby table, leaning his staff against the edge and then turning back to the bound monk. He loosened the bindings holding down the monk's arms.

Thom was distracted from hearing any more of their exchange, for the two women finally succeeded in releasing his chains, and the sudden demand on his tortured legs was too much. He barely kept in a cry of pain and would have collapsed to the ground if they hadn't quickly seized him and kept him standing.

"My poor Thomas," said the woman on his left and he recognized the voice of his beloved.

He turned his head, trying to see her with his good eye. In disbelief, he muttered, "Adele?"

"Yes."

"We need to keep moving or they will find us out," stated Kane. "Can the journeyman stand on his own?"

"He's too weak," replied Vivien. "He is almost as limp as a newborn, so we will need to help him dress."

Thom forced himself to support more of his own weight, even though his legs screamed from where Belden had lashed them with magical tendrils that had caused them to twitch and his ankles were rubbed raw from when he had been chained by them during his last torture session. "I...I can walk on my own. Just give me a moment to regain my balance. I was hanging upside down for nearly an hour before they chained me to the wall." He shuddered just a little as his eyes wandered to where a chain hung from the ceiling, his blood still stained the shackles and floor stones.

Kane followed Thom's glance and frowned as he recognized what had been done. "Belden always was wasteful in his actions."

"That from the man who killed and rendered every magical beast and being in the Sherwood Forest," stated Francis with anger. "Why should we cooperate with a killer like you?"

"Tell them," ordered Kane of Vivien as he stepped away from the monk.

Vivien complied. "You will cooperate because the Butcher of Sherwood Forest repented and joined the League of Barnabas. He was one of the cloaked magicians we saw at the monastery." She paused to look at the former sorcerer. "At first I did not believe in his repentance either, though Wizardess Bronwen swore to it. I remember him well from when we were both students here at the keep. I remember his turning. Yet he was the one who said we could not leave anyone in Dalrake's hands. He is the one who risked all to sneak in here and rescue you."

"She is correct, though admittedly my main goal was not rescuing the two of you. Where is the cell holding Levitanus and the abbot?"

Francis replied as he struggled to stand and don his monk robe. "Our common cell is three doors down, on the right."

"Ladies, get these two moving. I am going on. Extinguish the lights in this room as you come out. Oh, and give Belden's magic cache to the journeyman. The monk would be better able to use it, but I know he will refuse the gift." With that, Kane pulled up his hood, grasped his staff in a tight grip, and swept out the door, closing it behind him.

Adele helped Thom into his trousers and he was too exhausted to be embarrassed that she did. When she helped him put on his tattered shirt he hissed in pain, barely able to restrain a scream of agony. She hesitated with his robe, but he insisted on putting it on. He then sat on the torture chair and she helped to pull on his boots, which revealed to him that his left ankle was in much worse shape than his right one.

It took great effort to stand after that, put he made it to his feet with Adele's help.

Vivien retrieved the magician's box and repacked it in the dead sorcerer's knapsack, a black leather pack that looked expensive. She handed it to Thom, who took it and struggled it over his shoulder. His still raw back and shoulders screamed in complaint, but he did his best to ignore his body's outrage.

Next, she handed him the guard-mage cape and the adorned staff that had belonged to the dead sorcerer. Thom grimaced at them, but she insisted and even helped lay the cape over his abused shoulders.

Once done, Vivien nodded approval and then went over to help Francis buckle on the sword belt. Thom tried bearing his own weight but found his left ankle yelling in protest. He had to lean heavily on Adele but he was able to hobble toward the door; he hoped he could do better once he had walked a bit more because he was of no help now.

The four made their way to the passageway and headed in slow pursuit of Kane. They were still only halfway to the cell, when Kane stormed out and reported the cell empty. "Where could they have been taken?"

"Belden said the Sorcerer Horis would be getting them ready for Dalrake's questioning," replied Francis. He seemed to be regaining his strength and his voice sounded stronger too. "Neither of them has been tortured yet and I hear no magic in use nearby. Maybe Horis has them upstairs in a more comfortable setting for more gentle questioning. I do hear more magic in use further away…"

"That has nothing to do with them," said Kane, dismissing it. "Merlin and his companions have struck back at Dalrake and Mordred. There is fierce fighting in the western sector of the city, especially around the king's keep. I would think Dalrake would be too busy to do any questioning now. Maybe he has them waiting in some reception room. But where? We will be discovered soon if we skulk through these halls much longer. Do any of you have an idea where we should look next?"

"Shouldn't we first get Thomas and Francis away from here?" suggested Adele. "They are both seriously injured."

"I think not," replied Kane coolly, "I did not come here to rescue them for they are not even a part of us. Their rescue was your idea, apprentice. And I will not let them slow me down. If they cannot keep up, we will leave them behind. It is vital we rescue the wizard and the abbot; everyone else is expendable."

"You are a cruel man," stated Vivien.

"But he is right," said Francis, cutting off any further protests. "Thom and I will do our best to keep up. It is distasteful to agree with him, but Levitanus and the Father Abbot are the essential ones to rescue, for they know too much. Most likely the two are waiting in some sitting room with bored guards as Horis tries to convince them to talk. Still, I would suggest a quick look-through of the other rooms on this level of the basement before we go upstairs."

Kane agreed, so he and the women quickly searched behind each door off that passage, but found no one. Thom and Francis slowly moved toward the stairwell, using each other as support. They listened for anyone approaching as they got ready to climb upward. Thom asked if they should also search any lower levels, but Francis thought it unlikely that Horis would bother with the inconvenience.

.

THIRTY

Ruse

They came upstairs to an empty guard room where usually a journeyman sat on duty to monitor who came and went to the basement. Because those cells below would usually contain various magical beasts or magical beings sentenced to death for rendering, it was an area the guild guarded carefully. But this time they found no one sitting at the duty desk and no guards outside the doors either. Early morning light came through a pair of high windows to light up dust motes in the air, that started dancing furiously as their arrival stirred up the still air. Thom was surprised at the time; had lost track of the hours in the forever-dark dungeon and for some reason thought it was still before sunrise. Somehow, he had lost track of a few hours.

As they entered the guard room, Francis saw an abandoned cudgel and claimed it, handing the sword and its belt to Thomas. "You are more skilled with it than I am and now that your strength seems to be returning, I doubt you'll drag it on the ground."

Thom offered the knife in its place, which the monk accepted.

"Hurry up," ordered Kane in a harsh whisper, even though he was merely standing by the open door and looking around the corner. "And keep your voices down."

Thom thought it suspicious that the sorcerers would leave the area unattended. "Where is everyone?" he whispered.

"We found it this empty when we came in," said Vivien softly, as they all moved to follow Kane. "We saw hardly anyone after we made it through the rubble of the main gate. The guards there asked little of Kane when he led us inside. It seems that the sorcerers and their soldiers are focused on what is happening at Rowan Gate and the castle, many of them having rushed off to help there."

They exited the guard room, entering the wing of Clas Myrddin that had once held the guild's guards, but the barracks were empty too. Thom would have expected to see at least a few guards sleeping in the darkened rooms- those who had stood duty during the night- but there was no one in any of the cramped rooms they passed. Doors were open and some beds were disheveled as if sleep had been interrupted, but nobody was there. In one room the windows weren't shuttered and sunshine streamed in. Thom was still surprised to realize it was daytime. Was this the day after his capture or was it two days after?

"Where to?" asked Vivien as they made their way down the hallway. "The visitor rooms?"

Kane gave a slight nod, motioning for Vivien to lead the way. "Guide us there. I haven't been a regular here since my journeyman days, before I left to become a sorcerer."

Thom knew of the section Vivien had suggested. It was a trio of sitting rooms set aside for distinguished visitors who were waiting to meet with a magician. The guild frowned on outsiders wandering the halls and passages, where they might disturb someone in the midst of teaching a class or crafting an enchantment, so the servants were careful to direct any visitors to the appropriate waiting area. They were well-appointed rooms, unlike the one larger room where commoners were sent to wait on unpadded benches or the waiting area outside the council chambers.

As he walked down the hallway, Thom began to limp more and more as he used Beldin's staff as walking aid. The injuries sustained during his latest round of torture were starting to reveal themselves. Adele waited for him and insisted that he lean on her; he was grateful for the support. As they continued through the guard wing, he whispered his appreciation.

"Thank you for rescuing Francis and I."

"I'm so glad to have you free," she replied, then paused a moment. "When did you find out that your teacher was still alive?"

Thom grimaced, and not due to any physical injury. "His deceit was exposed while we were in the prison cell."

Adele nodded. "Kane told Vivien and I right after he revealed his own identity. He only told us in case we had to finish the rescue without him." She paused again. "How do you feel towards him?"

"I feel anger and hurt," he replied coldly. "He knew I suffered, thinking him dead all this time, and he did nothing. Not only did he fake his death, he lived a false life too. He taught me as a guild wizard, even though he had already founded the League of Barnabas in rivalry to it. I thought I knew him. I looked up to him as a father." He swallowed the rising anger, for now wasn't the time to rage. "He left me behind, but you didn't. You came for me. Thank you again, my dear Adele."

She smiled at him. "Of course I came for you, just as you would for me. But I didn't do much. It was Master Kane who killed three and Vivien who stabbed another. Even though Vivien seems to despise him, the two work well together. Kane is ruthless, but effective."

"But you're the one who insisted on rescuing us. I heard Kane; he's only interested in freeing the abbot and Levitanus. He would have left Francis and I behind."

"I still might leave you behind if you don't hurry up and stop the chatter," whispered Kane harshly. "Those two are vital to our cause. You and the monk are not. That is simple truth, even if it is harsh to hear. Now quicken your pace."

Thom did his best to comply, but each step seemed to jar one injury or another. Without Adele's help, he wouldn't have been able to go on. He doubted he could do much with the sword hanging at his side; he had no strength or endurance left in him. He hoped no soldiers would find them.

The five of them slipped through the seemingly abandoned hallways of Clas Myrddin. One servant did see them as they passed the entrance to some hall, but he quickly stopped his cleaning and rushed through a service doorway at the far end of the room. Thom hoped the man was merely avoiding them and not rushing off to report their incursion.

Just as they reached the hallway off which the sitting rooms lay, they heard with their inner ears a huge explosion of magic. All of them stopped and looked in that direction, even though they couldn't see anything.

"That was closer than Rowan Gate," whispered Francis. "Much closer."

Kane gave a grim nod of agreement, as Thom caught an echo of the explosion in the rhythms of the city's encircling magic.

Vivien stopped in front of the first door and looked to Kane for direction.

"Show no weapons yet," he whispered, making sure all heard and obeyed. "Be ready to quickly draw them, but I will use subterfuge first.

"Hoods up to hide your identities," he continued, doing as he ordered. "I want the monk and journeyman to delay out here because they are the most likely to be recognized. I don't want them to realize that we are here to free the captives; I want them confused so we can get the advantage. To them, I am still a sorcerer."

He nodded to Vivien to proceed, and she pushed the door open. She hurried through, Kane stalking through right behind her. Before Adele could follow, the two were already coming back out.

"Empty," mouthed Kane as he exited. He turned to Thom and Francis and leaned close so they could hear his whisper. "I want the two of you to hide in there while we investigate the next two rooms. Less of an opportunity for you to be recognized. Just leave the door ajar and listen in case we call for you."

Thom and Francis agreed, going in the sitting room. Vivien and Adele followed Kane to the next door, all them with their hoods up to conceal their identities.

As he stood near the slightly-opened door, Thom heard them barge into the next room and this time he heard voices in response.

He recognized Sorcerer Horis's voice. "What is the meaning of this?"

"I am here to take the prisoners to Dalrake," Kane replied. "You are ordered to Castle Camelot to help battle Merlin."

"Dalrake told me that he would be questioning them here," protested Horis.

"Plans change. He is delayed elsewhere as he leads our response to this new assault, which is why he wants these two taken to him. He wants them near for questioning as soon as there is a pause in the fighting. As for you, your skills are needed to support our soldiers. Get moving; I will see to it that the prisoners get to Dalrake."

"Who are you to order me to do anything?"

There was a pause when Kane must have lowered his hood.

Horis continued, "Kane, what are you doing here? I would think Dalrake would want you at the front for the bloody work."

"Right now, I am here. The longer you keep arguing with me, the longer I will be away from Dalrake myself. Get moving and take two of those men with you. I will only need two to control these old men."

"This is ridiculous," complained Horis. "How can I ever succeed in extracting any information when I keep getting interrupted? Dalrake shall hear of this."

Thom, listening in, remembered Horis' frustration the last time and was glad that he had been interrupted.

"You are right to complain," said Kane. "I have no desire to play his lackey either, but here I am to get these two and walk them over to his latest command post. Count yourself fortunate, Horis. Once you hand them over to me, you can forget all this intrigue and focus on stopping the guild."

"How goes the battle?"

"'Tis ugly," replied Kane. "I fear that wily Merlin may get us thrown out again."

Horis grunted in reply.

Peeking through the barely-opened door, Thom saw Horis and two soldiers leave the sitting room and stride away, down the hallway.

"He did it," whispered Francis from beside him. Thom could hear the surprise in his voice.

"There are still two soldiers in there," noted Thom. "Should we get ready to attack them?"

He started unsheathing the sword at his side, but Francis laid a hand over his.

"I think not," said Francis. "Kane may convince them to be our escort instead. Let's see what happens now."

THIRTY-ONE

Gate Fire

Thom and Francis pulled back when they heard the others coming out.

"Keep the prisoners moving along," they heard Kane order. "Students, tell the other sorcerer to join us and to bring his captive along too."

Francis silently urged Thom to get his hand away from the sword, whispering, "It sounds like Kane has decided that you are playing the role of a sorcerer and I am to be your captive." He motioned that they should both put up their hoods.

Thom let go of the sword and struggled to get his robe's hood out from under the guard cape and up over his head. He almost staggered against Francis as he lost his balance in his weakened state. He had to hold on to Beldin's staff with both hands to keep his feet, leaving the hood slightly askew.

Suddenly, the door opened as Vivien and Adele came in and motioned for them to follow. They also had their hoods up.

So Thom and Francis came out and started walking right behind the two soldiers escorting the wizard and the abbot. One of the soldiers glanced back but didn't seem alarmed that they had joined the group. It was all so calm that Thom wondered if Levitanus or the abbot even knew they were being rescued, but surely they had recognized Kane.

Kane strode purposefully through the halls, apparently heading for the main entrance to the guild house.

When they exited to the cobblestone courtyard, Thom felt a chill and it wasn't due to the morning coolness. It was here that he had almost died when he had been caught in the middle of a magical battle. He couldn't help but glance over his shoulder at the looming Sky Tower that soared up to the Road of Clouds far overhead. He half-expected to see a sorcerer at one of the lower windows getting ready to fling magic at them. But he saw no one up there and heard no crafting of any nearby enchantments.

"I think we are clear," he whispered to Francis.

"We still have those four," murmured the monk, indicating a quartet of soldiers standing guard in a cleared gap of the damaged wall that had once been the main gates.

Thom saw no magician dressed as a mage-guard like he was and he hoped they wouldn't be expecting him to start the shift for the now-deceased Beldin. He frowned, hoping the guards would be as obedient to Kane as the rest had been so far

But as they neared, one of the guards waved them to the side. "Make way for an incoming patrol." And they were forced to squeeze against the mounds of shattered stone so that a squad of six centaurs could clop in. They were accompanied by a sorcerer and a pair of human soldiers.

The sorcerer gave a nod to Kane and to Thomas as he passed.

Just then came a yelled order from the keep, "Stop him!"

All looked over to see Sorcerer Horis running out of the guild house with more soldiers following.

Thom grabbed for his sword, but didn't bare it yet. He knew he should be using his magician's staff somehow, but he still had no idea how such a thing helped with magic.

"You heard him," shouted Kane to the watch soldiers, pointing at the sorcerer who had just passed through the crumbled gate. "Seize him."

Chaos erupted, as they attempted to stop the wrong sorcerer. But while the men were conditioned to obey the nearest sorcerer's orders, the centaurs were more suspicious. After all, they had just completed a patrol with that man. They didn't grab anyone, but they did effectively block the way out.

The patrol wizard protested, demanding an answer from Sorcerer Horis, who had come to a stop with his own soldiers and was now kneeling behind them as he opened his magician's cache. Horis was too focused on his elements to answer.

The patrol sorcerer's two guards were uncertain what to do, so they simply stood aside. The soldiers that had been on gate duty were likewise bewildered, not knowing who to heed.

In the confusion, Kane tried to keep going, but the lead centaur blocked his way.

"No one leaves until this stampede calms down."

Francis drew near to Kane, so Thom followed. He was close enough to hear the monk's hushed words to the former sorcerer. "We must move now, before they have us surrounded. Centaurs are much harder to best, but beyond is our only escape."

Kane gave a slight nod, then yelled, "It is a trick! These centaurs are loyal to the king! Kill them now, before they gain entrance to the keep." He drew his dagger and attacked with fervor.

Francis obviously hated the man but the monk didn't hesitate to charge in beside him, swinging his cudgel.

Thom raised his sword, but the opening was too narrow to allow more than two to challenge the centaur, so he looked back to make sure no one was coming up on them.

He saw that the gate guards were unsure what to do, but like many humans they were distrusting of the temperamental and much-larger centaurs. One man actually stabbed at a nearby centaur, but caused nothing more than a slight nip. The angered centaur struck back, which caused two more of the guards to join in his defense. Even against three men, the centaur had them back up against the rubble. The fourth soldier hesitated, then moved to attack a centaur too; he lost his life before his sword met anything, dead to a centaur arrow from a different horse-man.

Thom suddenly realized that both the abbot and Levitanus were being led away. The two guards who had been escorting them had now set their bare blades to the backs of the two and were shoving them toward Horis.

Vivien and Adele were in pursuit.

Thom yelled out to Francis and Kane, "They are taking them back into the keep! We need to get them back!"

He tried running after, but with his injuries it was more of a rushed hobbling. He took only about five steps, when he heard the enchantment reach completion.

"Prepare for fire!" yelled Vivien over her shoulder, then she pulled Adele to the ground.

From behind the shelter of soldiers at-the-ready, Horis was handling a huge fireball.

"Ware the coming fire!" Thom yelled, hoping that Kane and Francis listened, then tried to find refuge among the broken stonework.

He was still too far from safety when a sword suddenly swung at him. He desperately deflected it with his staff. One of the human patrollers had decided he was a foe after all and was now attacking. Thankfully, he was a mediocre swordsman, so Thom was able to fend him off his first three swings, the hardwood of the staff holding up well under the blade. Then the fireball was released and Thom heard it rushing their way. Instead of trying to fight, Thom dove to the side, hoping to avoid being roasted.

When he hit the ground, he screamed in agony. Maybe it would have been less painful to have taken a sword cut. He hoped the soldier didn't skewer him as he lay at his feet, but then he heard the man running away. He knew the man didn't fear him, so he must have seen the fireball being thrown in their direction. Thom turned his face towards the cobblestones and covered his head with his arms, hoping it would be enough to spare him.

Fire roared through the ragged opening that had once been the main gate to Clas Myrddin; Thom felt the blast of heat as it sizzled past him.

The fire was intense but brief, for there was nothing for the fire to burn in that rubble.

Then he heard the screams and he corrected his thought. There was almost nothing to burn.

Looking up, his eyes went to a fire-engulfed centaur, his wails of pain like the screams of a horse in agony. Thom looked away in revulsion as the centaur collapsed to the ground in his death throes. His gaze rested on his recent foe, whose sleeve was smoking and hair singed. The soldier was no longer interested in striking at Thom; he was too busy trying to extinguish his smoldering clothes.

Thom scrambled to his feet, using the staff to help stand. He tried his best to ignore the throbbing from his abused body. Looking around, he saw that Adele and Vivien had survived and were just now untangling themselves from the stone debris that had fallen on them when the passing inferno had sped overhead. The two women seemed relatively unscathed, but Justin and Levitanus were not with them. Thom spotted the men being taken back toward the keep by their two remaining guards.

Just as he set off in pursuit, he was joined by Francis and Kane.

"Faster, Thomas," urged Francis, as the middle-aged monk ran by. "We have to get them back."

Thom lengthened his stride as best he could, but the pain was intense; his body was protesting this latest shock on top of the torture he had endured mere hours earlier.

"The bastard flamed at a half-dozen of his own centaurs and just as many human soldiers, just to get his prisoners back," cursed Kane, loud enough for a following Thom to hear. "What now monk? Have you any idea how we can free them?"

"Magic is hard to craft when pressed," replied Francis, "so we must charge after them."

Kane let out a bitter laugh. "That is true, but we are too few to press the attack. The soldiers I had duped into escorting us are wise to my scheme and scurried off with our prize. It is now just the five of us."

"But they are running from us now," argued Thomas, wishing he could just rest, yet knowing that he was needed even in his weakened condition.

"Horis retreats only to get his prisoners to safety," replied Kane. "He will turn back on us soon."

They entered through the doorway where the abbot and the wizard had been taken. Although they had their weapons ready for any guards, they found none inside. There was also no trace of Justin and Levitanus.

Looking behind him, Thom saw that Vivien and Adele were nearly caught up with them. The reason that they weren't being pursued was that the centaurs were angry about the magical attack and were now attacking any humans near them, forcing the remaining sorcerer and soldiers to defend themselves.

"Monk, which way do you think they've gone?" asked Kane.

"It has been too long since I've walked these halls; I was less welcome to Clas Myrddin than you," replied Francis. "Which way, Thomas?"

Thom considered, then pointed toward the wing that contained the council chambers and the masters' suites. "I doubt they'll return to the sitting room they were using earlier. They're probably headed that way, to the wizards' wing."

Just then the women caught up, running through the doorway.

"Why are you just standing here?" demanded Vivien. "Get after them or that sorcerer in the courtyard will toast your buns."

Thom decided not to respond; he knew better with that fiery journeywoman. Instead, he took off in the direction he had picked and trusted that the others would follow. It wouldn't be hard for them, since his pace was a mere shambling stumble.

THIRTY-TWO

In Pursuit

As he walked down a wide hallway, Thom heard someone open a magician's cache somewhere up ahead, even though he couldn't see anyone.

"He starts an enchantment," stated Adele.

"Your inner ear is well attuned for an apprentice," replied Vivien. "What you are hearing is the starting of a trio of Flame Circles, a nasty enchantment that will burn anyone who walks into it. I am surprised at the sorcerer's choice, because using such magic indoors risks burning the keep. In addition, it is not a subtle enchantment. Phoenix plumage are always loud."

"He isn't trying to catch us unaware," stated Kane. "I would guess that he has set his trap in every hallway leading to that wing of Clas Myrddin so that we cannot follow. The circles are a warning to us. Now we need to burn them out or go around."

"Are you asking for volunteers to trigger the snares?" asked Francis. "I know Beldin already tenderized me with his careful attention, but I'd rather not be roasted today."

Thom thought over his weeks of exploring these rooms, before they banished him to the basement, and he recalled some side doors that were often overlooked by others. There was one such route nearby. "Maybe we can sneak around his enchantments by passing through the library. There is a service hallway at the back used by the library workers to deliver tomes to the masters in their grand study."

"Good suggestion. I know the doorway you mean," said Vivien, pushing to the fore and leading everyone down the echoing hallway and then into the vast room full of books, scrolls, and maps.

If he had been in better condition Thom would have taken offense at the redhead's presumption, but he didn't have the strength to reassert the lead.

Adele noticed him lagging and came up beside him, offering herself as support. He leaned on her in relief, placing his arm over her shoulder even as she lightly placed her arm around his waist.

"Do you think we will be able to get them back?" she asked him quietly.

"For your sake, I hope we do," he answered honestly. "I'm not so close to the abbot and I have nothing but contempt for my old master, but if they are kept and tortured then the sorcerers will learn of the league and who belongs to it. I don't want you or your position in the king's castle endangered."

Adele smiled. "As if I'm not in danger right now. I'm just thankful that we were able to rescue you."

He squeezed her shoulder in gratitude. "I was overwhelmed when I realized you were there."

Kane interrupted, "Did my sweet face bring a tear to your eye too?"

He gave a short laugh at Thom's frown, then he looked away. "Where is this hidden passage, journeywoman? Time is pressing and I can hear that the guild is approaching."

Alerted by the infuriating man's remark, Thom took a moment to listen to the magic happening farther away. He was right; it did sound like they had moved on from Castle Camelot and were getting closer.

Kane continued, "We will soon be in the middle of a battle between wizards and sorcerers, and neither side will spare us. I want Levitanus and the abbot freed and away from here before then."

Vivien led them to the partially-hidden doorway that opened on an unlit hallway. "It seems the servants have neglected their duties; we will have to walk in the dark."

Kane took the fore now, a knife in his hand as he stalked down the bare passage. The rest followed, with Thom and Adele at the rear.

The passageway came out in a cavernous study, richly appointed with padded chairs and solid tables. Thick rugs covered much or the tile floor and large tapestries hung on the wood panel walls. Although Thom had never dared to pass through before, a librarian had told him that this was where the master magicians would often lounge in the evenings to read and discuss various texts. The passageway exited in a niche in the back of the room, half-hidden by a wall tapestry.

As Thom came around the corner of the tapestry, still leaning on Adele, he noticed that the room seemed forgotten by the keep's new occupants. It was dimly light by three tall windows overlooking one of the keep gardens, but the huge fireplace was cold and all the lamps were extinguished. Most likely, no one had used the room since the wizards had fled.

"Do you think we made it beyond the enchantment traps?" asked Adele in a soft whisper.

"It sounds that way," Thom whispered back. He saw that Kane was already at the study's closed door and listening for what might be beyond. "Let's see what the others have discovered."

They came up just as Kane turned to Vivien. "Journeywoman, what do you hear?"

"In the guild house? I hear the three Blaze Circles and an exposed cache, but no active mixing."

"Do you recognize the cache?"

Vivien gave him a skeptic look. "You can tell the difference between caches?"

Kane replied, "Only when I have recently heard a magician's particular assortment. We heard Horis' mix twice already, once in the courtyard and a second time when the Blaze Circles were crafted. The open cache we hear now is not his for this one holds more Phoenix powder and no Whispering Pine resin or Mermaid tears, so I must presume that at least two sorcerers are ahead of us."

Vivien nodded understanding. "I should have noticed such things myself. I will listen more carefully from now on."

Kane gave her a brief smile. "Not many have bothered to foster the skill. I had to after my horrible crime, when so many wizards and sorcerers were hunting for me. I needed to recognize who was flinging magic at me."

"The sorcerers pursued you as well?"

He nodded. "Dalrake and the others were furious at my wasteful slaughter of so many beings and beasts, but enough about that. I detest talking about my awful past and now is not the time anyway. Let us focus on what is ahead. Where do you think they are keeping them?"

"It could be in the council chambers or in one of the wizard studies or classrooms, since there are a few of those on this floor as well. Considering where those Blaze Circles seem to have been set, it sounds like the stairway to the upper floors has been blocked, so I doubt they were taken upstairs."

"A fair assessment, but it still leaves us an expansive area to search and as I recall the hallways here are wide and bare in furniture. That will not offer us much opportunity for stealth and I would rather not run into the arms of the soldiers that seem to be crawling all over the keep... I still do not know how Dalrake acquired so many guards apart from Mordred's liege men. I do know that we are not skilled enough to fight through by our weapon skills and we do not even know where the two are being kept."

Kane sighed as he swept his knapsack off his back. "Only our magical skills will get us through. We will need to make some noise and see what that stirs up. Journeyman Thomas, I want you to go back through the library and then down the hallway to the nearest Blaze Circle. I want you to send a Wizard Light into the circle and cause a reaction. It will not be enough to explode the Blaze Circle but will cause quite a light show and enough noise to hopefully mask what the journeywoman and I will be doing."

"I will do it," replied Thom. It was a simple enough crafting that he thought he could do it even in his weakened state.

"You set him up as a lure," observed Francis.

"A distraction," corrected Kane. "I need Horis and the other looking and listening in his direction so that Journeywoman Vivien can slip an Eagle's Spying into the area. We must find out where Levitanus and the Father Abbot are being held and we cannot afford to waste more time on this, for I think Dalrake and the others will soon be pressed to retreat this way. I have no desire to linger in the path of a moving battle where both sides despise me."

Francis frowned, "I will go with Thomas to make sure he can get out of the way of any counter attack they send his way."

The monk moved to Thom's side, offering his aid even though he was likely still in pain from his own torture. As he and Adele helped Thom to head back the way they'd come, Francis paused to look over his shoulder and met the former sorcerer's gaze. "Do your best to rescue the Father Abbot; he is dear to so many of us."

"I must rescue him," replied Kane, "for if he is forced to reveal the league, they will crush it and I cannot have that. The league is my only chance at redemption."

THIRTY-THREE

Fire around the Corner

The narrow passageway back to the library was even harder to pass through the second time, but Thom made it by leaning against Adele on one side and the wall on the other. His left ankle throbbed so hard that he wondered if he would be able to hear enough to properly craft anything.

He had to pause when they came out in the cavernous room and he lost the added support.

"Let me take over helping Thomas," suggested Francis, moving up to his side.

"But you were tortured too," protested Adele.

"Not as long as he was," replied the monk. "The three of you interrupted before it became that severe for me."

Thom wanted to protest that he didn't need any help, but that wasn't true unless he crawled the rest of the way. Hanging upside down from chains shackled to his ankles had caused too much injury. So he just stood there, holding the magician's staff and leaning against the edge of a reading table, trying not to whimper or moan.

"We shall both help," decided Adele, nodding for the monk to come along Thom's right side. "The less weight he puts on his feet the better."

They practically carried him the rest of the way, through the library and along the wide hallway beyond until they came to where the hallway turned. They settled Thomas on a settee near the corner and then Francis peeked around to see what lay ahead.

Thom carefully pulled the knapsack off his tender back and set it on the settee cushion. He opened the pack and peered inside. He found a velvet bag containing a mixing bowl and matching pestle and a magician's box that was made from a highly-polished, fine-grained wood. Thomas set the cache on the seat between his leg and the knapsack but he didn't dare open it. He wasn't even sure what he could craft, for he had no idea what elements were inside the lead-lined box.

"Are you strong enough to craft?" asked Adele, looking down at him with concern.

"I'll have to be." He tried to smile at her but it probably looked more like a grimace, since the pain wasn't letting up. "We need to do our part to distract the sorcerers and let Kane and Vivien slip by to rescue the others."

"You are so brave, my dear Thomas. You aren't even a member of the league and still you fight for it."

"I don't feel brave; I feel battered. Besides, you were the one who risked sneaking in here to free me. You're the brave one."

Adele shook her head at that, but before she could protest, she was interrupted.

"Let's just declare that you are both brave," whispered Francis with a wisp of a smile, having walked up on them. "The Blazing Circle is near, as you most likely guessed from its sound, and covers the width of the hallway. There is no way around it, so we will need to trigger it."

"Does that risk setting the building on fire?" asked Adele.

"Not likely," replied Francis. "There are no rugs, tapestries, paintings, or furniture nearby. As long as the magical clash isn't too great it should be fine, and I wouldn't expect much power in any enchantment from our abused friend here."

Thom nodded ruefully. He was doubtful that he could concentrate enough, except for maybe the simplest of crafting, and confessed as much.

"You do need to keep this simple," stated Francis. "The idea isn't to destroy the enchantment in front of us, but to trigger enough of a reaction that the noise and light will distract the sorcerers beyond. I would think Wizard Lights will be enough."

It was the most basic of apprentice-level enchantments. Thom considered and nodded. "I think I have enough strength to make a handful of lights."

"Not just you," replied Francis. "I think Adele should make them as well. I am certain that Vivien has already taught her how to craft them."

The monk's suggestion surprised Thom. "I would expect you to be the last person to encourage others to practice magic."

Francis gave a sad smile. "I had to do the same with you on the Road of Leaves, Thomas. Both of you understand that I dislike magic use, but I know that the League of Barnabas is much better than either of the other two magician assemblies."

A sudden realization came to Thom. "Each of the Founders now has his own group. Is the league just a personal toy for Levitanus?" If true, it would give him more reason to detest his deceptive teacher.

Francis seemed to consider. "I think not. Looking back, I see the touches that were his, but this is also the work of the Father Abbot, who is not a magician, and the many magical beings who are part of its leadership. The league shows his handiwork, but far less so than the Roads enchantments or the Magicians' Guild."

"I still do not like it," muttered Thom. "He isn't who he pretended to be for so long."

Francis gave a thoughtful nod to that. "Maybe some day he will give you an honest answer of why he deceived you even as he taught you, but first we must rescue him and the abbot. Are you ready?"

Thom assessed himself. His hands weren't shaky and he thought he could concentrate enough. His mouth was dry, but he could find enough spit to finish the enchantment. "I am."

"Then you go first. Once you are finished, I will wipe off the bowl and pestle and hand them to Adele to do her crafting. Leave out the vials for her to quicken her task."

Thom nodded understanding, setting his staff to lean against the wall behind the seat. He repositioned the mixing bowl and pestle that he'd already taken out, setting them against his leg on the settee. He then opened the magician's box and a cacophony of sounds filled his inner ear, many of them new to him. Cautiously, he picked out the three vials he needed and set them aside, closing the lid to silence the rest of the whispering songs of the other elements. He stared at the three vials and suddenly doubted himself. Were these the right ones? What order was he supposed to mix them?

Francis noticed his hesitancy and offered encouragement. "Good. Start with the powdered Azure Fireflies and go on from there."

Thom poured some powder from the vial, then stoppered it and set it aside. Next, he added powdered Meadow Dragons wings and then Glow Berries, adding some water and then setting it on his lap as he mixed the powders together with the stone pestle. Finally, he lifted the bowl, gathered the moisture in his mouth, and spat, tuning the magic to himself. Setting the pestle aside, he set the bowl back on his lap and began to form small balls from the thickening paste. The blobs began to glow through his fingers.

"Let me get these cleaned for Adele," said Francis as soon as Thom gathered the half-dozen misshapen globes in his hand. He took the bowl and pestle, wiping them out with a cloth he had gotten from somewhere. "Just sit there until I get her started."

Thom held the glowing spheres carefully, trying not to crush them or let them get away too early. Already, he could tell that they were floating within his light grip.

He watched as Francis set the now-clean bowl and pestle back on the settee for Adele to use. The monk gave her whispered encouragement on how to craft the enchantment and then he helped Thom to get to his feet. There was no way Thom could use the staff this time for his hands were full of magical lights, so he had to depend on Francis to steady him.

Pain shot up Thom's leg as soon as he put weight on that abused left ankle and he almost fell over, but Francis kept him upright.

Francis half guided and half carried him forward. "Keep your mental connection with your enchantment. Just a few short steps, until you can look down the corridor."

Thom did as he was told, concentrating on walking and on keeping the Wizard Lights glowing.

As they came around the corner, Thom saw the red glow of the Blaze Circle halfway down the corridor. It glowed like a pile of angry coals and the heat shimmer distorted the handful of soldiers that stood beyond it. He couldn't see any sorcerer robes, but one of them pointed Thom out, obviously noting his dark blue journeyman's garb.

"Can you toss them from here?" asked Francis. "The enchantment will flare when a Wizard Light passes over it and that will be an unbearable heat if we are too close."

It would mean that Thom would have to keep his concentration on the lights for the length of the hallway, guiding them true and not letting them fade out too quickly. It would be a strain, but he thought he could do it so, instead of answering, he lifted his hand to his mouth and blew the Wizard Lights away on their course.

Two of the lights veered away in the wrong direction, bumping into a wall, but when Thom tried to redirect them with his thoughts, the others wobbled too.

"Concentrate on the main group," urged Francis.

He did, letting the two wandering lights fade away. He lost one other before he had the remaining globes all moving in the general direction he wanted.

Three Wizard Lights slowly flew toward the Blaze Circle. Thom worked hard to keep his concentration on them, to keep the enchantment going. He wished he could speed them up, but this was the best he could do.

He heard Francis speak to Adele and sensed her near, but he kept his focus where it needed to be, on the orbs he had sent out and on his target that glowed redly and the men who waited beyond it.

He realized that the soldiers had stepped aside to let a sorcerer through, a sorcerer who was staring in Thom's direction. He wanted to keep his eye on the man, but then his remaining Wizard Lights began to sink and he had to keep all his attention on them before they dropped too low.

Francis was still at his side, helping to keep him standing steady, but the monk was also directing Adele in her crafting, urging her through her crafting, and soon another handful of Wizard Lights were heading toward the Blaze Circle, moving much faster and confidently than Thom's.

Thom felt a bit of pride at how well Adele had crafted, but then he had to refocus on his three glowing globes.

The first Wizard Light floated over the area covered by the Blaze Circle, causing that enchantment to angrily respond. Fire shot up toward the little ball of light, drowning its faint glow in the angry red flames.

THIRTY-FOUR

Blaze Circle

Thom felt the snuffing of that first Wizard Light, but he kept the other two flying down the corridor. He hoped this was making enough noise to cover whatever Kane and Vivien were doing.

He sent a second light over the Blaze Circle and it again responded in burst of flames that quickly shredded his tiny magic without causing any disruption to the greater enchantment.

"That is what would happen if any of us were to step into that circle," observed Francis, then he seemed to lean back to look beyond Thom and down the corridor beyond the turn. "Hold that last Wizard Light, Thomas. We have trouble approaching behind us."

Thom brought the last light to a bobbing hover, close to the Blaze Circle but not yet over it. This required even more concentration and he started to sweat a little from the strain.

"Walk back with me to the magician's box," urged Francis, "but don't let your magic falter."

Concentrating on two things was even harder. He had to depend on Francis to guide him because he needed to keep his eyes on the Wizard Light just to keep it burning.

"Adele, I need you to hold back on your Wizard Lights as well. We are going to have to cause a little explosion, so we will need to time their contact."

"But I don't know how to make them hover like Thomas does," she plead.

"Make them go in circles instead, just do not let them cross over that Blaze Circle," ordered Francis. "You also need to make your way over here. We all will need to scramble around the corner when we make the enchantments explode."

"I thought we were only trying to distract them," she argued.

"What could be more distracting than a keep-shaking explosion?" replied Francis in a light tone.

Francis stopped moving when they reached the corner and let Thomas grabbed the wall for extra support.

"That's it, Adele. Don't worry about those two you've lost. Three will be more than enough. Keep them circling," encouraged the monk, then he spoke more softly to Thom. "Do you have enough control to hit one of her Wizard Lights with your own?"

Thom took a quick glance at her spheres that were now moving in a hurried, tightening circle. "She's too fast. Can you get her to slow them down and bunch them together? Then I will more likely hit at least one of them."

Francis nodded. "I will guide her into slowing them down and then I'll have her ease them toward the Blaze Circle. You will need to collide with them just as they go over the other enchantment."

Thom didn't reply, concentrating on his one remaining Wizard Light, keeping it away from Adele's and from the sorcerer's magic until the timing was right.

Under Francis' guidance, Adele was able to slow down her Wizard Lights and gather them closer in their lazy circling. Then, slowly, she expanded that circle so that by the next rotation and globes would be passing over the Blazing Circle.

Thom watched her magic, as his own Wizard Light bobbed up and down. As Adele's trio came around, he took his Wizard Light higher, almost touching the high ceiling, and then sent it racing downward at her three lights just as they crossed over the area where the Blaze Circle sat.

The Blaze Circle flared, its hungry flames shooting up at the lights, but just before the fire reached the globes, Thom's Wizard Light struck one of Adele's and their magic began to react in a cascade of sparks. With his inner ear, Thom heard the enchantment rhythms suddenly turn erratic and then the far more powerful Blaze Circle also reacted, becoming a jarring sound.

Francis yanked Thom around the corner and yelled for Adele to follow.

The explosion shook the corridor and fire flared to the end of the hallway and licked a tapestry further down the passage, but not long enough to set it ablaze.

Thom staggered over to the settee and sat down again, feeling exhausted. He tried to ignore the ringing from the just-passed explosion and listened for the Blaze Circle. His inner ear caught nothing of its rhythms, and he already knew that his own Wizard Light was no more.

Adele came over to him but her eyes were drawn down the corridor behind them. "That patrol sorcerer is approaching and he has a handful of men with him. How can we fight them off?"

Thom shut his eyes as a feeling of defeat came over him. He had no more strength in him. "Oh God, help us," he whispered. "I don't want it to end like this."

THIRTY-FIVE

Colin's Lock

Francis looked around the corner. "Some of the soldiers appear to have been hurt or at least knocked off their feet by the explosion, but the sorcerer realized our plan and safely avoided the explosion. He seems to have fled for I do not see him anywhere in the corridor. As for the remaining soldiers, the heated stones and smoke will keep them at bay."

Thom stared at the monk, finding little hope in the report. The stone would cool and the smoke would clear, and then the soldiers would be at them.

"But what about the others coming up behind us?" asked Adele.

"We cannot fight them here; this hallway is too wide," said Francis, then he motioned at the closed doors across the corridor. "Thomas, are those still classrooms?"

Thom gave a slight nod. He had never been allowed to attend any of the classes, but that was what they were.

"We need to retreat to one of them," decided the monk. "Adele, carry the magician's box while I help Thomas."

They made it to the nearest classroom, but there was no way to bolt the door. Thom realized that pushing one of the heavy tables against it would not likely slow any pursuers much, but he couldn't think of any other way to close it off. He looked around as Francis eased him onto one of the worn stools in the hall. There was a bank of windows at the far end of the room, but he was in no shape to try scampering through, especially considering the drop on the other side. "What can we do now?" he asked.

"We have to seal the door with magic, since there is no bolt or latch," said Francis. "Were you ever taught how to craft Colin's Lock?"

Thom shook his head, wondering if he would be able to learn a new enchantment in his tired state.

"It is a simple enchantment that many older apprentices use to keep their few possessions safe from others, but I guess you had no need for such magic living in the wilds as you did. I doubt anyone ever tried to pilfer from Levitanus' country cottage." Francis motioned for Adele to set the magician's box on the highly-polished table in front of Thom. "Maybe the two of you will need to craft this one together, for Adele has the strength, while Thom has the skill."

"Why not do the crafting yourself?" asked Adele. "You know so much more than either of us."

"I swore never to do magic again and that isn't a vow I want to break. Although I help you two, I still find magic a vile craft that destroys far more than it creates. Even the little aid I give still feels wrong. Much like telling a drunkard where his dropped bottle rolled."

"Magic can still be just," argued Adele. "Same as war. I do not learn this craft to entertain or to gain riches. I learn it to help others."

Thom was too tired for this argument, so he interrupted. "What do you mean about us working together on an enchantment?" He knew that the greater enchantments often required magicians to combine their work, but he had never been taught how. It was tricky business, for an enchantment that went wrong could easily explode or cause other havoc. He worried about his own ability to concentrate and follow instructions; he didn't want to endanger Adele due to his exhaustion. "I can risk myself to a failed enchantment, but not Adele also. Doing the work together puts us both at risk."

"I should do this by myself," insisted Adele. "Thom, you can assist and make sure I do it right."

Thom was about to object but then saw the firm set of her jaw. She was right; she should try this herself. He nodded his acceptance.

Francis agreed as well. "Then she shall do the crafting and you will just guide her. Find her the following elements, and do so quickly for they will be at the door very soon: Rowan bark, White Stag blood, Rockbinder vine, and powdered Karkinos shell."

Thom opened the case and a cacophony of sounds rose up, for the box was nearly full with dozens of elements that let out their distinct rhythms. He found the powdered Rowan bark, the powdered Rockbinder vine, and the Karkinos, setting those vials aside on the table, but he couldn't find any White Stag blood. The iron in magical blood has a certain deep pulsation to its sound, so he was able to find six different vials containing blood of various magical beasts and beings, but not the right one. Two of them he recognized, but the other four were from unknown creatures.

He looked up at Francis, unsure what to do.

"Use the Goldhorn blood instead," suggested Francis. "That's the vial in your right hand that looks orangish in color. We only need a few drops of blood to bind it to the little bit of metal that is in this door, so a replacement should be fine. Colin's Lock is an enchantment that doesn't demand precise mixing."

And so Francis led Adele on how to craft a Colin's Lock, which she then carefully applied around the edges of the door, binding it shut.

As she finished, Adele asked, "Why would anyone want to use this enchantment? It seems a lot of work to maintain for such a passive magic."

Francis gave her a small smile. "You can release it now. This is one of those enchantments that tend to linger for hours or even days. During my time as a student here we would set a Colin's Lock on our wardrobes to prevent pranks or pilfering."

"Can it be undone or are we now sealed in here?" asked Adele.

Thom knew that it was an enchantment that would dissipate when the magician gave it a slight mental tweak, but he left it for his friend to explain.

Francis answered as he walked toward the teacher platform, where a large marble-topped table sat. "It will protect us long enough to hopefully fortify ourselves."

Thom wondered what he meant. They had no way to fortify this place.

The monk stepped onto the raised platform and went past the teacher's table to a small cabinet in the back corner. He looked inside and nodded. "As I thought. No one has cleared the classroom pantry."

He pulled out a wax-paper wrapped cheese, a small bowl of dried fruit, and a pitcher of watered wine with a couple of glasses. As he came back to Thom and Adele, he explained. "Crafting magic can be exhausting work. Although it isn't hard labor like smithing, it is an exacting craft that can often overextend students. They keep some food in each classroom in case anyone grows faint, so that the teacher needn't waste time by having to send a student off to the kitchen for nourishment. It isn't great fare, but all three of us need it."

Thom nodded, now understanding. They had to fortify their bodies, which were exhausted from torture and fleeing and crafting enchantments.

They ate quickly, fully aware that this was no true hideout. The patrol sorcerer had seen them retreat inside and now Adele's enchantment let off its distinct sound, sounding much like a slow, melodious heartbeat. Any nearby magician would be aware of their presence.

Eric Loren

THIRTY-SIX

Wormbore

Francis reached over and opened the magician's box and then closed it a moment later.

Thom gave him a puzzled look.

"They already know we are here, so let them hear the elements and worry that we are crafting more surprises."

"Do we *have* any surprises planned?" asked Adele. "I don't think we are helping any by hiding in here, and we have no idea where Kane and Vivien are or if they are close to rescuing the others."

"I've heard no other nearby magic after Vivien released her Eagle's Spying," replied Francis, not directly answering the question. "She did that rather quickly and was done by the time Thomas exploded the Blaze Circle."

Thom hadn't noticed any of that. Even now, he had to fight to keep his eyes open. He was so tired and probably would have fallen asleep as soon as he sat down except for the constant throbbing from his blistered back and his abused ankles. He took a moment to listen for any other active magic nearby. The other Blaze Circles were still active but he heard no other enchantments inside Clas Myrddin. He knew the Road of Clouds was far overhead, but that was outside of Camelot's dome of magic and so couldn't be heard here. The enchantment covering the city was faint and sounded... erratic. He looked to Francis. "Has another attack hit Camelot's enchantment?"

Francis replied, "Not too long ago. It sounds like it was somewhere near the Short Roads."

Thom stared back dumbly, too tired to understand what that signified.

"The magic battle around Castle Camelot has died down. Instead, it has begun around the Short Roads and it also draws toward us, toward Clas Myrddin."

Thom still didn't grasp the meaning, but Adele did. "The king and Merlin are driving Mordred and Dalrake back. They are winning back the city."

Francis nodded at her answer. "The sorcerers are losing ground faster than Kane anticipated. Some of them will surely come this way as they seek to flee by the Road of Clouds."

Thom understood now. "But how can we help the others? If Adele releases the door lock, we will likely find a soldier in the corridor ready to slay us, for I doubt the sorcerer passed by without leaving behind a watch."

"Then we will have to create a new way out," said Francis, studying the wall that separated this room for the next classroom.

Thom follow his gaze worriedly. "You are not thinking of a Wormbore enchantment, are you?"

"You have crafted a Wormbore before?" asked Francis.

"Certainly, but only through dirt, not stone." His master had taught him the enchantment one sunny afternoon, but had also called it as useless as using a butcher's cleaver to remove a splinter. "That the magician's box wouldn't have any powdered scales of Amphisbaena. My master claimed it had few other uses, so who would clutter their cache with such?"

"It is in there," refuted Francis. "I checked when I last opened the box. As is powdered Troll finger and Water of Strid."

"Troll finger?" asked Adele, sounding disgusted. "They kill trolls just for their fingers?"

"Possibly, but doubtful," replied Francis. "Their fingers break off regularly while digging through rock or hard soil. As long as a troll doesn't break it off at the final knuckle, it will grow back within a year. Gather a troll finger within a week of its severing and it will still have its potency."

"Sounds rather painful."

"They merely grunt when it happens, so I'm not sure how much it pains them." Francis picked up the magician's box and handed it to Adele. "Carry this for us, my lady. Come, Thomas. Let's get you situated so that you can more easily craft."

Thom let Francis help him to his feet, but he was still doubtful of the plan. "You think I'm capable of this?"

"You need to be," said Francis softly yet firmly. "I detest magic, but even I realize it can be used sometimes for a just cause. This is such a time. We need to get free of here and then rescue the abbot and your old master. We cannot leave them in the hands of Dalrake and his companions; the sorcerers would find out the secrets of the league if we did, and then they would crush the league and probably enlist the guild to help them."

"You think they would work together against us?" asked Adele.

"I do. As much as Merlin and Dalrake fume and rail at each other, they still cooperate in maintaining the Roads and the enchantment of Camelot. They may argue over who should have control, but both want the enchantments to remain."

Thom realized the truth in what his friend said. Maybe the League of Barnabas was the better option, but he didn't trust it either, not now that he knew his old master had a hand in creating it.

Francis brought him to the table nearest the middle of the wall, letting Thom lean again the highly polished wood while he moved a stool around so that he could sit facing the wall. Thom couldn't help but sigh as he sat down again, for his whole body throbbed with pain.

Adele set the magician's box in front of him, along with the wiped bowl and pestle. She set the knapsack on the end of table.

Thom opened the lead-lined box and carefully selected the vials he needed. He set them aside and then shut the box to silence all the other elements. He realized that he needed one more item, but Francis anticipated him. The monk had walked over to the wall and used his knife to chip at the stone and mortar. It took some work and dulled the blade, but he was rewarded with enough slivers and bits for Thom's need.

At that moment, Thomas heard another magician's box open somewhere in the corridor they had fled. The others heard it too, all of them glancing toward the enchanted door.

After a brief moment, Francis motioned for Thom to start. "What they are crafting will not attack us directly, but it gives us more reason to find another way out of here."

He didn't explain further and Thom was too worn out to try deciphering the elemental sounds.

"Go ahead," urged the monk. "Focus on the elements in front of you and start crafting."

Even though a Wormbore enchantment was fairly simple, Thom had to go slowly and work hard to keep his mind focused. Adele watched carefully as he worked. He mixed the powdered Troll finger with the crushed scales of the double-ended snake Amphisbaena and the stone and mortar chips. Once the mix was well done, he added the necessary moisture: Water of Strid and his own spittle. He realized his quantity might be too little for such a hard material, but it was too late to add in more. He kept going until the various sounds combined into the proper symphony of magic, nodding to himself when it was done.

In the near distance, he heard someone crafting another enchantment, but he had no time to try to understand what was happening. He needed to finish with his enchantment first.

"Help me up," he asked of Francis, realizing he couldn't walk over to the wall while carrying the muddy looking concoction. This was not something he would want to splash on the stone floor, for it would likely cause deep pocking.

With the steadying guidance of the monk, he made it over to the wall and started slathering the watery paste onto the wall in a roughly circular pattern. The hardest part was bending over to get the lower stones. He became dizzy while doing so, but kept hold of the potent magic and made sure to finish his task. Once his bowl was empty, he stepped back and did his best to hurry away, with Francis' aid. Adele stepped back too.

The enchantment made the wall glisten as it seeped into the stone, and then it began to slough off, taking the rock with it. By the time the magic died away, there was a slushy pile of rubble on the floor and a hole in the wall that was roughly the shape of a door, though it had a knee-high threshold that they would have to step over. Beyond was another empty classroom.

Thom's left ankle was so weak that it gave out as he tried stepping over the lip of his opening, but Adele kept him standing and Francis, who had already gone through, helped him cross over.

His weakness embarrassed Thom, but he wasn't about to just give up. As long as his weakness didn't hold the others back too much, he would keep going and do what he could to help.

THIRTY-SEVEN

Water Lightning

Francis left him leaning against another student table while the monk went to this room's door. Thom watched him carefully peek out at whatever was in the corridor. It was some kind of enchantment having to do with lightning. He couldn't fully discern what magical elements were in that particular chorus of sound.

"What's out there?" Thom asked.

Francis closed the door and came back. "I've never seen the like. It is a Water Lightning enchantment, but on dry ground. They've added some element that makes the whole corridor wet so that the lightning will work here." He shook his head. "Anyone who dares walk on that surface will die."

"What will we do now?" asked Adele.

"We need to break into the next classroom, for its door lines up with that of the library. Then we will need to find some way to cross over without touching the ground and sparking the magic."

Thom tried to stand straighter, but still had to lean against the table for support. "I...I don't know if I have the strength to craft another Wormbore."

"Then Adele will have to do it," replied Francis, looking to her.

She nodded.

So Adele crafted the next enchantment. Thom sat beside her and tried his best to offer help, but it was Francis who mainly guided her through the mixing and crafting. She did well, working with a confidence that refuted her ignorance of magic.

The Wormbore enchantment worked as expected and was even better than the one Thom had done because Adele was able to bend low and spread the liquidy paste close to the ground, leaving only a small lip for them to step over when they entered the next classroom.

As Francis had said, the door to this classroom lined up with the doorway to the library, but there still was a wide hallway to cross and that hallway's floor was covered in a thin layer of water that held small flashes of blue lightning in it. They now had to find a way to cross over so that they could rejoin Vivien and Kane.

"Can we throw something out there and trigger the magic?" asked Thom.

"I cannot see him from here, but some sorcerer continues to maintain this magic," replied Francis. "It will not stop just become something or someone has fallen into it."

"Can we explode it like we did the Blaze Circle?" asked Adele.

Francis shook his head. "Not from here, unless we want to kill ourselves in the process. The Blaze Circle was constricted to its small space which helped control the resulting explosion too. Not this. A magic clash with this enchantment might bring this whole wing of the keep down on us."

Adele went to the open doorway and gazed across the wide corridor at the library's open doors. "If only we could run a rope from one door to the other so that we could scramble across. But no, Thomas is no shape for that even if we could find the rope and places to tie it."

She leaned out and looked down the corridor in either direction. "Even the settee we sat on is just a charred heap now."

"Wood can't withstand lightning," stated Francis. "Only dirt and stone can stand up to such an onslaught."

Thom suddenly had a thought. He looked behind him at the teacher's table in this room. It was like the one in the other classroom, a long marble-topped table. "Francis, we should make a bridge over to the other side. Would that slab of marble be thick enough to break the surface of that lightning sea out there?"

The monk gave him a startled look and then smiled. "Brilliant, Thomas. Come, Adele, help me drag this table to the door and flip it over. I think it is thick enough that the enchantment will not wash over it. We will make a stone causeway to get us over to our companions."

They worked quickly and soon they had the marble table turned upside down and pushed out into the hallway. The Water Lightning flashed and crackled around it but the stone proved safe to step on when Francis tested it. Unfortunately, the table wasn't long enough to bridge the width of the corridor.

Thom had hobbled over to watch their progress but he wasn't able to offer much aid, for it was hard enough to just limp across the room to get here. He had brought the knapsack containing the magician's box slung over his shoulder and now he was leaning back on it against the wall. The aggravated pain of his shoulder and back were compensated by the relief off his abused legs and ankles.

He tried to collect his thoughts.

What could they do now? Then he remembered the other classrooms that they had passed through, all of them with a marble teacher's table. "You can bring another marble table through the hole Adele crafted. I think the opening is wide enough. If not, then she'll need to craft a widening."

Just then a familiar face appeared at the library door. Kane. He looked at the magic-covered floor and then at them. "What are you doing?"

"We are trying to set a bridge over to you so that we can join you," replied Francis.

"You do not want to cross over here. They have us blocked in. This enchantment flows in front of all the exits from our area and they have men outside the windows in case we try escaping that way."

Behind him stepped forward another in a black robe. Levitanus. "What are you doing with that table, Brother Francis?"

"You freed them!" exclaimed Adele. "Is Vivien with you as well?"

"Is the Father Abbot with you?" asked Francis at the same time.

"All four of us are fine," replied Levitanus, as both the journeywoman and the abbot came up behind him. "Now explain the flipped-over table, if you will."

Francis spoke up. "Your student, in spite of all his injuries, thought of a way to safely cross the Water Lightning. The stone will protect us. We just need to retrieve another table to lengthen our makeshift marble causeway."

"Well done, Thomas," said Levitanus.

"Give us a moment, for we need to get the table from another classroom and Adele may need to widen the Wormbore."

"Do not bother," replied Kane. "Time is too short. We will find a suitable table on this side and complete your bridge."

With that, the former sorcerer disappeared back into the library with the others. Soon they returned, hefting a large and very heavy granite side table. They succeeded in getting it turned upside down and then slid it out into the hallway. It was enough to cover the gap and soon all four scrambled across to join the other three. They pulled the teacher table back inside so that no one could follow them.

Once all were inside the classroom, they shut the door and took a moment to greet each other. Vivien and Adele hugged, as did Abbot Justin and Francis.

Thom just watched awkwardly, once again using the knapsack as a cushion so that he could lean against the wall. His old teacher nodded toward him but walked over to stand beside Kane, which was best. Thom had no desire to get near either of them.

Levitanus looked around and chuckled at the hole in the wall. "Apprentice Adele shows talent, if that is her work."

"Where do we go now?" asked Vivien, having finished her brief moment of tenderness. "They set that Water Lightning to keep us in place, but soon they will release it and come after us again."

"I doubt they are watching the windows on this side," mentioned Kane, striding over to look out.

"Thomas is in no shape for that kind of a drop," stated Adele.

"And we will not be leaving him behind," added Levitanus. "Besides, Justin and I are too old for climbing out windows."

The wizard looked through the hole that Adele had made. "Quite a bit of boring you three did. I say we continue it, on through to the students' dining hall. That will get us past that enchantment outside and then we can pick which exit best suits us. Vivien, you should craft the next Wormbore, but make this one farther down the wall. As much as I enjoy remodeling Merlin's keep, I would rather not have it come crumbling down on us."

"I will do so, but I have no Amphisbaena in my cache. I have not used it since my apprentice years."

"We have some," said Adele, reaching for the knapsack Thom was leaning against. He surrendered it to her and she took it over to Vivien.

Journeywoman Vivien crafted the enchantment and then had to do it once more to get them into the dining hall. As they came through the opening into the empty hall, they heard a new enchantment being crafted nearby.

THIRTY-EIGHT

Running through Clas Myrddin

Thom looked around the dining hall, remembering his last meal here, the morning the council had ordered him to the servants' level until they could find him a new master. He had broken almost all the commands that they had given him. Today, he had entered the areas of the keep they had set off-limits. Earlier, he had gone about the city without wearing his robes. And worst of all, he had now practiced magic numerous times. If they ever found out about any of that, they would likely banish him from the guild.

Adele was at his side, helping him walk into the hall. She was wearing the Sorcerer Beldin's knapsack now, for which Thom was thankful because its strap had aggravated a shoulder wound. She whispered to him, "What are they doing now?"

Thom focused his attention on her, leaving off his ruminating, then he looked at the others in their party, confused by her comment. "Who do you mean?"

"The sorcerers. What magic is that?"

Thom felt foolish. Of course she meant those chasing them. He concentrated on the sounds of the nearby enchantment and finally recognized it. "Someone has crafted an Eagle Spying... no, make that three have crafted such."

"They cannot get in here because the doors are closed," added Vivien, who had overhead their whispered exchange, "but it sounds like one of them is lingering nearby while another is going through the rooms across the hall- maybe the library where they think we are trapped. The third one seems to have gone on, maybe to the reception area or to the wing holding Sky Tower."

"That means at least four sorcerers are nearby," said Kane, "for the Water Lightning is still live as well. They are closing in on us. Should we just make a run for it?"

"We will go this way," stated Levitanus, indicating the back of the dining hall where a servant's passage led to the kitchens.

They found the narrow corridor dark, for no one had bothered to maintain the few wall lamps along this unadorned route. They entered without bothering to light any, for it was a straight corridor and they could dimly see the light of the kitchen below.

"Hoods up," suggested Kane, who strode at the lead. "No need to reveal who we are to the kitchen help."

Thom tried to do so, but groaned from the pain. Adele, who was at his side in that narrow way, reached over and pulled up the hood for him, then raised her own.

"Thank you," he whispered, feeling so helpless.

"You're welcome, my beloved." She gave a gentle squeeze around his waist, not so hard that it would increase his pain but enough to let him know she was there for him.

The kitchen they entered was almost empty. Apparently, many of the workers had fled since Clas Myrddin had come into the sorcerer's hands. The head cook saw the black robes and hurried to them, asking how he could be of help. He was far friendlier than the last time Thom had seen him.

"We are merely passing through," explained Kane. "Continue your work, cook."

"I will do so," he replied contritely, though his eyes were full of questions at the appearance of two masters, two journey-ranked, an apprentice, and a pair of monastics as well. Even as he stepped back toward his stove, he was staring at them.

Thom looked away before their eyes met, for he had no desire to be in another confrontation with the man.

They left the kitchen through a wide corridor that sloped up to the ground floor store rooms. The corridor ended at a barred door that was used for receiving food deliveries.

Kane opened the heavy door and peeked out. After a careful look, he whispered over his shoulder. "No one is in the service courtyard, but we will have to see what is around the corner."

They all exited to the cobbled courtyard. There were no guards in sight, but they kept close to the building in case any were standing watch in the towers overhead. Thom was surprised to realize it was only about midday, for so much had happened already. The sky above was patchy with clouds but clear otherwise.

The small courtyard ended at the end of the buildings to either side. A graveled path crossed there, heading toward the Stable Gate to the right and to the keep's orchard and garden to the left. The more traveled direction was obviously to the right, which was the route for those who came to sell their goods to the guild.

Keeping close to the buildings, the group followed that route as well, hoping to find the Stable Gate unguarded.

THIRTY-NINE

Ways Blocked

Thom was now leaning heavily on Adele, for which he had already apologized twice. He wasn't certain how much longer he could keep going. As soon as they were away from the guild house, he was going to suggest they leave him in the nearest inn or even in some alley so that he could rest. He really wanted to sit down and do nothing. To sleep, if the throbbing would let him.

"We will be exposed as we go around the stables, but that way is the nearest escape," said Levitanus, indicating the stone and wood structure that sat between the guild house and the outer wall. It was a small stable, but one well-appointed for the occasional centaur guest.

Kane strode purposely around that corner, followed by the others. Hopefully, any watchers would assume they were just another group of sorcerers. Only Thomas wasn't able to project such confidence, although he tried walking on his own. When he nearly fell, Francis and Adele came up on either side and helped him catch up with the others.

They moved along a stone alley that ran between the stable and the outer wall. Beyond the stable was another courtyard and the Stable Gate where two guards stood watch. The wooden gates were unbarred and partially open, but the two men stood in that opening, gazing at something out in the city.

"Do you think a Shroud of Obscurity will get us past them?" asked Kane in a whisper so as not to attract their attention.

"With so many of us? I think not," replied Levitanus. "Even if they did not feel our passing, they would surely hear it. Thomas and Brother Francis are both staggering from their torture; do not expect them to creep soundlessly in a shadowy mist."

"Then what about Tendra's Sleep?"

Levitanus nodded, "But you will need to be quick about it. There are almost no other enchantments in the area. They have extinguished their Blaze Circles and the Water Lightning. Only the trio of Eagle's Spying enchantments still roam the guild house looking for us and I think those purple orbs will rush in our direction as soon as the sorcerers hear you crafting."

"I will be quick," assured Kane, kneeling on the damp and mossy cobblestones in the shadow of the outer wall.

Thom leaned against the sunnier wall of the stables, still needing Adele's aid. He looked over at Levitanus, who was focused on the guards up ahead. He wondered why his mentor had even bothered taking him as an apprentice, since it had apparently been a decade of deceit. The man had been like a father to him, far more so than the abusive drunkard who had actually fathered him.

Adele noticed who he was watching. She asked in a whisper, "Do you miss your time with your master in magic?"

"My former master," he whispered back, his voice low but forceful. "He abandoned me on the Road of Waters, faking his own death to get away."

"What if he asks you to be his student again?"

"No!" he whispered harshly. "I've learned my lesson. I'll not let him trick me again. Let us talk of anything else."

She nodded understanding but didn't have any more questions. For a moment, Thom was caught by her beauty, even forgetting about his constant pain. The sunlight caught her face and he had the sudden urge to want to kiss her, but leaning toward her would only send him sprawling. He was already embarrassed enough that she was having to prop him up, he wasn't about cause more strain by leaning more on her merely to steal a kiss. So he just stared at her.

"Why are you looking at me like that?" Adele asked, wiping at her face. "Do I have something smeared on me?"

He smiled a bit, realizing he was thankful for her faithfulness in spite of everything. "No. I just love you so much."

"I love you too," she whispered back.

Just then, Kane finished his crafting and blew the enchantment in the direction of the two soldiers, who were now opening the gates wider, their focus still on something outside. A whitish mist moved from Kane's extended hands toward the two, like a cloud of steam, but didn't dissipate or rise skyward like steam would. The cloud stayed compact and moving toward the gate.

At the last minute, the cloud split in two and settled over the two guards.

It all happened so quietly that Thom heard them when they involuntarily took a big gulp of air, inhaling the enchantment. The man coughed and looked around in confusion, while the other collapsed immediately. His companion moved to help, but then fell too.

Kane released his enchantment and quickly cleaned his hands and tools, repacking everything in his knapsack and swinging it over his shoulder. He stood up and ran over to check on the guards, as the others followed him at a slower pace.

Thom, again leaning on Adele, was busy watching where he was placing his feet on the uneven cobblestones so he didn't see what happened next. He only looked up when Adele asked, "Why is he closing the gates?"

Kane was indeed shutting and barring the Stable Gate, having to move one of the sleeping guards out of the way to do so.

"What now?" asked Levitanus in a loud whisper.

"Dalrake comes," replied Kane, hurrying back to them. "The guards were opening the gate for a large group of soldiers and sorcerers. They fly the sorcerer's personal flag, so I would guess he rides with them."

"Where to now?" asked the Father Abbot.

Thom had a moment of clarity. "When the pixie Dorthos and I fled here, we made it out through the Garden Gate."

"Excellent idea," said Levitanus. "Follow me, everyone. We will go around the outside of the guild house to reach it. The garden is on the other side of the servants' wing."

So they hurried back around the stables and across the delivery courtyard, leaving the cobblestones and walking over hard-packed gravel that led around the next corner, between the guild house and the outer wall. There were no soldiers on the wall walk and it was unlikely that anyone would lean out any of the windows overhead, so they were safe for the moment.

As they rounded the far corner, they came upon the guild house garden. A stout wooden fence ran from the outer wall to the corner of the keep, with a wooden gate at the end near the building. They passed through the unlocked gate and found a small grove of fruit trees and berry bushes in front of them, the growth so thick and the branches so heavy with fruit that they couldn't even see the outer wall of the keep any longer and there was no obvious or quick route to their exit. They wouldn't be able to follow the smaller wall back to perimeter, for a huge raspberry bramble crowded against the wooden fence. There was no cobbled path on this side- just dirt between rows of fruit trees.

Thom noted a pile of branches that had been trimmed recently but he saw no workers anywhere. Next to the pile of branches was an empty wheelbarrow. Thom wondered if anyone had worked here since Clas Myrddin had been captured.

Just then they all heard behind them the quick crafting of Fireballs by different magicians. Thom judged it came from the area of the Stable Gate. Then they heard the Fireballs getting thrown into each other to cause an explosion.

"I believe the Stable Gate is now open," noted Kane with a little bitter note in his voice. "Dalrake never did like it when obstacles stood in his way." He pushed to the fore with Levitanus. "We need to move faster if we want a hope of escaping."

"Thomas cannot go any faster," said Levitanus.

"I need to get you and the abbot out of here," replied Kane, talking as he forged ahead down a row of the orchard. "The two of you are the ones who must escape; the rest of us are expendable. It is the two of you who know all the names and places and allies of the league. The rest of us do not. If necessary, the journeyman can follow behind at his own pace with whoever wants to aid him, but I cannot let him be the cause of your recapture."

Thomas didn't like what the ex-sorcerer said but knew it was true. Of their group, Levitanus and Justin were the ones who had to escape.

"I have abandoned him once already; I will not do so again," said Levitanus, looking back at Thomas.

"Kane is right," argued Thom as he tried ducking under a plum-laden branch. He only partially succeeded, as one twig scratched his head above his right ear. As he straightened, he added. "I will do my best to keep up, but do not let me hinder your escape."

"I will stay with you," said Adele to Thom.

"If we separate, we will be easier to overwhelm," argued Levitanus. "Let us keep going. The gate is not far. Once we are through it, then we can consider the best way for all of us to flee across the city."

Kane didn't argue further, but he kept up his fast pace through the orchard, a pace Thom struggled to keep. Without Adele's help he would have collapsed in one of the irrigation furrows, but instead he drug his feet through the rich clods of dirt and staggered in pursuit of the others.

They came to the garden's main path, a graveled way, and turned toward the gate. Thom saw the scorched trees from when a sorcerer had tried to stop him and Dorthos. What he didn't notice, at least at first, was the sound of magician's cache ahead.

"Do you hear that?" Adele whispered to him.

At the same time, Kane held up his hand for all of them to stop.

As Thom and Adele caught up, he heard Kane's passionate whisper. "Horis anticipated our coming."

"Are you certain it is him?" asked Levitanus.

"It is his mix of elements that I hear," replied Kane, "but I have no idea who might be with him. We will need to fight our way out, and I would prefer we do so with magic rather than weapons."

"Agreed," said Levitanus. "Apprentice Adele, let me have that knapsack. I am better at magic than you and Thomas is too weak to craft. I will put that magician's cache to good use."

Thom almost protested, not wanting to give anything to his old master, but Adele surrendered it freely. He swallowed his words, not wanting to argue with her. Frankly, his old master was right; he was too weak to do any more crafting.

Kane quickly pulled out his magician's box. As soon as he lifted the lid, Sorcerer Horis released his magic in his direction. Thomas doubted the sorcerer could see Kane, but he could hear the other magician's cache of elements, so Horis threw a pair of hefty fireballs toward him, lofting them into the trees overhead.

One tree crown caught fire, but it was still damp from Camelot's morning dew and so only burned sullenly.

A scattering of sparks landed around Kane, but he ignored it all as he focused on his crafting, making an enchantment Thom both recognized and feared, Hand of Lightning.

FORTY

Earth Shuddering

Thom was unsure what to do. Should he move back toward the keep or shelter among the trees? Vivien and Levitanus knelt near Kane, bringing out the caches of elements to begin crafting too.

Francis seemed to sense Thom's uncertainty, for the monk came over with the abbot. "We should keep some distance from the others, because the sorcerers will target all attacks on those." He pointed at the trio of open magician boxes.

"But we shouldn't retreat too far," argued Abbot Justin. "Once they gain an opening, we will need to hurry through before more sorcerers reach us."

"How are you feeling, Father Abbot?" asked Adele.

He smiled at her. "They did not abuse me or Levitanus. I may be tired, but I am not spent like Brother Francis or poor Thomas. You do well to help him, Lady Adele, although I am sure if Sister Harmony were here, she would be furious at your closeness to a man."

Adele laughed at the thought of the ever-offended nun. Even Thom smiled, remembering her waspish manner.

The abbot turned to Francis. "Now, where should we shelter, brother? We also need to spend time in prayer, for we need the Lord's help to get out of this over-boiling cauldron. Although praying with eyes open might be prudent on our part, for I expect the air to be bristling with magic soon."

They stepped off the gravel path, walking under the cover of cherry trees that were both flowering and full of green leaves and fruit- such was the fruitfulness inside the city's enchantment. Thom leaned against a low limb for support, allowing Adele a moment free of his weight. He watched the abbot and Francis start their praying and even tried to silently join them, but the sound of magic was too distracting.

"They're making a lot of noise," whispered Adele to him, and she didn't mean the praying brethren.

Thom nodded in agreement. Two sorcerers were already crafting in reaction to Levitanus, Kane, and Vivien. With so many enchantments being crafted, he almost wanted to cover his ears to block the noise, though he knew that wouldn't work to stifle the sound in his inner ear. "Dalrake and his party will surely come this way. If we don't get past that pair of sorcerers soon, we will end up surrounded."

From where they were, Thom could see Vivien and Levitanus, but Kane had moved farther down the garden path. Thom could follow his progress from the sharp rhythm of the lightning magic that crackled across the man's hands. He heard the ex-sorcerer release a double handful of lightning bolts and then heard a huge explosion, a cacophony of sounds. Apparently, Kane had hit an open cache, obliterating some sorcerer's collection of elements.

Fireballs came back toward them in quick response, setting more fire to nearby trees. Vivien and Levitanus continued their crafting in spite the flames because it is dangerous to interrupt the crafting of any enchantment. His was taking longer, but Vivien finished hers, crafting her own pair of huge fireballs. She stood up and heaved them toward the garden gate, just as Kane came running back into view, his robe smoldering a trail of smoke behind him.

"Over here," ordered Francis.

The ex-sorcerer did as directed and soon the monk was helping to smother the embers.

"Horis still lives, but I struck Connal's cache before he closed it. He flew into the wall like a bird drunk on overripe berries."

"We need to get past them quickly; this much noise will surely draw Dalrake." Francis paused to listen to what Levitanus was crafting. "What kind of enchantment is that?"

Kane gave his robe one final brush off and then looked toward Levitanus too. "Everyone get ready for some shaking. I have heard that enchantment only once before, when Dalrake helped Mordred by bringing down the castle of a recalcitrant baron. He named it an Earth Shuddering."

Thom's old master finished his crafting and then he slapped his hands against the ground. The soil reacted similar to when a rock is dropped in a pond. Ripples radiated out from Levitanus, slowly shaking the ground in all directions. Three concentric waves rolled out from the master magician, clearly seen as the land bulged up and then lowered again. The ground waves moved outward at about the speed of a fast-walking person so they could be outrun, but the sorcerers were backed up against the outer wall so they wouldn't have anywhere to flee unless they ran out the gate. The ground swells were too wide for anyone to leap over them.

Thom watched as the three circles rolled through the soil as they moved outward and came toward him. He held tight to the tree he had been leaning against as the land heaved beneath him. Once, twice, and then again, lifting and falling. Next to him, Adele staggered as she tried to keep on her feet.

Levitanus wiped his hands as he stood up. "Move! We need to follow the waves as they crash into the outer wall."

Vivien and Kane responded quickly. Francis was helping a knocked-over Justin back to his feet.

"Come on, Thomas," said Adele, her voice sounding tired yet still loving. "I want you out of this place."

He used the magician's staff to push off and then to keep his balance as he leaned heavily on Adele as well. He whispered, "Thank you."

The two of them followed the others as the garden continued to shake and quiver. They went as fast as Thom could, but with each step they fell more behind.

FORTY-ONE

Garden Gate

Thom looked down the garden path for the others, but they were just turning a corner behind a blackberry hedge. He and Adele did their best to hurry after them, walking through smoke from a still-smoldering tree. As they came around the hedge, they saw and expanse of short-cut grasses to the outer wall, with a gravel path going to the gate that the sorcerers were guarding. Both the field of grass and the stone wall were swaying as the waves of Levitanus' enchantment slowly rolled through.

There were six soldiers and two sorcerers there, none of them standing firm as the ground rolled and the wall shook. Sorcerer Horis was leaning against a soldier who was, in turn, bracing himself against the closed gate. Thom could hear no elements around the sorcerer, so his cache was either destroyed or closed.

The other sorcerer- Thom assumed he was Connal- was sitting on his rump, looking rather confused. Thom wasn't certain if that was because the Earth Shuddering enchantment had caused the sorcerer to tumble down or if he was still dazed from Kane's attack earlier. Connal's face and robe were smeared and stained. The sorcerer's cache of elements had been shattered and much of it burned off, but Thom could still hear hints of various rhythms and beats from the scattered powders that had survived. It was an odd, muted noise to his inner ear that came from the sorcerer's clothing and from the ground around him. There were two soldiers stumbling nearby, rubbing fiercely at their eyes at whatever the explosion had flung into their faces.

Kane, his wizard staff grasped with both hands like a weapon, was leading the charge at them; he looked determined to clear the way for Levitanus and Abbot Justin. Francis had his cudgel out and ready, while Vivien held her staff at the ready too.

Horis let go of the warrior helping him to balance and bent over the magician's box that was at his feet, but then he toppled over as another wave from Levitanus' enchantment passed underneath.

Thom guessed there would be no time for any of them to craft magic now.

"There are too many soldiers," said Adele. "How will we get past them?"

Just then a soldier stumbled toward Francis and the abbot. The warrior had his sword out but Francis quickly hit it aside with the cudgel he held. With another swipe, Francis knocked the man down.

"That is how we'll get past," said Thom, gesturing toward what had just occurred. "Levitanus' enchantment has made them all unsteady. I just hope we can catch up and get away too, before they recover."

He then tried hard to quicken his pace. His body hurt so much, but he didn't want to be the reason for Adele's capture. He sped up to a jarring half-run, although he yelped every time his left ankle had to carry his weight. If it weren't for the staff, he would have collapsed on top of Adele after the second step, but he kept going. With a yell of pain, he sped up even more so that they wouldn't be left behind to be captured.

His beloved Adele gave him a worried look but she said nothing, just quickened her pace to match his. He loved her all the more for that, for she understood his need to torture himself to get to safety.

In the next few moments, so many things happened so quickly. Kane swung his staff at Sorcerer Horis, with the jewel blazing as it connected with the sorcerer's head in a small explosion that flung him aside. Two soldiers came at Francis, one of them grazing the monk's side with a wild swing. Kane came from behind and killed one of the men, while Francis was able to stun the one who cut him. Meanwhile, Levitanus bowled over another soldier while that man was rushing toward the abbot. The final soldier ran right past Vivien as he attempted to engage Kane, which was his lethal mistake for assuming a woman was harmless. She jabbed him in the arm with her staff as he went by, her blow so hard that the grizzled warrior lost his grip on his sword. Kane swept in to finish him off.

Thom and Adele were still fifty yards off, when the others made it through the gate. Francis paused to look back, urging them to hurry up, even as he held his injured side.

"We're coming!" yelled Adele. "Go on without us. We will catch up. You need to get Levitanus and Justin away from here."

Thom nodded his head in agreement, too pained to say anything.

Francis gave them a pained smile, obviously feeling for his dear friends, but he too nodded and then exited the Garden Gate.

FORTY-TWO

Past the Wall

Thom and Adele struggled to reach the gate, even while they noticed Horis and two of the soldiers getting to their feet. Horis looked at them and then dismissed Thom and Adele as unimportant. He motioned for one of the soldiers to take care of them, while gathering up his box and staff and then taking the other guard through the gate.

The remaining soldier set himself up in the narrow opening, his sword at the ready. Levitanus' enchantment had dissipated, so he stood firm and ready. If the gate had been padlocked and wedged shut it wouldn't have been more fully blocked than it was now, for neither Thom nor Adele had the remaining strength or weapons to get past an armed and ready warrior.

Just then, two piercing cries filled the air as a pair of griffins dove at those who had gotten through the gate.

Tears of pain and frustration stained Thom's smeared cheeks. He saw no way for two of them to get free, but maybe the others would still get away. "God help them escape," he muttered, for it all seemed so impossible now.

As they got nearer, following the gravel path as it angled toward the gate, the black-haired soldier smirked and his pale eyes seemed to twinkle with an anticipated slaughter. He was likely twice Thom's age but, considering the journeyman's current state, was far stronger. He was also well equipped with a long sword and likely well trained.

They kept heading towards him, even though they had no idea how to get past. It wasn't until they were within twenty paces, that Adele stopped. "Do you hear it?" she asked.

Thom gave her a puzzled looked, his senses dulled by the pain, but then he caught what she meant. Multiple people had begun crafting magic on the street beyond the keep's wall. The soldier apparently had no ear for magic, for he showed no response to the nearby magic.

"I don't think we want to be anywhere near that gate opening," she added in a whisper, "but we should try to keep him there."

Thom nodded, then shouted at the guard. "Let us through and we will not harm you."

The man smiled. "Ya can't hurt me, weakling. I've been around ya magic-makers long enough to know that ya need to do your mixing and spitting and stuff. Ya ain't pulling any spell out of the your sleeve."

Thom paused a moment, then judged that the others crafting nearby were almost done. "This is your final warning. Drop your weapon and move aside, or you'll feel the wrath of magic." Thom had no idea if he would, but he hoped something would at least distract the fellow.

The man actually laughed. "Brassy youngster, ain't ya? Why don't ya come close and I'll make sure your killing is swift. As for the pretty lass, well…"

Beyond the wall multiple enchantments were thrown about and collided, setting off explosions. Suddenly, the man was but a silhouette as a huge orange fireball appeared behind him. One moment he was laughing and threatening, and then in mid-sentence he became a human torch.

The explosion missed Thom and his beloved, but he still felt the wave of heat. Only Adele and the sorcerer's staff kept him on his feet. She had looked away, so she hadn't seen the man's demise, but Thom had. The soldier's smirk had turned into a look of horror as he caught fire, and then he had been thrown into the air by the explosion, to land totally engulfed in flames among the quickly withering grasses.

The gruesome sight caused Thom to heave, but his stomach was too empty to bring up anything more than a mouthful of bile. He spat it out and then the smoke wafted his way and he caught the horrific smell of burnt flesh. He gagged again.

Adele started coughing in reaction too. She had finally turned to look at where the man's body still burned. The sight of it seemed to freeze her.

"We need to go on," Thomas said gently. "We need to find out what has happened beyond the wall."

He noticed that the griffins were still attacking, swooping at something, and that gave him hope that at least some of his companions were still alive.

As the two of them walked toward the smoldering gate, they noticed that no one else stirred on this side of the wall. Sorcerer Conel just laid there, most likely dead. The remaining soldiers were either corpses or unconscious. Thom didn't think any of them were in the explosion's path because none showed any burning, but none were left to stop him and Adele from passing.

They made it to the gate and looked out at the cobblestoned street beyond Clas Myrddin, to find destruction and chaos.

FORTY-THREE

Griffin Attack

Thom saw that his companions had been separated. Francis and the abbot were just up the street, lying flat on the cobblestones and partially hidden by a knocked-over pushcart that its owner had abandoned. Various fruits were splattered on the cobblestones around them. A cloth canopy that had been the fruit seller's shade, was crushed among the ruined product and gave partial covering to the monk and the abbot. Thom wasn't sure if they were dead, unconscious, or just trying to keep from being noticed by what flew overhead.

Horis and his remaining soldier were on the other side of the cart. The reason the two hadn't yet retaken Francis and Justin was obvious: a griffin had become interested in them. The sorcerer and the soldier were trapped against the underside of the cart that lay on its side, finding a little shelter between the large wheels, their backs pressed against the cart.

Thomas looked around and finally spotted the rest of his companions, under the attack of another griffin. The beast was diving and swooping toward the mouth of an alley across the wide road. It screamed with frustration, for the narrow opening and the tall buildings to each side kept it from its prey. Kane, Vivien, and Levitanus sheltered there. At the moment, Kane stood at the ready with his staff and long knife while the other two knelt over mixing bowls crafting magic.

"How can we help?" asked Adele, looking over the same scene. "There are just too many and they will soon be unleashing more enchantments."

She pointed down the street, to where Thom could hear more magic being crafted. Three sorcerers were at work while a double-handful of soldiers kept guard. Thom couldn't tell from where he stood, but most likely Dalrake was one of them. The soldiers were still mounted, but the magicians knelt on the cobblestones very close to a pair of shuttered shops.

"Can we distract them?" she asked.

Thom shook his head. "Not unless a griffin swoops in and scatters those horses." They would likely be either trampled or skewered before either he or Adele could ever get near the sorcerers. He looked again toward Francis and Justin. "If we are to help anyone, it should be to get the abbot away from here."

"You'd rather face a griffin than a baker's dozen of horses?" asked Adele, sounding a bit amused even in their hopeless situation.

"I was more thinking of only one soldier instead of ten."

"True enough." A smile wisped across her lips, but was soon gone. "If we hug the wall as we move closer, maybe the griffin won't notice us. Can you do that?"

Thom nodded, though he had his doubts. He let go of her and put one hand against the rough stones while the other held the walking stick. He started up the street, staying in the wall's shadow. Adele walked right behind him.

He kept going until he was parallel to the overturned cart. To one side were Francis and the abbot, hunkered down under a crushed canopy that had once shaded the cart. They were surrounded by spilled fruit. The two just lay there unmoving, but then Thom saw Francis's head move slightly as he kept an eye on the griffin overhead. He realized they were doing their best to be still and unnoticed by the winged monster. It seemed to have worked for now, for the griffin had lost interest in the sheltering monastics and was now trying to get at the sorcerer and the soldier with him.

On the other side of the cart, sheltering against the cart's underside between the tall wheels, the sorcerer and his companion used a staff and a sword to try to ward off the beast. That the griffin was even focused on them told Thom that it wasn't under anyone's magical control. The monster was loose and ready to kill the nearest prey.

"Soon, it will swoop down on them," he said softly to Adele, not wanting to attract the beast's attention. "Once it is busy feasting, we can get the abbot and Francis out of there."

"Why would it attack them? Doesn't it belong to the sorcerers?"

"They may have used an enchantment to lure it here, but that is still a wild creature. I think it's hungry and those two look like nice morsels."

At that moment, the griffin swept in and actually snatched the soldier with its claws, completely unfazed by the sword he swung at it. The padded paw flattened the man as he screamed. The huge lion-eagle pulled him away from the cart, scrapping him across the cobblestones toward itself.

"Should we try to help them?" asked Adele as they watched the griffin pull away with its prey, away from the sorcerer who was trying to hit it with his staff.

He was impressed with her compassion, but he still shook his head. "The soldier is sure to die no matter what we try, while Horis would kill us himself if we got near to him. No, leave them to their monster. We need to hurry to Francis and the abbot while both Horis and the griffin are distracted."

She nodded in return. "Let me lead in this, Thomas. You should wait here, while I help Francis get the abbot away."

He knew better than to argue, for she was right to have him stay back. If the griffin turned from its kill, he wouldn't be in any shape to get out of its way.

Just then the soldier screamed in terror, as the beast lifted its claw and bent its head near. Both Thom and Adele looked away as the powerful beak snapped shut on the struggling man.

Thom struggled to regain his composure, surprised that he was so affected by the death of one of his torturers. He took a deep breath and focused on what they had to do. It was time for Adele to move, while the monster was eating its kill. "Go quickly, and watch out for the sorcerer as much as the monster."

She nodded in agreement, obviously distressed by the bloody killing too.

So he stood there, leaning heavily against the cool wall, as his beloved Adele ran across the cobblestones to where Francis was trying to get the abbot to sit up. Thom wondered if Justin was injured. He looked at the sorcerer and found him still focused on the griffin as it crouched over its kill.

Thom wondered what they would do once they had the abbot and Francis away from that spilled cart. The wall's shadow really didn't offer them any shelter, but he saw nothing better nearby. He doubted they could make it across to the others. Would they have to retreat back into the garden?

Adele reached the others and knelt by the abbot's side. That the elderly man wasn't getting up immediately, informed Thom that he was definitely injured. He resisted the urge to rush over and help, knowing that he was in no shape to rush anywhere and had no strength to help carry anyone either.

Frustrated, he again looked around for any place where they could shelter, but he saw nothing close. The nearest alley held his other companions, who were still busy with the second griffin and a trio of sorcerers. The nearest cross-street was beyond the mounted soldiers, making it unreachable. There were no shops or houses on this side of the street, only the blank wall of Clas Myrddin's outer wall. All the buildings on the other side were shut and most had been boarded up too, so there would be no fleeing through a shop. Thom still saw no obvious escape from sorcerers and hungry griffins.

At that thought, he looked over at the lion-eagle and saw that it was done with its meal. Instead of looking at the humans nearby, its eyes were on the other griffin, who was screaming its rage at some attack Kane had done. The beast raised its eagle-like head and called out to the other one, then it spread its wings and took a few hops to get airborne, flying off to see what had angered the other.

Thom sighed in relief, knowing that his Adele and the monks would more likely escape now. He was about to yell an encouragement to them to hurry, but then he saw Horis.

The sorcerer had his cache out and was already crafting some magic. Thom had missed the sounds in all the excitement, but now it was obvious. There would be fireballs thrown soon, and that could mean death for others.

Thom yelled warning to the others as he started limping toward the sorcerer.

Adele and Francis were bent over the abbot, trying to help the injured man to his feet. They didn't look up at Thom's shouting.

Eric Loren

FORTY-FOUR

Fire and Flight

Thomas kept going, slow and painful in his steps, moving toward the kneeling sorcerer. He leaned heavily on the magician's staff as he stumbled over the cobblestones, but he wasn't about to let Horis hurt his friends.

"Beware the sorcerer!" he yelled again. This time both Adele and Francis looked over, but they were now holding up the abbot, who seemed barely conscious. He doubted they would be able to do anything about Horis now, who was on the other side of the flipped cart.

Thom quickened his pace as he heard the crafting of a Fireball enchantment, imagining the flames engulfing his beloved Adele. He walked faster, even though his left ankle had gone from throbbing to a sharp pain with each step. He was determined to stop the sorcerer, although he worried that he wouldn't get there in time.

Even as Thomas stepped carefully over the spilled fruits, he saw Horis bend lower and spit into his mixing bowl, attuning the magic to himself, then the sorcerer plunged his sand-coated hands into the goo.

With a weak shout, Thom stumble-ran at him. He swung his staff and hit Horis in the neck. The blow wasn't hard, for Thom was near complete exhaustion, but it hit just as the sorcerer had ignited the fireballs forming in his hands. Instinctively, Horis reached out with his hands to stop his fall, sending both fireballs to shatter on the pavement he was about to hit. Flames scattered all over the ground.

In a feat of extraordinary strength, Horis caught himself from falling his body's length into the flames. He did so by plunging his arms into the fire and pushing off the blistering hot stones. Within the blink of an eye, the sorcerer was rolling away from the magical fire. And he kept rolling, trying to get away from the coming explosion and to extinguish the bits of clothing that had caught fire. His hands had been protected by their coating but his arms hadn't been and were likely badly burned, yet he was still alive.

After hitting the sorcerer, Thom came close to falling in the flames himself. Instead, he slammed into the tipped-over cart and grabbed the spoked wheel to keep from hitting the pavement. He looked fearfully at the fire splattered all around Horis' mixing bowl and knew an explosion was imminent, but he had no strength left to flee.

"Come on Thomas," said Francis, suddenly at his side. The monk handed back the staff Thom had dropped when he grabbed the wagon wheel. "We need to get behind this abused cart before that mixed batch ignites."

His friend led him around the cart and settled him on the cobblestones next to a still-dazed Justin. Adele was on the other side of the abbot, helping to sit up.

"Brace against the cart," Francis urged all of them, "or else it will bash against us when that enchantment explodes."

They did so and then the fires finally heated up Horace's remaining mix hot enough for it to combust. The force didn't move the heavy cart as much but the blast of heat was intense for a moment, then it was followed by more explosions of various colors and dark smoke that smelled like rotten eggs. Thom suspected that last was Horace's cache catching fire.

The explosion also caused a screech of outrage from the griffin that had been silently gliding back toward them and had been caught in the explosion's force. Thom looked up as the monster veered away, shaking its head as if it had gotten a beak full of that fetid smoke.

"The beast is angry now," stated Francis. He looked over the smoldering cart to where the magician's box still burned. It didn't seem to worry him, but he did frown when he looked skyward at the griffin. "We had best find shelter quickly, before it circles back for revenge and another meal. Sorcerer Horis is already scampering to the shelter of his comrades."

"Where can we go?" asked Adele, still holding up the abbot. "Has the second griffin left off its haranguing of the others?"

Francis shook his head. "We can't flee that way."

The monk looked behind them, but he saw the same thing Thom saw- an empty road with barred doors and no side streets or alleys for the rest of the distance to the end of Clas Myrddin's wall. It was too great a distance for Thom and certainly too far for the barely-conscious abbot. The journeyman spoke up, although he didn't want to. "Maybe you should leave me behind and the two of you carry the abbot as far as you can down the road. You might make it around the corner of the keep or maybe to one of those shops' overhangs that will shelter you from the griffin."

"No!" exclaimed Adele.

Francis shook his head. "That wouldn't work and, besides, I have no intention of leaving you behind."

"But where else can we go?" asked Thom. "I doubt that this wreckage will deter a griffin any longer."

Francis looked around and Thomas could see the frustration on his face.

"We go back," said Adele from where she still knelt beside the abbot. "The tangle of fruit trees in the garden will likely keep the griffin at bay or at least force it to stalk us from the ground, which would give us a chance to escape once night arrives and that is only a few hours away."

Francis chuckled as he shook his head. "Escape by running back into the prison I just fled? Tis insanity, young Adele, but it does seem to be our best chance. Can you help Thomas while I aid the Father Abbot?"

"For my beloved, I would carry him on my back if needed," she replied. "We will get them safely away from here."

"God helping," added Francis.

Adele helped Thom up to his feet, then left him leaning on the now-burning cart while she helped Francis get the abbot to stand.

Thom looked down at the cart's grounded trace and noted the flames eating at it. It was no immediate threat; the griffin would devour him before the fire reached this end of the cart. He knew he should be wondering where the griffin was, but he had no strength to scan the skies for it. In truth, all he wanted to do was sink to the ground and sleep. He was so exhausted that his throbbing wounds were almost a comfort to him. The pain kept him at least a bit aware and proved that he was still alive, though he wondered if the throbbing from his head and side and injured ankle would ever end. He wanted to linger here, but it was time to move again.

The pain in his ankle increased to a sharp pain as he began to walk, leaning heavily on both Adele and the staff. He couldn't help but whimper with each step of his left foot.

"Is the pain too much?" asked Adele, sympathy writ all over her countenance.

He swallowed, trying to show himself brave to his dear one. "I… I will endure. I have no choice; we have to hide before the griffin returns."

"Maybe it won't return."

Before Thom could reply, they both heard a griffin's cry far overhead.

FORTY-FIVE

Retreat

The griffin swept in quickly, coming at the now-burning produce cart from the south.

Thom and his companions had just reached the dubious shelter of the keep's wall. At the sound of the beast's screech, Thom stumbled. He heard it behind them but dared not look over his shoulder while walking, in fear that he would lose his balance and tumble to the cobblestones.

Francis ordered them all to stop and hold still, explaining in a hushed voice, "Movement will bring it right to us. Right now it is focused on those dancing flames and rising smoke because that is where it was singed, but it will quickly want a fleshier target and we are only a wing beat away."

Thom stopped. He leaned hard against the wall once again, trying to catch his ragged breath between throbs of pain. He felt Adele's hands still on him, keeping him from falling over. He was too tired to try look, but Adele told him what was happening.

"Keep still. It is hovering over the burning cart and now it's looking around."

After a pause, there was a sharp intake of breath. "It sees us, Thomas!" she said in a sharp whisper. "No... wait... it is now looking at Sorcerer Horis because he's running toward his comrades."

There was another brief pause and then suddenly she patted his shoulder. "It flies after Horis. We need to go now. Can you still walk?"

Thom didn't have the strength to reply, so he just started sludging toward the Garden Gate. He had to, since they had put him at the lead and they wanted to stay pressed close to the wall as they moved. If not, he would have let them go on without him.

"Can you two move faster?" asked Francis.

"Thomas is at his limit," replied Adele.

Thom had to agree with her, but he was determined to lead them to safety. Left foot. Right foot. Left foot. Right foot.

"Horris escapes again," muttered Francis.

"Why did the griffin stop?" asked Adele.

"You heard that enchantment?"

"I did but I don't recognize it."

In a muddle, Thom wondered why he hadn't heard anything. But, then again, his ears seemed full of the pounding of his aches. He stumbled but caught himself. He stopped trying to think about anything else. Left foot. Right foot. Left foot. Right foot.

"One of those sorcerers saved Horis by enchanting the beast," stated Francis.

"It is under their control again."

"Will they send it after us?"

"I pray that they have forgotten us. It looks like our companions have moved deeper up that alley, for I can no longer see them and that other griffin is perched on a rooftop farther back, looking down and screeching at something that is frustrating it- most likely Vivien, Kane, and Levitanus. The sorcerers seem drawn to that sound and it seems that the other griffin is now flying in that direction."

Thom didn't understand much of that. Instead, he was shocked when his hand finally touched the rough and scorched frame of the Garden Gate. He had made it!

Almost, he collapsed in relief, but Adele quickly grabbed him and held him up. "We aren't there yet, Thomas. We need to go inside the garden and get under the trees."

He muttered something to her, but even he didn't know what. He tried to sigh, but it turned into a painful cough.

"We need to keep going. Do you understand?"

He nodded, pausing to catch his breath, then started walking again. Since they were no longer trying to hide against the wall, she came up alongside him and that helped greatly.

"You are practically carrying him," observed Francis. "Do you want to switch?"

"The abbot is no better," she observed.

"But he is lighter. Thomas is a tall and muscular young man."

"I will be fine. Let's just get them to shelter."

Left foot.

Right foot.

Left foot.

Right foot.

* * *

Thom noticed nothing more until he revived while sitting on green grass with his back against a tree. Water was in his mouth and causing him to choke. Adele hovered over him with a waterskin in her hand.

He coughed and spat most of it out, letting it dribble down his chin and onto his shirt.

"Try again," she urged. "You need water after all your efforts."

He looked up at her and gave a little nod, letting her tip its end into his mouth again.

Thom drank, swallowing two mouthfuls, before turning his head away to let her know he had enough.

"Do you remember where we are?" Adele asked, brushing a rogue strand of hair out of his eyes.

Thom thought a moment and then became alarmed. He looked around for the griffin they had been fleeing, but neither saw nor heard it. He did see Francis and the abbot sitting under the next apple tree, both with head bowed in either prayer or slumber. "We... we are back in the keep's garden. Shouldn't we get out of here... that is if the griffin is gone."

Adele smiled, stroking his cheek lightly. "We are safe for the moment. The sorcerers and their monsters seem to have forgotten us. Both Francis and I heard more magical clashes, but he thinks it isn't with our friends anymore. He suspects that Merlin and the other wizards have arrived and are now challenging the sorcerers."

Thom thought about that for a moment, finding it hard to think clearly as he became more aware of all his injuries. "I... I don't believe that we'll be safe with the wizards either. I'm not sure why I feel that, but I do."

Adele nodded understanding, but said, "Where would we go? You and the abbot can barely move. I think we will have no choice but to seek the guild's help."

Francis looked up from his praying. "Thomas is right. We aren't safe around the wizards any more than we are around the sorcerers."

"Surely, you jest. I thought they would be more like allies to us, at least in this conflict."

Francis shook his head. "Then Vivien would have brought you into the guild. Adele, you are a rogue magician in their eyes and they will hunt you down if they learn of your skills. The guild doesn't tolerate any outsiders, be they sorcerer or wizard or just someone who dabbles in magic crafting. The sorcerers band together only out of fear of the guild. When it comes to the guild, it is wiser to expect death not deliverance."

"But you left their ranks and they haven't killed you."

"I renounced magic and my revulsion toward the craft is well known. I'm also a monk, so I won't have any children or the temptation to apprentice them to my old craft. As it is, the guild barely tolerates me and only because I have never truly opposed it openly." Francis shook his head. "Once the abbot and the journeyman have recovered a little more, we will need to get out of here. Right now all is in chaos, but we do need to leave before the wizards realize that we are here. Somehow, we need to get the Father Abbot and young Thomas back to the monastery."

"How will we do that? Even if there were no war in the city, they are both too weak to walk that far."

Thom saw Francis whisper to the abbot and then settle him back against the tree trunk. His friend then stood and looked at Adele again. "I will find a handcart and then we will push them across Camelot."

"Then I should go find it," said Adele. "Thomas wasn't the only one tortured."

"True, but they did much more to him than to me. I still have a bit of strength left. You stay, Lady Adele, and keep these two safe. I plan to raid the guild house's stable and you would not know where to look in there for the cart storage." He smiled and Thom thought it was meant to assure Adele. "If you went, you might accidentally walk in on a centaur snoozing or disturb a pegasus at its feeding. This is no normal stable house."

"Go quickly yet carefully," she replied. "I need your help to get these two to safety."

Francis nodded and set off through the orchard, heading back toward the stable.

FORTY-SIX

Burning Sky

Thomas slept.

He couldn't help it, in spite of all the danger nearby.

He was just so tired.

A loud explosion of magic is what finally woke him up. Startled, he looked about in fear, for it had been like a shout into his inner ear. He saw Adele with her hands over her ears, cringing in pain at the sound that still echoed in his own head.

Thom sat up, fighting down a bit of nausea. The initial magical "scream" had ended, but he still heard the jarring sound of a magical reaction and even a kind of tearing sound. It came from somewhere overhead. He looked up, but could see very little of the evening sky through the dense leaf cover.

With the worst of the sound now passed, Adele let go of her ears and stood. She moved out from under the tree's thick canopy and looked skyward. As Thom watched, he saw her gasp and shake her head.

"What is it?" he asked.

"The sky... it's burning."

"Do you mean there are fireballs in the sky?"

"No. The sky itself seems to be on fire."

Thom couldn't grasp what she meant but knew that he had to see it for himself. "Help me up," he pleaded as he struggled to get his feet under him.

Adele did, but it wasn't easy because he outweighed her. He was gasping for breath by the time he stood, leaning on both the staff and his beloved. Slowly and carefully, she helped him across the uneven ground to where they could see the heavens clearly.

"There," she said, pointing to where he should look.

Thom was already gazing that way, for his inner ear couldn't shut out the clashing noises. It did look like the sky was burning, but he soon realized that it was something to do with the usually-invisible enchantment that covered the city. Listening more carefully, he realized it was no steady burn, but an ongoing series of small explosions. It seemed that the city's dome of magic was being eaten away by an ever-growing circle of explosions that was burning a hole in the enchantment. He could neither hear nor see any magical onslaught, but the intricate enchantment that protected and hid Camelot was falling apart.

"The enchantment over the city has been attacked by magic again," he whispered, "and this time they may have started its complete destruction."

"Will the whole sky explode?" Adele asked.

"I have no idea," answered Thom, suddenly feeling his weakness catch up with him. "Can you help me back over to where the abbot is resting? We may need to flee soon and we should try to wake him."

When they reached the abbot's side, he was already awake. He turned his face upward toward them. Even in the darkening shadows of twilight, Thom saw the blackened eye and the large bump on his forehead.

The abbot spoke in a tired voice. "I overheard you. Is this the end of Camelot?"

"I... don't... know...," answered Thomas haltingly, struggling to catch his breath. It was frustrating, for he felt as weak as an ancient invalid.

"What do you hear with your inner ear?"

Adele answered, "That tear continues its discordant cry, like the wail of some inhuman thing. I don't hear much else in the way of enchantments; maybe all are too startled at what has happened."

The abbot nodded then grimaced at the pain that nod brought, one hand going up gently to his bump. "Neither wizard nor sorcerer wants the enchantment over Camelot to end. They will fight ferociously over which magician rules here, but they both support this city and its magical roads."

Thom agreed, but had no energy to say so. Instead, he leaned against a low apple tree branch to take the weight off his throbbing ankle. Adele helped him to settle against the rough wood and then went over to help the Father Abbot to his feet. It took some time for her to help Justin, for the older man was unsteady on his feet, but he was finally up and hugging the tree too.

We are a fine pair, thought Thom, hoping that Francis would show up soon with a handcart where they could both sit down. Just as he thought that, he heard a rattling sound behind them. Turning carefully, he looked over a crook in the branch and spotted something moving through the dusky orchard. He caught a glimpse of a robed man through the leaves and then a brief view of a high-wheeled push cart as it jumbled across irrigation ditches and dirt mounds.

When Francis arrived, he informed Thomas and the abbot that they would have to wait before climbing in. "Let us get it out on the gravel path first or else we'll get bogged down in this damp soil."

Thom nodded his understanding, though he felt no pleasure at having to trudge any farther.

They tried asking him about the torn enchantment overhead, but Francis shushed them, urging them to get moving. "We can talk once we are free of here. We need to get away while everyone is distracted."

"I will help Thom to the cart," said Adele, "so that he can hold on to its side and keep steady. Maybe the Father Abbot can walk between the poles while you and I hold them from outside and bear the weight of the cart."

"Good idea, Lady Adele," said Francis.

Adele had already moved to Thom's side to help him get moving, when all of them heard others.

The voices came from the gate.

FORTY-SEVEN

Riders Passing

"We are found out!" hissed Thom.

Francis raised his hand in caution. "Maybe not. That sounds more like an argument than a stealthy hunt. Let's hide behind the cart and see if they pass us by."

So they did, keeping to the growing shadows where they could barely see the gravel path that led from the gate to the door into the servant's wing.

Mounted humans rode down the path, going slowly since the way was meant for walkers not riders and so the overhanging limbs needed to brushed aside at times. The riders were arguing as they approached.

"Horis, why do you insist on this way? You are in no shape for such a vigorous route."

The sorcerer's reply was weaker and more muted than Thom had ever heard the cruel man use. "Dalrake wants us to take our prisoner this way."

"But the guards cannot accompany us on the Road of Clouds..."

"Don't you think I know that, Sellic?" interrupted Horis, "but Dalrake says this is the best route for keeping him hidden from Merlin."

"Surely Merlin already knows that he is still alive," argued Sellic.

Thom, peeking around a corner of the cart, could now see some of the party beyond the orchard.

"We take the Road of Clouds," replied Horis firmly.

"Sorcerer Horis, what about us? I've heard that only magicians can walk among the clouds."

"You will escort us to the top of the tower, then you and your men can find your own way out of Camelot. I would suggest King's Harbor, but there is also the Short Roads. If you ride hard, you might be able to join up with the forces retreating with Prince Mordred, but know that as soon as he passes through the Short Roads, the Keeper will yank that route to another city to keep Arthur from pursuing his son. You don't want to be caught between a frustrated king and a closed Road. So it probably would be best to go for the harbor. You should easily be able to catch a ship before morning."

"Yes, sir," replied the soldier, not sounding very hopeful. "We will do that."

"What of the journeymen?" asked Sellic. "The Road of Clouds is only for masters..."

"According to Merlin," remarked Horis. "That's his rule only."

"I believe the Founders all agreed to that rule," replied Sellic, sounding peeved at Horis, "and they made it for good reason."

"Nonetheless, we will bend that rule for we need the journeymen to control him and also to aid me. We… with caution… and then …"

As they moved on, Thom could no longer make out what was being said, for the horses' hooves made too much noise on the gravel. He turned to look at the others, who seemed mere shadows in the growing darkness of evening. "They have Levitanus and are taking him up Sky Tower."

"It is the safer route for them," noted Francis. "If they had taken the Short Roads, they would have found themselves in the midst of Mordred's estates and I don't think Dalrake wants to share the wizard with him. Taking the Road of Clouds is the better retreat for them, for they can redirect the route by the force of their will. Dalrake and his fellow sorcerers can go almost anywhere within the realm by taking to the skies."

"Poor Levitanus," said the abbot. "The sorcerers will grow tired of his obstinace and will surely treat him harshly."

"I should go after them and try to free him before they get up the tower," stated Adele.

Francis placed a restraining hand on her shoulder. "No. Chasing them wouldn't be wise. We still need to get the Father Abbot and Thomas safely away from here."

"But Dalrake will get his answers out of Levitanus somehow and then the league will be exposed."

"Most likely, but the league can't remain hidden forever. Dalrake will already have his suspicions."

She looked to Justin for support, but the abbot shook his head.

"I hate the thought of abandoning him," said the abbot, "but there aren't enough of us to challenge them, especially with two of us so weakened."

"Where is Dalrake?" asked Thom, suddenly wondering where the leader of the sorcerers might be.

"He is otherwise occupied. Listen carefully, Thomas. There is some powerful crafting happening toward the center of the city. That is more than Keeper Bronwen can muster on her own. I think it is both Dalrake and Merlin working to repair the city's enchantment before it completely fails."

"I hear it now," affirmed Thom, noting that it must be an impressive crafting to be heard at such a great distance.

"Why would they work together?" asked Adele. "They are enemies."

"Not in this, they aren't," said Francis. "The Founders built the Roads as well as the enchantment covering Camelot. These two have no desire to see it end."

"Maybe they will wait for Dalrake inside. We still might be able to get Levitanus freed before they ascend the tower."

"They will take him all the way up," argued Francis. "They might wait before starting along the road, but they won't pause until they are up there."

"What should we do then?" asked Adele.

"We leave as soon as we can," replied Francis, "and we pull these two back to the monastery. I think we should wait until the soldiers leave before we come out of this orchard."

"Should we take their horses and ride back?"

Francis grinned at her. "My mule Ears would be jealous if I ever rode a horse.

Besides, I would guess at least two men stayed with the animals to keep them restrained and safe. Those men will not want to lose their mounts and get stranded in Camelot, and we don't have the strength to wrestle the horses away from them. No, we will hide here until they ride back out, then we will leave too."

That made sense to Thom, so he turned to Adele. "Can you help to… cart? I can sit on its edge. Easier to get up from there than from… ground."

She helped him to maneuver between the resting poles and sit on the cart's tilted bed. Francis settled the abbot next to him and then they all waited, still sheltered among the trees.

Finally, about twenty minutes later, the soldiers rode back out, leading five without mounts. As soon as they were gone, Adele helped Thom and Abbot Justin to their feet and around to the back of the cart where they could hold onto it for support. She stood between them, to help push while Francis lifted the heavy arms and began pulling the cart through the orchard and finally onto the gravel path. He set the arms on a low-cut hedge to keep it level and then helped Adele settle the two onto the cart's bed. Once the abbot and journeyman were in place, Francis and Adele lifted the poles and began pulling them toward the Garden Gate.

Thom found the ride jarring but was relieved to be off his feet. He sat against one of the sidewalls, with his knees pulled up and the magician's staff lying next to him, trying to stay awake. For some reason, it felt odd not having a knapsack on his back. He looked over to where the abbot leaned against the other sidewall, sitting with crossed legs and holding the cart's side with one hand. With every jolt Justin grimaced and often raised his other hand toward his injured head but stopping short of actually touching the large bump.

Thom felt helpless as Francis and Adele pushed them around the final curve of the path. He looked up at where the burning hole was in Camelot's enchanted covering and noted that the explosions were over and now it only had a glow to its edge, like that of a banked fire. It also seemed smaller. Could it be that the master magicians were able to repair it so quickly?

Elsewhere in the sky he saw the Road of Clouds glowing too, but that was from the last rays of the sun, for sunset had finally come. He saw nothing of the griffins.

Looking up made him feel lightheaded, so he lowered his gaze and instead focused on the battered gate that was directly ahead. It was a comfort to know that they were almost away from here, and this time there was no magical battle in the streets beyond nor any diving griffins. But then he noticed something else that caused him to grip the cart's sideboard even harder.

"The are two people standing in the gate's shadow," he whispered loudly to Francis and Adele.

FORTY-EIGHT

Sky Tower

Francis and Adele stopped pulling and set the cart down. The sudden tilt caused both Thom and the abbot to grab tighter to the sides to keep from sliding forward.

One of the figures in the evening shadows stepped forward a bit, crossed their arms, and spoke. "Well. Well. Look who is still alive. Last I saw of you, Betrayer, a griffin seemed ready to make you into a meal."

"Butcher of Sherwood. I am glad to see you alive as well, for all of God's creations are precious," replied Francis. "Is that Vivien with you?"

She stepped forward, walking past the ex-sorcerer and heading for them. "Indeed, it is I. It seems that the Father Abbot is more battered than when we left you, but at least you still have him. We lost Levitanus."

Adele gave a cry of delight and ran up to Vivien, giving her a hug which the journeywoman returned. Thom wasn't certain due to the poor lighting, but he thought Vivien looked a bit stiff and embarrassed by the friendly affection.

Kane strode over to the cart, looking in on its passengers. "Father Abbot. I am thankful that you are still free, although that wound needs attention. Journeyman Thomas, you are a tough one. Most would have died after all you went through, let alone remain clear eyed and aware of their surroundings. Well done, young man."

Thom didn't know how to respond to that, so he simply nodded.

"The sorcerers have Levitanus," said Francis. "They have taken him to the Road of Clouds."

"I feared as much," replied Kane. "Do you know how many hold him?"

"Two sorcerers and two journeymen passed us a few hours ago with him," answered the monk. "I don't know if any may have already been waiting inside Clas Myrddin. Sorcerer Sellic seemed hale and ready, but Sorcerer Horis is wounded, having suffered burns after Thomas clubbed him and knocked him into his own enchantment."

Kane chuckled. "The journeyman is practically on death's door and still he had enough fight in him to inflict injury on Horis? Good for him!" The master magician paused to give another look at Thomas and then spoke again. "If he weren't so exhausted from torture I would gladly take him with me, but he would only be a burden."

"You are going after them to rescue Levitanus," stated Francis.

"I must, and Vivien is going with me."

"A journeywoman on the masters' road?"

"You just told me that the sorcerers are taking two students with them as well.

Besides, her skill at the craft is a master's level. Her gaining of black robes is a mere formality that was delayed by the unfortunate death of her mentor." Kane paused to meet Francis' gaze. "I could use another master like yourself, but I know you have sworn off all magic."

"Even if I wanted to break that vow, my place is here in Camelot," said Francis. "With the Father Abbot injured, I must help the evacuation of the monastery."

"You think we've already been compromised?" asked Kane. "I doubt that Dalrake has gotten any answers out of Levitanus yet."

"But Dalrake already suspects much, which is why he held the abbot and even kept Thomas and I alive in spite of his hatred for us. He may not know the extent of the League of Barnabas, but he is a crafty one. He will suspect much and he will have told Merlin about some of it."

"Merlin?"

Francis nodded. "They have been together repairing the rift." He pointed at the glowing circle in the sky overhead. "Do you think Keeper Bronwen could have stopped that on her own? I think those two Founders have helped her. Even now it no longer burns and has begun coming back into harmony. I think the two are at the Keeper's tower with her now."

Kane frowned, then nodded. "Most likely, but Dalrake hates Merlin. Why would he share anything with him?"

"They both want all of this to continue," said Francis, opening his arms as if to embrace the city and its magical ways. "When Levitanus faked his death, he removed his magical influence on all of it and forced so many to scramble to stabilize the various enchantments. His apparent death is what emboldened Dalrake to try seizing Camelot again, so finding him alive must have been like a bite to the bone for Dalrake... a wound he'll nurse for a long time and will never forget. You know him better. Is my assessment correct?"

"Dalrake will suspect great schemes," admitted Kane. "He might even wonder if it was some elaborate trap that Merlin and Levitanus plotted."

"Does he know that Levitanus was recaptured?" asked Adele, who had come to stand near Thomas.

Kane looked over and nodded. "He was there when Sorcerer Sellic captured him with an enchantment. We couldn't get him free in time."

"Francis is right," announced Abbot Justin in a weak voice. "All who are of the league must flee the monastery. Just because the king and his wizards have recaptured the city, does not shelter us. We must assume that Merlin will learn enough to be suspicious of us."

Kane nodded again and shifted the pack hung over his shoulders. "So be it. Vivien and I will go up Sky Tower and pursue the abductors, while the rest of you go to the monastery and start its evacuation."

"Should we try to send any others to join you?" asked the abbot.

"No, Father Abbot. Bronwen will not be free for some time and none of the others are near." He paused to look directly overhead at where the trail of clouds led away from the tip of the highest tower. The corridor of clouds was still lit by the setting sun, even though everything in the garden was already in the darkness of coming night. "Vivien and I will be moving fast so that we can catch any shifts in the Road. Who knows how far ahead of us they are by now?"

He signaled to Vivien, waved his farewells to the rest of them, and soon the two of them half-ran down the gravel path.

Just then those remaining heard a great cry in the sky. Looking up, they saw a huge winged bird flying their direction.

"Don't move!" shouted Francis. "Let's hope the gloom of sunset hides us or else it could carry us all away, cart and all."

Thom frowned at his friend's exaggeration, but then he realized the bird was much bigger than he thought. At first he thought it was a mother eagle followed by two eaglets, but then he realized the followers were lion-eagles. Griffins? What could be so large as to make griffins seem like fledglings?

"What is it?" he asked, "and are the griffins chasing it?"

"That is a roc," replied Francis, "and there is no bird bigger. It can easily carry off a pair of horses in those claws. I had no idea a roc was in the city. Such a great beast wouldn't run from griffins."

"There is someone clinging to its back," said Adele.

Thom looked again and saw something there but couldn't see well enough to declare it a person.

"Even more reason for us to do nothing to attract their attention," replied Francis. "I think Dalrake is about to join the others on their retreat to the Road of Clouds."

The roc was swift in spite of its great size; the two griffins labored to keep up. The bird flew directly at the keep's Sky Tower and only at the last moment did it choose to circle Clas Myrddin once as it sought the best landing perch on the keep's highest spire.

Thom felt his heart beat faster as the huge beast flew directly over them. It certainly was large enough to carry them all away in those huge claws.

The roc finally decided where it would land and backwinged to a gentle stop on the ledge of Sky Tower's final walk before the spire pierced through the city's dome of enchantment. From far below, Thom and the others watched, for the animal was almost directly above them. It carefully approached, slowing its forward motion to almost nothing. The roc grasped the ledge almost daintily with its massive claws, but still some of the stonework broke off and plunged to the ground. It did not fold its wings, for the place was a precarious perch, but it remained still enough for the man on its back to leap off it and onto the tower's landing.

"Why didn't it fly to the pinnacle of the tower?" asked Adele. "Surely that would have been a more secure perch."

"That would have meant piercing the enchantment," replied Francis, "and that wouldn't be a wise thing to do even if the dome of magic were fully restored."

As soon as the man was off its back, the roc flew away, some more stonework crumbling as it pushed off the tower. It flew away, back toward the center of the city. Thom wondered how the beast ever got into the city in the first place, for it seemed too large to pass through Rowan Gate. Maybe it flew up the Road of Waters and to the harbor.

Once the roc was gone, the two griffins landed and then squeezed their way inside the tower's upper entrance.

"The danger for Kane and Vivien has just greatly increased," observed Francis. "May God bless their quest to rescue Levitanus."

"Amen," replied Abbot Justin weakly yet fervently.

Thom nodded in agreement. He had no love for his deceitful old master, but he also had no desire for him to be tortured into telling his secrets.

FORTY-NINE

Respite

Francis and Adele succeeded in pulling the handcart all the way across the city. Instead of going to the monastery, they went to the attached convent and banged on that stout gate. It took some time, but finally a nun appeared on the wall walk above it and demanded to know who was disturbing their midnight prayers.

"Sister Harmony, let us in. It is Brother Francis and I'm bringing back the maiden you were supposed to be chaperoning. I also have two wounded men with me, one of whom is worthy of your respect."

"What? Who is wounded?"

"I'll not shout names except yours, Harmony, but get down here and crack the gates. We need to get inside now."

"The Mother Superior will hear of your demanding ways, and the Father Abbot will learn of it as well." She stayed put on her roost directly over them.

"Get down here, sister. I wouldn't be rattling your door if this wasn't important." Francis pointed at her and then at the barred gate in front of him. "Be quick about, for these two need aid."

Harmony glared down at them for a moment longer, but then did as he bade. When they finally passed inside to the convent's courtyard, the sister saw who was in the cart and gasped. "You didn't tell me it was…"

"I said no names," interrupted Francis, "and that still holds. Do you understand me, sister?"

She blinked her confusion. "Why?"

Francis made sure the gate was barred again behind them, then finally answered her. "There is much turmoil in the city right now. Now, fetch the Mother Superior and your best healing sister. These two need prompt attention."

"And Brother Francis is also wounded," added Adele in a shout toward Harmony's quickly retreating back. She then turned to Francis with a warm rebuke. "You cannot keep ignoring your own injuries."

Thom agreed with her, though he didn't have the strength to say so.

* * *

Thomas awoke in a soft bed instead of on a hard pallet. The comfort soon fled, though, as he felt a sharp pain in his ankle. He looked down and tried to pull it free, but the healing sister had a firm grip on his leg.

"None of that, young man. Wizardess Bronwen heard of your injuries and sent this poultice over. I'm not too keen on magic, but if it will help your bones to mend, I'm not about to refuse it. The servant who delivered it called this Cream of Caladrius." She held up a tiny tin that contained a milky white goop. "Now hold still, for I'll not waste it by smearing the bedsheets. Once I'm done with the cream, I'll replace your splint and you can go back to napping."

The nun seemed rough in her efficiency, but Thom realized that she was probably as gentle as she could be with his abused foot. Soon she was done, his ankle smeared and wrapped and braced in the bed. The blanket she had flipped to the side was patted back in place. She took a moment to look at his pupils and ask him some questions about where it hurt, which was followed by some poking and squeezing to make sure nothing else was broken. Before leaving his side, she pointed out a covered bowl of soup on the nightstand and encouraged him to eat as much as he could.

She moved to the other bed in the spacious room, which held Abbot Justin. Thom was glad to see that the abbot was awake and was holding a conversation with her.

Having no desire to eavesdrop, he looked elsewhere, inspecting the convalescing room he now occupied. It was a large space, spartan yet clean. It held four beds, though the other two were empty. The small windows set high on the wall showed that it was daytime outside, but Thom had no idea how long he had slept. He did feel hungry, in spite of all his aches, so he scooted himself against the headboard until he was in something of a seated position and then reach over for the soup.

He was nearly finished when the others arrived. Francis went first to his superior, while Adele came to his bedside. Following Adele was Sister Harmony, still looking sour and watching carefully to make sure all remained chaste. Thom was a bit surprised to see that Adele was wearing an apprentice magician robe.

"How are you feeling?" she asked, reaching out to him and then stopping when the nun cleared her throat.

"Better." He set the almost-empty bowl on the side table. "How long has it been since we arrived here?"

"This is the second morning. You slept all of yesterday and through the night."

Thom nodded his understanding. "Is it time for us to leave?"

Adele smiled. "No, I don't think the sisters will toss you out just yet. But once you are recovered, they will move you over to the other side of the wall, to the monastery's guest house."

"That's not what I meant. Should we not be helping the brothers and sisters to flee Camelot?"

"Whatever for?" asked Harmony, butting in.

Adele hushed her, since the healing sister was still in the room, while Thom whispered an explanation.

"Dalrake and the sorcerers may have fled, but it is likely that the Magicians' Guild has learned about the league and they will hunt all of you as rogue magicians."

"Nonsense," remarked Harmony, her whisper not much quieter than her usual voice. "We are God's servants here. The magicians would dare not sully these holy grounds."

Adele ignored her and instead leaned closer to Thom and whispered her own response. "We still have some time. Merlin still works with Bronwen on repairing Camelot's enchantment. Francis thinks many of guild are also at the City Keeper's Tower, helping them. Meanwhile, the king and his men are distracted by stragglers from Mordred's army and a few bands of renegade centaurs. Even worse, three griffins are still loose in Camelot and they are no longer constrained by the sorcerers who brought them."

"That does give us some time," agreed Thom, relieved that he wouldn't have to flee this day.

Adele came even closer and sat on the edge of his bed, taking his hand in hers. Sister Harmony hissed in warning, but she ignored her. "I thank God that you are alive, my dear Thom."

"I'm alive because this time, as in so many times before, you rescued me." He smiled up at her in his deep affection.

She laughed. "We do seem to fill our lives with peril, don't we?"

He shook his head. "No, it is only that we live in perilous times, you brave and beautiful woman."

Before the nun could restrain them, Adele leaned forward, careful not to press on any of Thom's many wounds, and they exchanged a strong kiss.

Eric Loren

WAYS OF CAMELOT
4-Book Arthurian Fantasy Series

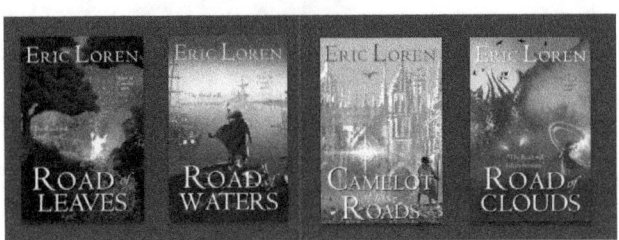

1- Road of Leaves
First Book of the 4-Book Ways of Camelot Series.. Available in paperback and e-book.

2- Road of Waters
Available in paperback and e-book

3- Camelot of the Roads
Available **September 15, 2023** in paperback and e-book.

4- Road of Clouds
Available **October 15, 2023** in paperback and e-book.

Eric Loren

About the Author

Eric Loren

Eric is an American author of fantasy, science fiction, and dystopian novels.

His writings include the Ways of Camelot series, the upcoming Tag Warren series, and the Cirian War saga.

The son of immigrants, he can speak his parents' tongue, though with a decidedly American accent. He studied our collective past and our present (holding a degree in both History and Religious Studies), and still enjoys learning about the world's diverse cultures and beliefs.

Eric currently lives in California, enjoying the sunshine and natural wonders of that unique state. He is married to his beloved Amy and has two wonderful sons.

Learn more about Eric at his website:
http://ericloren.com

www.ingramcontent.com/pod-product-compliance
Lightning Source LLC
Chambersburg PA
CBHW070747180626
46818CB00007B/3021